ABOUT THE AUTHOR

PATRICIA DONOVAN grew up in Christchurch, New Zealand and graduated from the University of Canterbury with a Master's Degree (with honours) in English Literature. After graduation she worked in corporate communications in Australia and New Zealand and is the author of a best practice guide to the profession. She is a member of the New Zealand Society of Authors and the New Zealand Writers Guild, and *The Madison Gap* is her second novel.

www.patriciadonovan.nz

ALSO BY PATRICIA DONOVAN

The Remarkable Miss Digby

THE MADISON GAP

PATRICIA DONOVAN

MARY EGAN
PUBLISHING

Published by Mary Egan Publishing
www.maryegan.co.nz

This edition published 2021

Designed by Mary Egan
Cover designed by Anna Egan-Reid
Produced by Mary Egan Publishing

ISBN 978-0-473-56567-1

for Pen

Nothing is absolute. Everything changes, everything moves, everything revolves, everything flies and goes away.

— **Frida Kahlo**

1

Projects on my desk at work were mounting up, their deadlines niggling like a persistent cough, but I put them out of my mind, switched off my Mac, and left the agency early. I had a valid excuse, to my mind anyway. Chrissy was coming to stay and I wanted to be there when she arrived.

She was due at four. By eight, she still hadn't arrived. Conor and I gave up waiting and decided to eat.

I don't pretend to be much of a cook and usually get home too late after work, and too whacked, to make dinner. Left to my own devices, I'll shove a ready-made meal in the microwave, something from Fresh Meals or Youfoodz, but since this was Chrissy's first night with us, I'd gone out of my way on the dinner front and made an effort. I poured Conor a glass of Merlot and lifted my beef casserole from the oven. Then I took a bottle of Chablis from the fridge and filled my own glass.

Conor put his arms around me and nuzzled the back of my neck. I turned to kiss him and he drew me close. 'Do you think we've got time before she gets here?'

'She was due four hours ago.' By now it was well after eight, almost eight-thirty, and even if we'd had time, I wasn't in the mood for making love. I was annoyed with Chrissy for being so late and not even bothering to phone. Would a text be so hard? I'd taken the lid off my casserole too soon and now it was drying out.

We were just sitting down to eat when we heard the squeal of brakes in the street outside and a jarring crunch of metal against metal. Conor and I rushed outside to see what had happened. There was a sign on the pavement in front of our house, declaring the parking spaces for residents only, and Chrissy had crashed right into it. The pole was now a steel disorder obstructing the pavement. It was going to annoy the hell out of the young mother I sometimes saw on weekends, wearily pushing her toddler past our gate in a stroller.

Chrissy stepped away from her Mazda with insouciance, as if creating a spot of wreckage in the neighbourhood was just the entrance she was aiming for. She wore a figure-hugging dress made from some green slinky fabric, and high spikey-heeled ocelot-striped shoes. She'd let her hair grow long since we'd last seen each other and the loose ponytail suited her.

I was wearing grey baggy track pants, a faded pink hoodie that had been too often through the wash, and an old pair of espadrilles. Chrissy was chic as a Ferrari and for an uncomfortable moment she made me feel like a second-hand Holden.

We hugged after which Chrissy kissed me first on one cheek and then again on the other, an affectation, for us Antipodeans anyway, that I thought she found as awkward as I did.

Her breath smelled of booze and over her shoulder I couldn't help noticing how much gear she'd brought with her. Usually she arrived with a single faux-leather overnight bag, but this time there were two, on the back seat, and both so full Chrissy hadn't been able to close them. More clothes lay in a jumbled heap: trousers, shirts, jackets, and dresses, some of them still on their hangers. It looked as if Chrissy had lifted them straight from her wardrobe and plonked them any old how into the back of her car.

On the passenger seat was a half-empty bottle of green chartreuse.

'Don't tell me you've been drinking.'

Chrissy shrugged. 'And you haven't?'

'I'm not driving.'

My sister laughed and proffered her cheek to Conor.

2

There was just enough room in our house for a guest. Conor and I lived in one of Glebe's roughed-up terraces of shabby single-storey homes built in the 1890s. From the outside it looked as if nothing had been done with them since, but I knew from months of rackety construction and skips of building rubble on the street that a couple of our neighbours had remodelled their interiors. Conor and I told each other at regular intervals that we'd catch up with those neighbours just as soon as Conor got around to drawing up plans for the build and our bank balance had a growth spurt. Until then, my husband's study with its flaking paint and threadbare carpet doubled as our spare bedroom.

The evening before, when we'd rearranged the study to accommodate my sister, Conor had taken the cushions off the sofa bed and made a funny face, blowing his cheeks out and rolling his lower lip in a phony pout. He was given to adopting comic poses. 'This is getting to be bit of a habit, Lexi,' he said. 'Do you think she's preparing for a final bolt?'

Bob Dylan was on the radio, singing *Paint Your Masterpiece*. I turned the sound down and regarded my husband. We'd been married for nearly two years and while Conor was cruising comfortably into marriage 201, I was on marriage 101 and still feeling my way along our respective boundaries, discovering by trial and error what needed to be negotiated and what didn't. 'You don't mind her being here, do you? You'd say, wouldn't you?'

'I'll cope. It's only a few days, isn't it?'

'Probably.' I hadn't been entirely honest with Conor about how long Chrissy might stay and was feeling a bit bad about that. When she'd phoned the week before, I'd had a hunch she was depressed, and told her there was a bed in our house for as long as she needed one.

This weekend visit was her fifth, actually it may have been her sixth, since I'd moved into Mitchell Street two years before. Chrissy referred to these visits as stopovers in her life's journey, and sometimes as respite care. 'Diversion' was another word she used, from the moodiness of her writer husband, she said, and the boredom of living stuck out in the Blue Mountains.

I was always happy to see her because those breaks from her own routine enlivened ours. Our routine was this: Conor and I went to work early and arrived home late, sometimes as late as seven or eight if Conor went to the gym and I went for one of my long walks around Jubilee Park. After that we'd usually collapse on the sofa, Conor with a beer and me with a cup of tea or glass of wine, then eat something unmemorable for dinner and either catch up on the news or watch a movie on Netflix. Then we'd go to bed and read our respective books. I nearly always had a novel on the go or, if I was too tired to read, I'd just flick through one of my old art books for a while. There was a stack of them under the bed, pre-loved hardbacks like Christiane Weidemann's *50 Women Artists* and Christopher Allen's *Art in Australia*. Conor usually read journals on architecture and urban design, or brought his iPad to bed and carried on scanning the news. We'd read for an hour or so before lights out at eleven, or books down at ten and the lights dimmed for browsing each other.

Whenever Chrissy came to stay, she cooked at least one night, dishes that *were* memorable, such as a coconut curry with shrimp, or chicken with caramelised oranges. On another night she'd insist on us all going out to a restaurant or a show and I loved that she did this. The only discordant note during her visits was the noisy phone calls she made to her husband each night, but other than those, my big sister added colour. Looking back, you might say I was in her thrall.

Conor tossed a cushion at me which brought me back to the task at hand: preparing Chrissy's room. I wiped the shelves in the wardrobe with a damp cloth, put sheets on the sofa bed and tucked them in, shook out a duvet and arranged two pillows, then sat back against them to admire Conor clearing his desk.

If you can refer to a man as well made, this pretty much sums up Conor. He's tall and solid but not the least bit overweight and all the separate parts of him seem perfectly, securely fitted and well proportioned. He has grey friendly eyes, a slightly crooked nose – broken in his teens during a footy match – and he's particular about always being clean-shaven. His hair is dark brown, almost black, which even though he's only in his early forties, is already flecked with grey.

He knocked up his papers into neat stacks and filed them under project names in three cardboard file boxes, names like Bankstown Concepts and City Stadium, and then he swept his drafting compasses, set square, and rulers into a drawer. I liked that about Conor; without being too fussy about it, he was tidy, except in the kitchen where he had a blind spot, and diligent about anything to do with his work. He was fairly easy-going, never letting anything get him down and, in this way, he was good for me because I have a tendency to take things too seriously. Conor's optimism made sure the mood in our house was always upbeat. And his confidence in the future, our future, gave me faith in it too.

When he was finished, I got up from the bed, smoothed the duvet, and straightened the print of Picasso's *Dream* which we'd found in an op shop in Paddington and which Conor had hung on the wall behind his desk. On the desk, as a final touch to make Chrissy feel welcome, I placed a small milk jug filled with creamy, fragrant freesias.

It was a nearing the end of April in 2017 when my sister came to stay.

They were troublesome times.

Everyone was still trying, and failing, to understand how low America had fallen, and we were all equally bemused by Britain's morbid decline into a fatal case of Brexit. At home in Aussie, the population reached twenty-four million, and in March, street gangs on a violent rampage through Melbourne spoiled the Moomba festival. Wherever you looked, anger flowed like molten lava. It's still roiling and it's not hard to see why. Too many people aren't getting enough of what they need while the careless elite continue with impunity devouring way more than their fair share.

It seemed to me during that uncertain time that there was no one you could rely on any more and it took an effort not to fall into an apocalyptic mood.

I frequently had to remind myself that despite the sorry plight the human race was fast sinking into, there were some things still right with the world, that in the increasingly jagged soundtrack of our lives, there were still songs worth hearing. I recollect it was only a few weeks before Chrissy's arrival that Bob Dylan was awarded the Nobel Prize for Literature.

3

Two days after she arrived, Chrissy asked me if we minded her staying longer, a fortnight, by which time her car would be fixed, or maybe three weeks, she wasn't sure.

'Stay as long as you need,' I said and made a mental note to get her a temporary parking permit. I waited for Chrissy to explain why she wanted to remain in Sydney longer than the usual four or five days, but she said nothing. Finally, after a few minutes watching my sister put her clothes away in the wardrobe and in the drawers of Conor's desk, I asked her if everything was okay. 'There's nothing wrong is there? Is Peter home?'

'Oh, he's . . .' Chrissy waved her hand vaguely back and forth in the air and didn't say any more.

I expected her to confide in me but still she didn't explain and I had no choice but to let it pass. I assumed she'd tell me in her own good time.

Two weeks later, three guys from the Council, wearing yellow high-vis jackets, came and replaced the parking sign. On the same day, Chrissy retrieved her car from the panel beater. She drove back to Mitchell Street via a garden centre where she filled the boot with bags of topsoil and compost. Across the back seat were five trays of seedlings.

'I'm going to fix up the garden for you,' she said.

'There's no need.' I meant this. Our back yard was as ramshackle as the rest of the house but cleaning it up, let alone planting anything there, hadn't been a priority for Conor and me. That's not to say it wasn't on our to-do list, but until we got around to it, the yard's only purpose was to store our rubbish and recycling bins, Conor's old bicycle, and the two kayaks we hadn't used since we married. There was a crumby old Hills Hoist there as well, installed yonks ago by long-dead occupants, which I used and reviled.

As far as I was concerned, gardening was a medieval pursuit designed for people with too much time on their hands and I couldn't see the point of growing vegetables when the Glebe Markets were just up the road.

I gave Chrissy an old grey and white chequered shirt of Conor's to wear while she was gardening. The collar and cuffs were frayed and there were a couple of buttons missing, but my sister, as she did with whatever she wore, managed, effortlessly, to give it style, tying the shirt tight at the waist, lifting its collar against her neck and rolling up the sleeves.

Conor and I didn't even own any tools, not so much as a hand-held gardening fork, but, along with the seedlings, Chrissy had purchased a small spade and a mattock. She set to with the mattock and began turning over the soil while I dragged our old hose out from under the house and did my best to straighten out the kinks in it.

'Do you remember, Chrissy, when I was in Grade Two and you helped me win that garden prize? We planted sweet peas, all along the back fence.'

'Yes, and I tried to persuade you to put in flowering kale but you were having none of it.'

This time, now that she was in charge, my sister got her way. The seedlings she'd bought were all edible plants: broad beans, broccoli, and spinach, along with a young apple tree, and a variety of herbs. The only ones I recognised were mint and parsley. 'You know I'm notoriously bad at this,' I said, 'especially herbs. They always die on me.'

'Perhaps I'd better stay on then.'

I couldn't tell whether or not she was being serious. 'Conor will need his study back.' I mumbled this in an apologetic sort of way because much as we wanted to make Chrissy feel welcome, I couldn't help thinking that maybe a fortnight was long enough, a month at a stretch. I wanted both of them to be happy and could already see myself being torn between what I saw as competing demands on me from my husband and my sister.

Fortunately, Chrissy hadn't heard me or if she had, she chose to ignore it.

Within a couple of hours, she'd turned over enough soil in the yard to start planting. She dug a deep hole, placed the apple sapling in it and then pressed in a generous mix of soil and compost.

Chrissy gets her green thumbs from our mother and watching her brought to mind a photo I use as a bookmark in the dog-eared *Oxford Concise* I've had since my school days. The photo is of Mum and me in the front garden at our house in Bendigo. It was taken in 1995, about six months after Mum's first mastectomy, and her short hair is just starting to turn grey. In the photo she wears maroon and navy tartan wool slacks, black rubber gardening shoes, and a buttery-coloured cotton blouse with the sleeves folded back to her elbows. She's tilling a straight groove with her spade along the edge of a bed of yellow and red roses, and I'm standing next to her, watching, barefoot, in pink shorts and a blue and white striped top.

During idle moments, I revisit my conversations with Mum and whenever I study that picture of us, I imagine her explaining to me the life-cycle of worms or the nutritional quality of stinging nettle. I was probably equally uninterested in both topics. What I strive for most when I think of my mother is to bring back the sound of her voice. I'd give anything to hear it again.

We are not the only people in that photo. In the background, sitting on the concrete steps up to our front door, is my older brother Robbie. I was six years old at the time that picture was taken which would make Rob what? If I remember rightly, he's less than eighteen months older than Chrissy so he must have been seventeen. It's absurd that I don't know for certain my own brother's age or even when his birthday is. What I did know for sure was that it was shortly after that photo was taken that he left home to join the army. So much time had passed since then that he'd become a blur to me, a photo negative waiting to be developed.

'Where's Robbie? Do you know?'

'Whatever makes you think of him?' By now Chrissy was planting the spinach and she eased the seedlings from their little pots without looking up.

'I often think of him. He's our brother. I wish I knew him. Why did he leave? And how come he's never contacted us?'

'You don't want to know.' Chrissy's voice was trenchant.

'Of course, I want to know. Tell me.'

'What I said.' Chrissy avoided looking at me, fussing now instead with another of the seedling trays. The atmosphere turned a little frigid.

Bringing up the subject of our brother had made her crabby so I let it drop.

This wasn't the first time this had happened. When Conor and I married, I'd wanted to invite Robbie to our wedding and asked Chrissy if she had his address and she'd had the same gelid reaction. There was a broken bridge in our family and I was completely in the dark as to why, or how to mend it.

4

I like to believe we Madisons were just your average Aussie family although what 'average' actually means baffles me. My father drank more than he should, but you could say that about a lot of people. Including me. We weren't special. Dad was an engineer with the City Council, Mum worked in the local library, and we lived in a modest house in an unassuming town a hundred and seventy kilometres from Melbourne. Bendigo's only claim to fame as far as I knew was its gold-rush past. Ned Kelly might once have passed through, on his way to robbing a bank somewhere, but that was more than a hundred years before I was born. While I was growing up, nothing interesting happened in Bendigo, and certainly not in the suburb of Epsom which was where we Madisons lived. The way I saw it, Bendigo was ever the bridesmaid to Melbourne's bride.

In Mitchell Street, Chrissy spent a week working in the garden and at the end of it, on Saturday afternoon, Conor built a raised bed for her to put the herbs in, but by then Chrissy's enthusiasm for the job had petered out. The soil and compost set aside for the bed remained sealed in their bags and the herbs were never planted.

From time to time, when I looked out our kitchen window or went into the back yard to put clothes on the line, I'd see Chrissy's abandoned project and remember that long row of sweet peas in Bendigo, how intense their colours had been – pink, purple, navy, and crimson – and their heady fragrance. We'd worked on that garden together when I was just a little kid, still at primary school.

By the time I got to high school, I'd lost interest in gardening completely and was restless for more adventurous pursuits. Both my siblings had left home by then and I suppose I was lonely, and impatient to follow them into the world. I'd stand at my bedroom window staring into the night and rage against the slowness of time. I was bored as a wallflower and in a furious hurry in those days to grow up, for my life to start. I really believe that at times I would happily have exposed myself to risk or danger, although I couldn't for the life of me have specified what, maybe go downtown and sit in a pub by myself, smoke clove cigarettes at the bar, even go so far as to let a strange man kiss me, because at least that would have been *living*. It would have been a grown-up thing to do.

This is what I remember of my feelings in those days.

Instead of doing my homework I'd study my reflection in the black pane of my bedroom window, and rejecting the pudgy adolescent face staring back at me, and those messy blonde plaits and even messier fringe, I'd conjure up the fascinating, elegant person my adult self would surely be.

I hadn't known then how to live in the present.

And when I moved in with Conor, I basked for months in a sense of having arrived. He'd bought the house in Glebe in the nineties, years before house prices put people like us into a banker's noose. Gentrification was yet to fully flex its bank account in our street and like most houses in the vicinity, ours was blighted by a sagging corrugated iron veranda behind a low rickety picket fence in dire need of paint. The front door opened to a long narrow hallway with all the rooms off to the right. The main bedroom was the first room you reached, then the study, and then down the corridor to the living/dining room which we'd furnished second-hand from eBay with a rumpty old chesterfield upholstered in bluey-green tartan, an oak dining table with curly legs and numerous blackened cigarette burns, and six mismatched chairs. The kitchen and bathroom were at the back, overlooking the yard.

I loved every mothy inch of the place.

As far as I was concerned, Mitchell Street was perfect, close to the city and with a couple of decent bookshops just down the road and where there were numerous cafés with great food. There was even a boutique art gallery where one day I hoped I might exhibit my own work. We were practically in Darling Harbour's lap; in one direction there was only a thirty-minute walk into the CBD and, in the other, an even shorter walk to Jubilee Park where one day, when we got one, I'd be able to walk the dog. The Glebe Markets were close by and the whole area, to me anyway, had a laid-back vibe and I was happy there.

During my first year of marriage my happiness seemed to me like a miracle, although there were times when I believed that in some obscure way those teenage day-dreams of mine had presaged my later life. Which is more real anyway? Life as a married woman, living in Sydney, or the life I'd lived in my imagination when I was a girl in Bendigo? As I grow older, time seems more and more to me to be a rather squashy concept; is there some law that says the events of our lives must follow linear time? Might it not be that I've already in some pre-ordained manner, experienced events that are in my future? I was a graphic designer and the wife of a second-generation Irish architect, living just the sort of life I'd once imagined, but what if I'd imagined something else – a career as a nurse, say, and co-habiting with an immigrant Turkish surgeon – might that not be what I became? Or might that not be what waits for me in another life?

These were the sorts of questions and fancies that sometimes occupied my mind during nights when I couldn't sleep, when I was jangling, I suppose, from all the espressos I'd consumed during the day.

5

When we'd decided we were a couple for keeps, Conor and I had
made a pact not to make a big deal of our birthdays unless they
marked a new decade. We agreed that instead of spending on
birthday presents, we'd save our dollars for more important things:
renovations on the house, a couple of kids, and their education.
Chrissy didn't know this. She'd been with us for about a month
when Conor turned thirty-four and she decided a celebration
was required. While I was at work, my sister baked a chocolate
coffee cake and after dinner, lit a circle of green, white, and orange
candles stuck in the coffee icing, and nudged the cake, blazing like
Christmas, across the table to Conor. She gave him a gift as well, a
DVD, and insisted we all watch it that night.

While I cleaned up after our meal, Conor made coffee for the
three of us, and Chrissy carved gooey slabs from the cake. By the
time I finished in the kitchen she'd arranged herself like an artist's
muse at one end of the sofa in the living room and was lighting up
a cigarillo. She patted the cushions next to her, inviting me to sit
there. Conor sat in the armchair across the other side of the room,
the ankle of one long leg propped on the knee of the other. This was
a habitual position of his that I disliked because who wants to see

the sole of a man's shoe, even if it is an Italian brogue? I was going to tap his foot as I passed but he always got a bit shirty when I did that so I refrained. He caught my vibe anyway and put both feet on the floor.

The cake was delicious.

The DVD was anything but. It turned out not to be a film at all, but an eight-part serial. We settled down to binge on the first few episodes. I don't remember what it was called and very soon lost interest. It was a rubbishy show from Brazil about a girl who runs away from her rich parents and gets a job in a brothel. The sex scenes started almost immediately. I gave Conor my spare-me-the-tedium look and I know he noticed because he raised his eyebrows in acknowledgement, but then kept his eyes glued to the telly.

At first, it was harmless stuff, just a bit of erotica, nothing you'd call X-rated, but the story soon turned gross when a creepy old guy in a wheelchair arrived at the brothel, wearing a movie camera strapped against his forehead. He was accompanied by a minder, a rottweiler in a blue serge suit who waited at the back of the room while the girl was slathered in gold paint and dressed in a broad red collar studded with bling.

'Why are we watching this? It's revolting.' Was I the only one who could see things were going to turn nasty?

'Your provincialism is showing, Lexi dear,' said Chrissy. 'Think of it as art.' She gave Conor a conspiratorial glance and I was gratified to see he didn't react.

The barb hit home though and I don't know which dismayed me more, that my sister would treat me so condescendingly or the ease with which she punctured my self-image as a woman of the world.

'Art be dammed,' I said. 'It's porn and I'd rather not have it my living room.' I looked to Conor for support but he was still studiously avoiding looking my way.

Chrissy lifted her head and blew a plume of smoke at me. I tersely waved it away.

The old geezer began mewling with pleasure as he watched his bodyguard knock the girl around.

'It's horrible.' I tried again to catch Conor's eye but he only glanced at me. This put me in a bad mood and I got up and pointedly, noisily, cleared away the cake and the coffee cups, then went to bed with Jonathan Franzen's *Purity*.

Conor and I nearly always ended the day together and I expected him to follow me, but two hours passed before he came into the bedroom.

'It didn't get any better,' he said.

'And that took you how long?' I was cheesed off with him and although I stopped reading, didn't look up from my book. 'Why did you ignore me?'

Conor sat on the side of the bed and pulled off his jumper, then took off the brogues. He removed his watch, took his reading glasses from his shirt pocket, and placed them on his bedside table.

'What was I supposed to do?' he said. 'Your sister was sitting right next to you and … how shall I put it? She obviously prefers to dress commando.'

'Poor you, too much of a good thing.' I didn't believe him.

'No, really. She's *sans* knickers tonight and I'm telling you, Lex, she meant for me to see.'

'Conor, get real.' I snapped my book shut, turned off the bedside lamp and thumped my pillow. 'Chrissy free-buffing is one thing but making a show of it, to you of all people, is another. She's my sister for god's sake.'

Conor finished undressing, got into bed and wrapped himself around me. 'You know, she never really struck me as the sisterly type. Know what I mean?'

In a way I did. There was often something detached about my sister, that wry arched brow of hers, her lowered eyelids, as if she were deliberately avoiding intimacy. I might be wrong. Maybe it was just because she was so much older than me, practically a different generation, that I sometimes got the feeling she regarded me as someone of no consequence.

I didn't answer Conor. He knew I got a kick out of dissecting people's behaviour, to figure out what makes them tick – it was a game we played often together – but it felt disloyal when my sister was the subject.

Conor's penis was hard against the small of my back. I moved away. He put his hand on my thigh and gave my night-shirt a little tug. 'C'mon love, it's my birthday.' He burrowed into my neck. 'I'm all turned on.'

'Not by me apparently.' I pushed his hand away and shifted further away on my side of the bed. 'It's late, go to sleep.'

We heard Chrissy moving around in her room. She was humming, something by Adele, I think. It might have been *Someone Like You* but the walls between us muted the sound so I couldn't be sure.

The following morning, running late for work and preoccupied with concern for the deadlines I had to meet that day, I'd almost forgotten what Conor said about my sister's flaunting her crotch at him.

That's the sort of person I was then, and still am for that matter. While I said that as a teenager I hadn't known how to live in the present, by my late twenties I did. They say that living in the present is the secret to happiness and I'd schooled myself in it, although now I'm no longer entirely convinced that it's an attribute worth having. Living in the present makes me forget things better remembered. It makes me forgive things unforgiveable.

6

A few days after Conor's birthday, I recalled Chrissy's behaviour that night, and the music coming from her room, and it occurred to me there hadn't been a single phone call from Peter. She'd brushed me off when I asked if everything was okay between them. Maybe they spoke during the day while I was at work, or maybe in her room at night, quietly, so I hadn't heard. But that would have been unusual, and out of character.

During her previous visits, my sister had spent at least an hour on the phone with her husband every night and didn't care whether or not we heard. In fact, sometimes I think she wanted us to hear. 'Pete, Pete, listen to me. You know I'm not sleeping well,' she'd complain, or 'I did so leave a message about that job, it's hardly my fault you missed out', and 'Can't you for once say something nice?' Her grievances piled up like rubbish during a garbage strike, each one more rancid than the one before.

If she'd stayed any longer than a week, those calls would have driven me round the bend. Our house wasn't large enough to get away from the disruption of such heated one-sided conversations. They began quietly enough but then Chrissy would start shouting at Peter until one of them hung up. These calls punctuated each day of Chrissy's visits after which Peter, if he was in the country and not on assignment overseas somewhere, would drive down from Katoomba and they'd hide themselves away for an hour or so, make up and spend the rest of the evening snogging one another before leaving early the next the morning.

This time we appreciated the quiet and Conor was chuffed when Chrissy ironed his shirts for him. I never did. I wouldn't have darned his socks either or replaced the button on his shorts, but Chrissy did.

One evening, during that tepid hour when I get home from work and want nothing more than to put my feet up with a glass of wine, I went into the kitchen to prepare pasta for dinner, something quick and easy so all I had to do was add pesto sauce and heat up some garlic bread. Chrissy came in behind me, picked up the packet of tagliatelle, gave it a disparaging glance and put it back in the fridge. 'Haven't you got anything better than this processed stuff?'

It was with that remark that my sister staked out the kitchen as her territory. I didn't mind. In fact, I appreciated it. And why shouldn't she take over the cooking? She was better at it than I was and even though her stay was now entering its second month, neither Conor nor I had asked her to contribute to the housekeeping.

I stood back and watched as my sister turned on the oven and foraged in the fridge. She took out a bag of chicken breasts and began chopping the meat into chunks.

'Have you tried cooking with rabbit?' she asked. 'Our butcher at home usually has it and it's just as good as chicken, and cheaper.'

I shivered. Chrissy gave me an interrogative look.

'Someone just walked over my grave,' I said. The feeling passed as soon as it arrived. 'How's Peter? We usually see him by now.'

'Oh, didn't I say?' Chrissy's knife hit the chopping board like a flesher's cleaver. 'He's in South America, covering a medical conference over there, something to do with some virus or other.'

'Who's looking after the dog?'

'Sophie. She's home.'

'I was worried you and Peter might have had a falling out.'

'Of course, we haven't. Why would we?'

As I've said, Chrissy's arguments with Peter were legendary so I felt during this conversation as if my sister and I were talking along parallel lines. 'When will he be back?' I asked.

'Why do you care?'

'Why ever would you think I don't?'

Chrissy packed a baking dish with the chicken, added blue cheese and broccoli, and poured in a creamy sauce before covering it all with tin foil. She put the dish in the oven. It already smelled good.

'Pete's only too happy to get home and find I'm not there. He can get on with his latest opus or whatever, before he has to start punching out more column inches for some newspaper or other.'

'Journalism pays the bills at least.'

Chrissy ignored my comment.

Outside it began to drizzle and I hoped Conor wouldn't get caught in the rain. I smiled to myself, thinking of the evenings I used to surprise him with the house in darkness apart from candles and a trail of pistachio nuts guiding him along the hall to the bathroom where I'd be waiting in the bath with champagne and our favourite bath toys. Think vibrating sponges. As the memory came to me, I realised how much I missed our intimate evenings alone together in the house.

The drizzle thickened into a steady rain, the sound of it on the roof turning to a steady thrum. I closed the kitchen window.

'We were wondering how long you're thinking of staying?'

'You're sick of me.'

'No, we're not, but what about your job? Won't they be expecting you back?'

'Are you telling me what to do?'

'No, I just meant …' The last thing I wanted was a quarrel.

'I quit. It was only part-time anyway.' Chrissy had worked at the local bush hospital in Katoomba, as an administrative assistant. I think she worked on the payroll or did when she started there, but I wasn't sure what job she'd moved onto after that. Whenever you asked Chrissy about her work, she'd adopt a bored pose, tapping her mouth over a feigned yawn, and be incomprehensibly vague, so I'd long ago stopped asking.

What I did know was that she was doing better than the family once expected. My sister was clever enough to succeed at whatever she put her mind to, and after she'd finished high school, Mum and Dad urged her to study for a profession. She toyed with accountancy, then law and in the end, when she was nearly twenty, enrolled in a business course at Bendigo TAFE, but didn't see out the first year. She began that last foray into tertiary education by moving into a shared house with some fellow students and they spent their nights partying and their days recovering, a careless lifestyle that was probably behind Chrissy's failing every exam that year. Dad refused to pay Chrissy's fees for a second year until she passed the first, paying her own way, so she went back to washing dishes and three months later moved to Sydney.

Watching her slice beans, I tried to envision Chrissy as a lawyer but all I could see was one of those white horsehair wigs, faceless, with pontifical speech oozing from it like sand and gravel from a concrete mixer.

Chrissy took chartreuse from the freezer – she'd stocked it with three bottles of the stuff – and drank a swig straight from the bottle. 'Here I am, going to the trouble of making you guys a decent meal. I thought you were happy to have me here.' She opened the oven door and a gust of hot air filled the kitchen.

'We are, I didn't mean …'

'Does Conor want to me to go?'

'You know we'll both go along with whatever you want.'

'There's no pleasure in cooking where I'm not wanted.'

Sometimes Chrissy put me in mind of the King of Hearts who tells the Mad Hatter: 'Don't be nervous or I'll have you executed on the spot'. She made me feel like I used to feel as a child during one of our father's boozy blowouts, when he was hiding out in the shed nursing his adversities, and Mum and I crept around the house as if barefoot across splinters of smashed crockery.

That night I had an unpleasant dream: I was hanging washing on the clothes line, that huckery Hills Hoist in our back yard, when a little black and tan dog crept through the neighbour's fence. It was fluffy-cute and I was about to go and pat it when it began to change, growing larger and larger until it turned into a huge ravening beast. I dropped whatever I was holding, pegs I suppose, and maybe a bathroom towel, and ran for the house, dodging garden pots and nearly falling over a kid's tricycle before I reached the safety of the back door.

I heard myself whimpering and woke up.

It was three am. I couldn't get back to sleep. Instead I stared at Conor's back and asked myself why it was so important to Chrissy whether he wanted her to stay or go. I reflected on Chrissy's first evening with us, when she'd rebuffed my question about Peter. I imagined her lying on her bed in the room next door, in Conor's study. What did she think about?

7

At work I was under increasing pressure.

Farras Leven, the advertising agency which employed me, had taken on a new client, a food and beverage company which was going through a massive expansion. I was tasked with designing the packaging for their new range of snack foods, but my heart wasn't in it. This wasn't entirely because I already had more work on than I could comfortably handle. Thinking about Chrissy, and about me and Chrissy, was keeping me awake at night and blunting my enthusiasm at work. More and more often, as I sat staring at the screen, I felt like a wall being papered over.

Scoring a six-month internship with Farras Leven is what brought me to Sydney in the first place, along with the fact, too, that Chrissy lived nearby. That was after I'd completed a Bachelor of Fine Arts and spent another couple of years working part-time jobs while I tried and failed to make a living as an artist. That's what I'd really wanted to do then, and still do, paint full-time, but unless you're a Damien Hurst – 'though I'm not into sharks and skulls – or a Banksy, art doesn't pay the bills. Graphic design does. When he took me on, Barry Leven promised training and a career path in advertising that paid well and sounded interesting. And it was. After my internship I spent eighteen months in the agency's creative department, learning design, a bit of copywriting, and production. I was then given the job of art director and at the end of 2016, a few months before Chrissy turned up, promoted again to creative director. These advancements didn't signify much in terms of management – apart from the owners, Farras Leven's structure wasn't hierarchical – but it meant Barry sometimes let me take the lead on an account. That's if he didn't want it for himself or if my colleague Marley didn't snaffle it before I did.

The agency was on the top floor of an old grain store in downtown Sydney and our rooms had high exposed beams and floor-to-ceiling mullioned windows. A kitchen and sitting area with black leather sofas took up one end of the floor while a rarely used ping-pong table dominated the other. The two owners each had a big office along one side, with their own adjoining meeting rooms, while on the other side of the floor there were four smaller offices for staff working on research, IT, finance and media buying. Between those two rows of offices, in the middle of the floor, was a large open plan area, with one long wooden desk, five work stations on either side. That's where I spent my working hours. We hot-desked so I never knew from one day to the next which Mac I'd be working on. I always struggled with that. There was nowhere to put stuff, like a pot plant and my little framed picture of Conor, or the fidget desk toy my friend Lauren once gave me. During my first year at the agency, I'd try to arrive at work early enough each day to get the same desk but this didn't always work. Finally, I gave up and accepted there was no place in the office for personal effects and that one work station was much the same as another.

Barry Leven was our general manager. The other owner, Gray Farras, did all the schmoozing with clients and I never had much to do with him. When I did, he was cordial, asking me politely whether or not I was happy in the work and inviting me to offer suggestions for change. I was never entirely sure if he genuinely wanted an answer. It did occur to me a few times to suggest a permanent desk of my own but I knew the limits of my influence and said nothing.

Gray was sixty and charismatic with eyes so blue and shrewd you didn't notice how short he was, only one metre sixty, and he was always immaculately groomed. He wore tailored suits in black or charcoal with narrow silk ties in muted greys, blues, and browns. His skin was smooth and his hairline receding but what hair he still had was thick and white and tied back in a short trim pony tail. The word in the agency was that he visited a barber every morning at seven, before he came into work.

Day to day it was Barry we answered to, but it was Gray we all wanted to impress.

Barry's office had glass walls through which he kept a gharial eye on us.

When he called me in to discuss the new account, he presented me with a sample of bags the client had in mind for its snack foods. I picked one up. It was manufactured from layers of foil and plastic and I detested everything about it: the trashy gold and red colours, and, especially, the fact that it couldn't be recycled.

'Why don't we offer them something in paper?'

'Not our brief.' Barry Leven looked more like an Oxford don than an advertising exec. He was the same age as Gray, or thereabouts, and every bit as astute, but sartorially he was Columbo to Gray's Poirot. He wore corduroy jackets and ill-fitting twill trousers and his greying hair roamed across his collar as if unsure which direction to take. If you didn't know him, you could be fooled into thinking he was in the wrong business, but there was nothing about the ad industry Barry didn't know, and his brown eyes would turn tack-sharp if he thought you were slacking.

'Paper can be just as good, better in fact,' I said.

'Sure, but it costs too much, and takes up more space on the shelf.'

'If we can't encourage our clients to think sustainably, who can?'

'I shouldn't have to tell you, Lexi, our business is design and branding; we don't decide what the packaging is made of.'

'Isn't brand about culture?'

'Just come up with some designs, will you. By the end of the week.'

I couldn't let it go. 'Turtles see plastic bags as food. They mistake them for squid and eat them. Then they die a horrible death. Did you know that?'

Barry pointed at his office door. I left but not without the last word. 'All these bags and trays and bubble wrap ... and don't get me started on straws. We don't need any of it and we're drowning in the stuff.'

Barry didn't even look up; he was preoccupied with a loose thread on his cuff. If he kept it up the whole sleeve was at risk of unravelling.

I took the samples back to my desk, crushed the bags and let them fall to the floor. As I stood there staring at the mess and depressed about how much junk was ending up in the ocean, I had an idea to make sure those bags got used again. My designs would include instructions on the back about how to turn them into something else. But what? Tote bags? Wallets for kids? Doggy poo bags?

Whether or not this proposal went down well with the client, I didn't at that point care. It would at least let me tackle the project with a lighter conscience. I would be happier working on it and, if nothing else, at least I'd be giving the client options. That was my short-term goal anyway. Longer term I aspired to see the agency take a stand on sustainable packaging and, if I could pull it off, with me leading the way.

8

One day when I arrived home from work – this was during the first week of June – Chrissy wasn't there. Usually, she was in the kitchen or, if she'd finished preparations for dinner, in the living room, smoking and cruising her iPad. I went into her bedroom and looked around. I half hoped she'd left her phone there so I could see if there were messages from Peter. I was also entertaining a vague notion that observing the room where she spent time alone might somehow shed light on her intentions.

Her evasiveness about her plans was getting to me, but what bothered me more was the uncomfortable idea that my sister might be taking advantage of me, because by now I was beginning to understand how much Chrissy relished her older-sister status. She behaved as if there was some implicit understanding between us that she knew more than I did about, well, everything. Perhaps this is the nature of siblings, particularly when you are born years apart from one another, that no matter how old you get, that gap is always there.

The bed was unmade. Clothes had been discarded, any old how, in a mess on the floor and across the bed. I picked up the blue dress Chrissy had worn the day before and held it against myself. The fabric was a mix of silk and linen, the skirt knee-length and narrow.

I stood in front of a mirror Chrissy had placed against the wall and held the dress up to see what it might look like on me. I already knew the answer. It looked better on my sister than it ever would on me.

Anyone seeing us together would know we were closely related. We share the same even features, blue eyes, and shoulder-length hair. We even have the same quirky cowlick on the crowns of our heads. But while my hair is thin and blonde, Chrissy's was thick and coppery. She was taller too, a little more than one metre seventy, while I'm a metre sixty. Unlike me, Chrissy turned heads. Her height and that hair gave her a leonine aura that I know men find seductive. And why wouldn't they? She *was* sexy.

There was a bottle of perfume on the desk. Burberry. I removed the stopper and dabbed a little scent on my wrist. It was smoky and ever so slightly masculine which appealed to me. It occurred to me that it might be a fragrance Conor would like as well.

I put the dress on a coat hanger and hung it up. Then I took it out again and dropped it back on the floor where I'd found it. I didn't want Chrissy to know I'd been in her room.

There were three cashmere cardigans on a shelf in the wardrobe and unlike the rest of her gear they were neatly folded with layers of tissue between them. They looked as if they had never been worn. I ran my hand over the one on top of the pile. It was soft, taupe-coloured and looked expensive. Tucked between two of the cardigans, and placed so far at the back it had to have been deliberately hidden there, was a National Bank cheque book, which was odd because Chrissy banked with Westpac. And how old-fashioned; I mean, who uses cheque books any more? I took it out and opened it; it was in the name of Peter's business, Peter Everson Ltd. My brother-in-law was a free-lance journalist and he'd also written a couple of biographies that as far as I could gather had been well received. The top butt noted a withdrawal made the week before, for cash. Two hundred dollars. I flipped through more of the butts. There were weekly withdrawals over the past five weeks of two and three hundred dollars. It took me only a few seconds to understand that Chrissy had been regularly withdrawing funds from Peter's account.

I supposed she and Peter had a shared account and were joint signatories to it, yet this was Peter's work account. It didn't make sense. My sister had told me once, emphatically, that she and Peter kept their finances separate. She'd advised me, when I was engaged to Conor, to do the same, that it's a matter of dignity for a woman to manage her own finances and to never to fall into the trap of letting a husband assume economic power. I'd been grateful for that advice and followed it.

I put the cheque book back between the cardigans and closed the wardrobe door. Why hide it there? Was she hiding it from herself, to put a lid on her temptation, perhaps, to use it? If that was the case it clearly wasn't working.

I opened the wardrobe door again, exactly as I'd found it. Chrissy's financial affairs were none of my business.

9

A few days later we had friends over for dinner. Janet and John – these really are their names – are Conor's oldest mates. Whenever I hear their names together, I can't help thinking of those children's books: *Off to play we go* … The three of them grew up together in the same neighbourhood in Lithgow, went to the same schools, and John and Conor both studied at the University of New South Wales.

We invited Steve to make up the numbers. Steve's wife Lauren is my best friend from high school and he was on his own for the weekend while Lauren took their two kids down to Melbourne to visit their grandparents.

It was Saturday, 10 June. I remember the date clearly because it was Queen's Birthday weekend and Conor and I always did something special during that weekend for our friends; it had become an annual event. Sometimes we all got dressed up and behaved like royals which meant we ironed our table napkins, put plums in our mouths, and used a butter knife. Conor and I enjoyed preparing the meal together and made a point that day of not letting Chrissy anywhere near the kitchen.

I made a Basque chicken casserole with loads of onions and green peppers while Conor experimented with dessert, layering apples, tamarillos, and blueberries into a baking dish and covering the fruit with a mix of rice flour, coconut, brown sugar and pumpkin seeds.

We pushed the sofa against one wall and the armchair against another and let the dining table take centre stage. I decorated it with a centrepiece of red bottlebrush flowers and lots of green leaves and branches of a plant I don't know the name of but which has red cheerful berries. Each white plate had one of our mustard-coloured napkins on it, decorated with a small leafy bunch of four or five black grapes. We were yet to buy decent cutlery so what we had was mismatched. Ditto with the wine glasses. We always said that what mattered most was what we poured into them and Conor had bought six bottles of a very decent dry white from the local vintner.

That night we all dressed Chinese. Conor put on his grey linen jacket with frog buttons and I wore a blue and silver vintage cheongsam. Chrissy spent most of the afternoon in her bedroom, emerging around five-thirty in narrow black pants with a velvet jacket which shimmered between wine-red and purple. Her lipstick was somewhere in between those two colours. She'd put her hair up like Kim Basinger in *The Informers* and looked just as gorgeous.

Everyone was in good spirits and it was a lively evening, helped along no doubt by the amount of wine most of us drank. As always, we launched into a spirited debate about current events but that night the conversation seemed more animated than usual, and the banter between Chrissy and Steve in particular was electric.

We'd finished the main course and as I cleared the plates from the table in readiness for dessert, Chrissy shared her views on population growth. 'By twenty-fifty,' she said, 'there'll be nearly forty million people in this country, sitting on top of each other in a dust bowl.'

'Doesn't bear thinking about,' said Janet. She'd taken up the Chinese theme and was wearing black jeans with a green and gold embroidered Mandarin jacket. It suited her. Janet's dark hair was cut in a page-boy style which drew attention to her large brown eyes. Scarlet lipstick made a bright narrow line of her mouth.

Janet's a social worker and spends a lot of time working with under-privileged children, volunteering regularly at the Kids' Cancer Centre. I went there with her once, thinking I could make myself useful, but seeing those kids with their big sweet dying eyes, hooked up to tubes and machines, made me desperately sad. I went back for a while, once a month on a Sunday morning, but not to those wards. I always left Janet to play with the kids while I helped out in the kitchen at Ronald MacDonald House where pity didn't render me useless.

'Maybe we could neuter babies at birth for a few years, just until the numbers become more sustainable,' suggested Chrissy.

'Don't say that,' I said, 'I'm looking forward to meeting my grandsons.'

'We'll need to have kids first,' said Conor. He crooned a couple of schmaltzy lines, something dippy like: 'Ooh, ma baby … ooh, ma songbird, can you feel me throb tonight? … do be mine.'

'Not in front of the kids.'

'Being childless is a gift to the planet.'

That was Chrissy and if she really cared about the planet, I thought, she'd stop throwing money away on designer clothes and buy recycled instead.

'We could move across the Tasman. Plenty of room over there, not to mention water.'

'There won't be if *we* all turn up.'

'I doubt we'd be welcome,' said Chrissy. 'Why would they want immigrants any more than we do?'

'You don't like immigrants?'

'I just think it's time everyone stayed home.'

'You're implying you don't like them,' said John. He raised his eyebrows and assumed an air of mild puzzlement.

I've never quite understood what John does for a living, something to do with engineering. He works for an oil company and is away one week in every four. He has receding hair and blue intelligent eyes, and his demeanour is serious until he bestows on you a broad engaging grin. That night he wore what he always wears: chino pants in grey or beige, a plain white or blue shirt and navy reefer jacket.

'Not at all,' said Chrissy, assuming the tone of a pedagogue. 'I'm suggesting that I don't like people who don't belong in Australia coming here and making this place their home when it isn't.'

'That's what an immigrant is, someone who comes here.'

'Would you say you're a racist then?'

'C'mon guys, stop riling my sister.' I was curious to see how Chrissy would handle the stirring, but she was my guest after all, and my sister, which in my book meant that if there was to be any baiting to be done, it was my prerogative to do it.

'I care what happens in this country.' Chrissy took out one of her cigarillos and with an ironic glance around the table, set a match to it.

'Where did your forbears come from?'

'Scotland,' I said, 'on Dad's side and England on Mum's.'

'I rest my case,' said John. He leaned back in his chair and linked his hands behind his head, as if the subject were now closed to any further discussion.

Conor fetched more wine from the fridge and replenished glasses. I decided it was time for some music and got up to find our iPad. I'd recently added Amber Coffman's *City of No Reply* album to the playlist and put *Nobody Knows* on, not too loud, just enough to soothe the tone of the conversation. It didn't. Amber Coffman was no match for Chrissy's intransigence.

'All I'm saying is what a lot of people are saying, that enough is enough.' Chrissy's jaw tightened and she exhaled loudly, blowing out a last plume of thick smoke before stubbing out the cigarillo, even though she'd only just lit it.

The mood became a little strained and for an awkward moment no one said anything.

'Chrissy may have a point,' said Janet, ever the diplomat. 'We

42

might ask the Aborigines what they think and I wouldn't blame them one little bit if they told the whole lot of us to clear off.'

'And take our rubbish with us,' I said.

'And of course, if there were fewer of us, we might get better service.'

'Amen to that. I was put on hold for forty minutes the other day, forced to listen to some juvenile on the radio caterwauling inanely about her love life. God, I hate that drivel.'

'And nor does connection always lead to communication. They're all from India or somewhere equally incomprehensible.'

'Are we back to discussing nativism?'

'"When I use a word," Humpty Dumpty said, "it means just what I choose it to mean – neither more nor less,"' recited Chrissy.

Steve finished the quote: '"The question is," said Alice, "whether you can make words mean so many different things."' He twirled his glass until its contents slid perilously close to the rim and then raised his eyebrows genially at Chrissy as if to say: here we are then, the two of us, kindred spirits.

There was obviously a spark between them and I could see Chrissy unbend under Steve's admiration. I was tempted to remind her that he was married, and to my best friend. Just as I was wishing Lauren was with us, Steve's phone jiggled on the table. He glanced at the screen. 'Lauren,' he said. 'I better take it.' He picked up his phone and went into the kitchen to talk to his wife.

'When I finally got through to the call centre at the bank yesterday,' continued Janet, 'the girl on the other end told me I'd have to phone back on Tuesday, that she wouldn't be able to call me because her mum was having knee surgery and she was taking the day off. Why tell me that? For all she knew, I was going into hospital myself, for a last futile dose of chemotherapy.'

'Or electric shock treatment,' said Chrissy and with a perfectly straight face she added: 'Alexandra knows all about that sort of therapy, don't you Lexi?'

Where did that come from? Why say such rubbish? I smarted from Chrissy's remark because who doesn't understand the power of words? Put them out there and they stick, whether or not they're true. No one cares about truth any more. But I wasn't going to let my disquiet show. 'Ever the tease, my sister,' I said loudly, 'and I hereby declare her comment fake news.'

'Speaking of banks,' said Janet, moving the subject back to safer ground, 'soon my mother won't even be able to write a cheque.'

'God, who uses those any more?' I couldn't resist the opportunity to put a little heat back on Chrissy, and, thinking of that National Bank cheque book in her room, asked her pointedly: 'I know Peter's old-fashioned, but do you guys use cheques? Or share an account?'

If my remark hit home, Chrissy showed no sign, not so much as a slight frown. What had I expected? That she'd blush? She ignored my question and instead pushed her chair back and stood up, just as Steve returned to the room. 'Why don't I make coffee,' she said. 'Want to give me a hand, Steve?'

The rest of us carried on complaining about the decline in customer service until Chrissy returned with coffees for most of us and a peppermint tea for Janet. She then offered Steve one of her skinny cigars and suggested they go outside together to smoke. Steve doesn't smoke but went with her anyway.

The party lasted another hour until just after midnight when Janet and John left.

Conor and I left the debris of the party for the morning and went to bed. We didn't see Chrissy again that night but we heard her. First it was Steve, keeping his voice low, then Chrissy who didn't. Then silence for a while until we heard the tell-tale rhythmic banging of the sofa-bed against the wall.

I prodded Conor. 'She's sleeping with him. Conor, are you listening to me? My sister is having it off with Steve.'

'Doesn't matter,' mumbled Conor. 'Go to sleep.'

It so mattered. My sister had no compunction about taking my best friend's husband into her bed and I'm not a prude, but I do have some moral scruples. And what about Steve? He and Lauren were Catholics. They went to St Joseph's most Sundays and presumably to weekly confession as well. What happened to 'Thou shalt not commit adultery'? How many Hail Marys would Steve have to recite to square this offence against the sixth commandment? If it were up to me, I'd have him on his knees scrubbing the entire nave of St Mary's Cathedral with a bald lavatory brush.

Chrissy's love-making was uninhibited. She was a bear on heat and at one point actually growled like one, a long low throaty vibration. If her intention was to advertise what a great time she was having, or how good she was in bed, it was wasted on me. I nudged Conor again. 'What on earth will I say to Lauren?'

'Nothing. You don't always have to control everything, Lexi.'

We both lay staring at the ceiling while from next door the evidence of sexual exertion reached a reverberating crescendo.

'Why did she say that stuff about you having shock therapy? You haven't, have you, Lex?'

'What do you think?' I closed my eyes and took a few mindful breathes, slow and deep. 'She was trying to be funny. God knows why. She never used to be like that.'

I couldn't see any reason why Chrissy should start teasing me and hoped it didn't become a habit. Maybe I'm the only one who thinks this way but, to me, teasing is always at someone else's expense, and always corrosive.

'She's got a chip on her shoulder I never saw before. Why do you suppose that is? Conor?'

There was no answer. 'Conor, are you listening?'

He wasn't. My husband was sound asleep, snoring slightly.

'Does she think I can't see those sneaky little insults in her silly jokes?' I reached across my bedside table and turned the light off. 'Anyone would think she resented me, which is absurd.'

10

It was dawn and barely light when I heard Steve get up and leave the house. I lay in bed and waited while Chrissy closed the front door after him, used the bathroom and returned to her room. I slipped out of bed myself then and, still in my pyjamas, cleaned up after the party.

I crept about, taking the empty bottles out to the recycling bin in the back yard, carrying plates and glasses from the dining table to the kitchen bench, washing them in the sink, wiping everything down, moving around as noiselessly as I could so as not to wake Conor or prompt Chrissy to get up and help. I preferred to do the job alone; cleaning up after a party is one of those tasks more efficiently done without too many hands, and the activity stopped me from thinking too much.

After I finished tidying up, I had a long hot shower and dressed in loose track pants and a tee. It was seven-thirty. Conor was still asleep. I left a glass of orange juice on his bedside table, picked up my sketchbook and pencils, and, soundless as a mousing cat, left the house.

Not only did I want some time alone, I also didn't particularly want to be there when Chrissy got up. Even though my relationship with Steve was superficial, my friendship with his wife was anything but, and his staying over put me in an awkward position. What would I say to Lauren? And of more immediate concern, what the hell could I say to Chrissy? Would she behave as if nothing untoward had happened? I knew the answer was yes before I'd even finished asking the question.

Well, two could play at that game.

I wouldn't say anything either. Wasn't it Rumi who said: Now I shall be silent, and let the silence divide that which is true from that which lies?

My autopilot kicked in and took me up to Glebe village where I caught a bus into town. I got off at St James Station, crossed Hyde Park and went up Prince Albert Road to the art gallery. I was the first one through the door when they opened and I spent more than two hours there, lingering in front of my favourite painting – Ralph Balson's *Girl in Pink* which I find perfectly dreamy – then over a cup of tea in the cafeteria where I doodled for a while in my sketch book before settling into a serious study of a family of Japanese tourists. The result was a fairly decent drawing, so the morning wasn't entirely wasted.

I tried not to think about Chrissy but my subconscious kept chewing at it all until what came to the surface was a decision to just stop worrying about it, or her. Chrissy was Chrissy and I wasn't her keeper. Conor was right: even if it were possible for me to do so, I couldn't control everything. At the same time, it was impossible not to feel irate with my sister for abusing my hospitality. That's what I primly believed she'd done. By sleeping with Steve, she'd debased herself and, in the process, my home.

After leaving the gallery, I walked home, picking up my pace until after twenty minutes I broke into a run and kept running until I reached Glebe Point Road and my clothes were drenched with sweat.

When I got home it was after midday. There was a note from

Conor on the kitchen bench. 'Having lunch at Badde Manors. See you there.'

See who there? Conor? Or Conor and Chrissy? Only a few minutes earlier I'd jogged past the café, on the other side of the road. Had they seen me? And if they had seen me, why not give me a wave?

I left the note where it was and made myself some toast, slathered it with hummus, and brewed a pot of chamomile tea.

Then I went online and looked up medical conferences in South America. There was one, or had been one, in Rio de Janeiro, a week-long conference in early April. That was two weeks before Chrissy had arrived to stay so telling me that's where Peter was had been a lie. What else had she lied about? Had she quit her job or had they given her the boot? If she and Peter had finally split, why not just say? And if Peter's cheque book was in our house in Glebe, where was Peter?

11

At work, the pile of projects on my desk never seemed to get any smaller, the files littered with an accumulation of red fluorescent post-it notes. They had to wait. The agency owed me a mental health day and I decided to take it. I texted Barry and hoped he'd appreciate it was the first time in years that I'd taken a sickie.

Conor was always slow getting ready for work in the mornings which usually didn't bother me. His timetable was his and mine was mine and we set off for work at different times, Conor at seven-thirty to catch a bus while I left at eight or eight-fifteen to walk into the CBD. That morning, when I took a sickie, Conor's slowness was exasperating because I wanted to get away, without him knowing where I was going, and before Chrissy was up.

Whenever we were due to go out somewhere it was always me who waited for Conor to get ready. His sluggishness on those occasions was painful. I'd be dressed and ready to leave while he was still dickering with the contents of his wardrobe and if I had to wait too long – sometimes it was as long as twenty or thirty minutes – the momentum of the outing would sag like a deflating balloon and with it, my anticipation.

At seven-fifteen, Conor was still trying to decide between a white business shirt and bluey tie with his charcoal suit, and an almost indecipherably striped shirt, open at the neck, with an inky blue blazer that was vaguely tweedy.

'Any meetings with clients today?'

'No.'

'Then hang loose and wear the blazer.' He looked great in that blazer, a young Samuel Beckett.

Conor always bought new and, while he never said, I could tell he had to make an effort to accommodate my insistence on buying only second-hand clothes. Maybe he was waiting for me to grow out of my wardrobe recycling, but no chance.

He went with the suit. He often asked for my advice and then did the opposite. I fell for it every time and every time I'd be convinced that if I'd told him to wear the suit, he'd have put the blazer on. Who says men aren't contrary? That morning I was too preoccupied to feel cross. I was taking the car and driving to Katoomba, to find Peter.

At last Conor left. Chrissy, mercifully, was still in bed. I threw my warmest jacket and thickest woollen scarf into the car and set off for the Blue Mountains. If Peter was there, I'd talk to him, find out what was really going on, maybe bring about a reconciliation if that was what was needed. If Peter wasn't there, then maybe his daughter Sophie would be and I could talk with her.

It felt good to be out of the city for a change and on the open road. The sky over the Great Western Highway was pearly grey and vast and when I put my foot down on the accelerator to pass first one truck, then another, I had to concede Conor had been right to blow some of our savings on a decent SUV. It hadn't taken much to persuade me to contribute and I was only too happy to trade in our old Toyota. I like nice cars, especially fast European ones, and I appreciated the Audi's power almost as if it were my own.

No one knew my plans for the day. I'd said nothing to Conor and that was sort of fine, but guilt at going behind Chrissy's back swelled in me a little, like an incipient boil. I had to keep pushing from my mind something Mum once said: if you can't talk openly about what you're doing then maybe you shouldn't be doing it. The whiff of Mum's counsel pervaded the car like ripe cheese. I turned on the radio to blank it out, searching through the stations until I found Smooth FM.

Ignoring my hunger was more difficult. I'd skipped breakfast and at Lawson nearly stopped at a service station to buy something to eat, but was afraid that if I even so much as paused, I might change my mind about the whole venture and turn back to Sydney.

I switched stations to The Edge. *Bohemian Rhapsody* came on and I turned up the volume and sang along.

Funny how the right words often come along just when you need them.

Queen's lyrics bolstered me and I kept going, slowing a little near Wentworth Falls to take in the view and remember to breathe. The Blue Mountains cover more than two and half thousand square kilometres and when you're there in that hinterland you can almost forget that the country was ever colonised. It's one of those places that make you want to stop talking, where Conor and I have walked far enough to start hearing what the silence has to say, to fill our lungs with pure air, and feel inspired by the vista of Kings Tableland and the Jamison Valley.

There were no cars in front of me and for about fifteen minutes I exceeded the speed limit. By mid-morning I was in the centre of Katoomba which was bustling with tourists. I stopped briefly to buy coffee and a sandwich before carrying on to the western outskirts of town where Chrissy and Peter lived on a two-acre block. I'd always held the view that my sister had the best of both worlds: a roomy home in a rural idyll and my place in Sydney to visit whenever she needed an urban fix.

Maybe Chrissy didn't it see it that way. Maybe she was one of those unenviable types for whom the grass on the other side is always greener, or that, while I believed she had everything a woman

51

could possibly want, the reality for her was that she was disappointed with the way life had turned out. I hoped this wasn't the case. I'd read enough novels – stories of unrequited love, and of thwarted ambition – to know that disappointment frequently leads to trouble.

12

After pulling into the drive, I turned off the ignition and sat looking at the Eversons' house. It was a single-storey white and grey wooden bungalow with a deep covered veranda along the front. To the right was a grey wooden fence, a garage and behind that, a cedar shed which Peter had converted into his office.

Cold air bit me when I got out of the car. Katoomba is nearly nine hundred metres above sea level and as I walked up the path to the front door, gravel and twigs crunching under my feet, the place felt arctic. I put my jacket on, zipped it up to my neck, and wrapped my scarf tightly around the lower half of my face.

I made a quick recce of the property. There didn't seem to be anyone around. There was no sign of Peter or Sophie, or of Peter's dog, and no answer when I knocked on the door. When I tried the handle, it was locked. I went around the side of the house, looking in all the windows, but the place was empty.

Peter's office was locked as well. I wiped dust off the window with the side of my hand and peered through it to see inside. Peter's old Olivetti was there but uncovered which was unusual. I knew Peter to be tidy almost to the point of obsessive compulsion. If he were away for even half a day, he'd put the cover on his precious typewriter.

Chrissy ribbed him for not getting a computer, but Peter said using the Olivetti helped him pace his work. He said it stopped his typing getting ahead of his thinking, and it was what he always used to produce a first draft.

He was as old-fashioned about that typewriter as he was about still using a cheque account for his business expenses.

There was no sign of the laptop he took with him when he was on a job somewhere. He must have returned home from that conference in Rio and gone away again almost immediately.

There were no cars around either. Sophie drove an old white Corolla but it wasn't in the driveway and Peter's Volvo wasn't in the garage.

I walked through a coppice of gum trees to the swimming pool.

Time seemed to slow down, as if I were walking through a foreign town, somewhere I'd never been before, and unsure of my way. The silence of the trees around me was suddenly oppressive. The pool hadn't been covered for winter and was full of leaves and rotting sprigs and rubbish, but I saw Chrissy had got her way at last and the area along one side of the pool was newly paved and furnished with faux wicker chairs. An old yellow beach towel had been left out and was mouldering on a square white plastic table.

Chrissy's herbaceous border along the drive was overgrown and gone to seed.

It had been almost a year at least since Conor and I had last visited Chrissy and Peter and there were other changes as well as that new area by the pool. A row of eucalypts on the south boundary had been cut down for firewood which was stacked in a stockage along the fence. Someone had begun replanting the area with trees I didn't recognise. They might have been a variety of ash or maybe birch. There are times – this was one of them – when I regret not paying more attention to Mum's tutelage; she knew the names of all the trees and shrubs and flowers. There were mounds of freshly dug soil and a dozen saplings already in the ground. Nearby a spade was propped against a wheelbarrow full of more seedlings which had turned brown and brittle and were probably dead.

I wandered back towards the house. The whole property looked as if it suffered from a mental illness. There was a sorrowful undertone. Something felt wrong and I was peeved with Chrissy for not being straight with me. She was my sister. We should be able to talk about things. Chrissy's obfuscation. Peter's absence. His cheque book. It was a struggle not to put two and two together and find them adding up to something sinister.

I went back to where the saplings had been planted. They were held in place with those skimpy plastic stakes you get from garden shops. I knelt down and dug around under some of the trees. Their roots hadn't yet taken hold and the ground was wet with recent rain. I grabbed the spade and turned over the clumps of dirt but there was nothing to find and I felt bit of an idiot for letting my imagination get the better of me.

In the trees, a kookaburra chuckled and its hilarity perked me up a little.

I came to my senses and told myself to stop being so mistrustful. It was not impossible that Peter had had to leave in a hurry. He was often called away on an assignment with very little notice. And presumably Sophie was at work during the day and socialising at night. She was twenty-two after all and unlikely to have much interest in gardening or keeping the house clean for her step-mother. I wished I had her phone number or email address. I considered leaving a note for her but decided she'd probably think I was being indiscreet, or resent my meddling.

My boots sank into the soggy ground as I stomped back over the mound and between the saplings, packing down the dirt I'd displaced and hoping the roots weren't irreparably damaged.

During another circuit of the house I peeked in all the windows again. They were old wooden casement windows and I tested each one to determine whether or not a stay was loose enough for me open. One was. I eased my hand through and prised the stay off its catch, swung the window open and climbed inside.

I was in Sophie's bedroom. Very tidy. She'd inherited her father's fastidiousness. The single bed was made, tucked in with hospital corners, and an assortment of toiletries was neatly arranged on a desk near the window and, apart from a pair of sports shoes by the wardrobe, there was nothing on the floor. On the bedside table there was a Samsung tablet, a book of short stories by David Malouf, and a framed picture of Sophie's mother.

All I knew about Peter's first wife was that her name was Madeleine, that she'd been a journalist like him, and died of ovarian cancer when Sophie was still a toddler. It was about three years after Madeleine's death that Peter met Chrissy. The photo was black and white, and arty, the backdrop muted to create only a suggestion of trees and lawn so that Madeleine took your eye and held it. She was sitting on what looked like an old apple crate and with her profile to the camera. She had a slightly turned up nose and was smiling, just enough to show a dimple in her cheek, and her dark hair was drawn away from her face in a chignon. She wore capri pants and an open-necked blouse, and exuded an air of refinement. As I examined the photo, I fancied Madeleine turning to face the camera, to acknowledge me and say: 'I am still here.' I resisted the urge to be nosy, take the photo out of its frame and see if there was anything written on the back.

A sudden crack outside made me jump. I leapt up from the bed where I'd been sitting and stood to one side of the window and snuck a glance outside, thinking someone had arrived, but there was no-one. When I looked out properly, I saw that a large dry branch had broken away from a eucalypt and fallen to the ground.

Trees crowded the house on three sides and I wondered why Peter hadn't taken them down. They kept the house cool in summer, but the risk of fire storms in Katoomba was an ever-present threat and living with all those trees would have made me nervous.

I smoothed the bedspread where I'd been sitting, left Sophie's room, and moved quickly through the rest of the house, in a hurry now to leave. There were two other bedrooms, one unused and the other, the master bedroom where Peter and Chrissy slept. I didn't do much more than look in from the doorway. It was motel-room spruce but the air was stale, as if months had passed since anyone had occupied it.

All those empty rooms seemed under a pall, and dreary.

As I passed the living room, I noticed a mobile phone on a side table. I went in and picked it up, tried to turn it on but the battery was flat. I stashed it in my pocket and left the house.

I was nearly back at Lawson when I changed my mind about the phone, turned the car around, drove back to the house and put it back where I found it. Breaking and entering was one thing, larceny was another and things were bad enough without my turning into a felon.

Sneaking around someone's else's home, even it did belong to family, had turned me into someone I didn't know, someone I didn't like, and it filled me with self-disgust. It took me an hour to shake off this feeling.

When I got to Parramatta Road, I pulled over and parked the Audi next to Victoria Park. My muscles felt tight after the long drive and I was tense. I got out of the car and walked briskly at a steady pace three times around the perimeter of the park and waved my arms about to get the blood moving. At one point a dog appeared from nowhere, part setter and the rest bitzer. For a while he trotted along beside me and I pretended he was mine before I heard a beckoning whistle from somewhere behind me and he scampered off to join his owner.

I felt better for the walk. Walking always soothes me. The sheer monotony of putting one foot in front of another, a motion that requires no thought and which soon takes on the rhythm of a mantra, frees my mind and I experience a liberating sort of detachment.

Sometimes at work, when I'm stuck for ideas, I'll leave the agency and go for a walk around the block, taking a notebook with me, and every time, within ten or fifteen minutes, ideas come to me. It's as if the act of walking itself is all that's needed to quieten the day's clamour enough for clarity to shine through.

By the time I got back into the Audi it was dark, but there was still time to get home before Conor. It was a Wednesday. He always went to the gym after work on Wednesdays and sometimes after that, to a pub with his mates for an hour.

As for Chrissy, she might be home or she might not. It wouldn't have surprised me to learn she'd sussed out Conor's drinking hole and met him there, casually. A coincidence, she'd claim. Just passing, I could hear her say, and saw you through the window. Even if there wasn't one.

The lights across Darling Harbour bounced off the water and twinkled, as if to reassure me and tell me that all was well with the world.

13

My anxiety over what was happening at home was bleeding into stress at work. Three weeks went by and I hadn't finished the packaging designs for our new client. Barry paced up and down in front of my desk.

'Not like you to miss a deadline, Lexi. What's up?'

'I've got a lot on.' I hadn't slept well the night before and was feeling so shattered that a kind word right then might have made me cry, although I needn't have worried; kind words rarely made an appearance in Barry's vocabulary.

'Don't stuff this up,' he said. 'You've got three days or we risk losing the most lucrative account we've picked up in a year.'

Barry picked up a pendulum wave toy on the desk next to mine and played with it. 'I'm holding you accountable.'

I wanted him to put the toy down, stop those metal sticks hammering each other; they might as well have been hammering me.

'Have I ever let you down, Barry? You know they'll be ready.'

For the next three days I worked from eight in the morning until seven or eight in the evening, barely stopping to eat. On two of those evenings, Marley went out and bought sushi and a bottle of lime and soda for me, and meat pies and beer for himself.

Marley Staines had been with Farras Leven almost from its inception and we'd worked together on a lot of accounts, me on the graphics and Marley writing copy. He's genius with slogans. Marley's the guy who came up with 'Drive Safe Arrive' and 'Fresh Food, Fresh You'. He's in his early fifties, with wavy brown hair streaked with grey, and steady brown eyes that make you think he's always weighing things up, filing away facts and phrases in case he needs them in the future. I've never seen him dressed in anything other than jeans and a collarless white shirt, or go anywhere without his Dell tablet. He's overweight but his corpulence didn't seem to bother him or if it did, not enough to give up beer. There was a joke in the agency that Marley's paunch always arrived at work a couple of minutes before he did, but it was always affectionately meant. We all respected Marley's talent too much to really disparage him.

He was more than a colleague to me; he was a friend, generous with his time, and always ready to share his expertise.

'Start with your slogan,' he suggested. 'Get the right catch-line and it'll set the tone. It'll energise your work too, but, hey, you already know that.'

I opened up a file on my Mac and swung the screen Marley's way to show him my initial drawings. 'I'll owe you forever.'

It took him less than a minute to come up with my slogan. 'Clever,' he said. 'That's your watchword.'

'That's all? Just 'Clever'?

'Think about it.'

'I am, I am.' And I was. It was obvious, and on the ball, and I laughed.

'How do you do it, Marley?"

Marley gave a small self-deprecating shrug. 'What's to know? The company's called Cleverly something isn't it?' He knew perfectly well it was. The client's name was B K Cleverly Holdings Ltd.

'You could call the bags Keepers, or SustainAsack though that sounds clichéd,' Marley added, 'but clients love to see their own name in lights. Either way, always good to get that "k" sound in if you can. Don't know why, but it just seems to resonate with the punters.'

'I'd kiss you Marley if I wasn't worried about health and safety.'

'Happy with my status page the way it is, thanks.' He swallowed the remaining half of a bottle of Steinlager and left me to get on with my work.

Marley didn't have a status page. I knew that much. He didn't even have a Twitter account let alone Facebook and would tell anyone who'd listen that the whole social media thing was a scourge on the planet, an end to civilisation as we know it. When I think of Zuckerberg's apparent disregard for the alarming and dehumanising consequences of Facebook, I have to concede that Marley is probably right.

The cleaners arrived as Marley left. They were a husband and wife team, Joe and Sonya Banovic, and super-efficient. My presence wasn't going to stop them getting on with their job and the drone of Sony's vacuum cleaner, followed by Joe's floor polisher, put paid to my doing any more work so I packed up and left as well.

I knew exactly how my designs should look and was determined to go the extra mile and realise my concept for making the bags irresistibly re-useable. I went over to Janet's place and borrowed her sewing machine, using the snack bags to make up a wallet, a small tote bag, and a small box as well which I reinforced with some old Christmas cards. Janet helped. She's an activist with People Against Plastic and wanted to make a difference as much as I did. The bags we came up with were all strong and bright without being tacky and I'd made sure the client's brand was prominent. I'd hoped to make a bijou kite as well, and test it in Jubilee Park, but I ran out of time. My artist's impressions would have to do.

At the end of the week I showed my work to Barry. He turned each sample over slowly and positioned them one by one in a row on his desk. Then he squeezed his thumb and forefinger against the bridge of his nose and sniffed loudly. 'You might have finished on time if you'd stuck to the brief.'

'Shouldn't we give our client options?'

'This sustainability thing is important to you, isn't it?'

'It's important to everyone. Some people just don't know it yet.'

Barry continued examining the samples and I continued talking. 'There's so much plastic out there we're absorbing it without realising. Even the poor blameless fish are forced to eat the stuff.'

Barry combed the fingers of both hands through his hair, making it even messier than usual, and gazed out the window. I waited for him to speak, but after a whole minute passed and he didn't say anything, I got impatient. 'Are you listening, Barry? It's in our food chain.'

Without looking at me, he began to fiddle with the samples, pushing them around the desk. He took the lid off the little box and filled it with paper clips.

'See?' I said. 'Even big kids will like them.'

Barry finally acknowledged my efforts. He sat back, folded his arms, tilted his head back and looked briefly at the ceiling and then at me. 'I can't guarantee it'll fly but you've done a great job, Lexi.'

'You'll back me then?'

Barry leaned back in his big black swivel chair and clasped his hands behind his head. He lifted his chin slightly in what may or may not have been an affirmative nod. 'Leave it with me.'

14

When Chrissy had first arrived and I'd assured her she could stay as long as she wanted, I'd presumed that we'd pick up where we last left off, spending at least one full day each weekend together exploring boutiques downtown, trying on clothes some of which Chrissy would most certainly buy, or we'd discover a new café and linger there companionably over flat whites and paninis.

We did resume a few of these activities, but only briefly. During the early weeks of her stay with us, there was the odd day now and then when we wandered through the Paddington markets or perused second-hand bookshops together. She gave me one of those new cashmere cardigans too, saying the colour suited me better than it did her. This wasn't true. The cardigan was shamrock green, Chrissy's favourite colour, but I wasn't going to argue. It was gorgeous and I was stoked to get the gift, regarding it as validation of Chrissy's big-sisterly affection for me.

Those were the good days. On the bad days, Chrissy was aloof and treated me as if I had no place in her life any more. I didn't know which woman was the real Chrissy. Perhaps I never had. Perhaps I was expecting something that had never been there.

And yet, we'd once been close.

When I was a little girl, Chrissy sewed my costumes and painted my face for school pageants. One year I was Émile in *Émile and the Detectives*, another, Cinderella. Chrissy in those days had been my fairy godmother and I adored her.

In her bedroom in our house in Bendigo, there was a narrow glass-fronted cabinet, every shelf crammed with a beguiling medley of big girls' stuff: nail polish, eye shadow, mascara, lipstick, perfume, and she let me, under strict supervision, try it all. She also let me delve in her wardrobe, a soft enticing muddle of so many clothes I could never tell where one garment ended and the next began.

In Bendigo, she'd often go into town and try on clothes, examining the style and cut, then buy fabric and make them for herself at a fraction of the cost. I'd lounge on her bed and watch as she fitted an unfinished dress, tucking it in here, taking it up there, arranging the fabric over her hips and her breasts, before turning to the mirror to assess the result. She never minded my being there and sometimes let me help. After confirming first that my hands were clean, she showed me how to make a dart, to fit a zip, and pin up a hem while she stood on a chair and turned slowly round and around, like the rotating ballerina on a music box.

The first thing I always did when I got home from the agency was change out of my work clothes, which were whatever I'd managed to find in op shops smart enough for the office: a dress that had had only one owner, or tailored trousers and blouse, with a jacket still in fashion. I'd kick off my heels and put on something slouchy, usually jeans and a t-shirt. I need to be in old sloppy clothes before I can really relax.

Chrissy was different. She could wear chic gear all the time and appear both decorous and comfortable, regardless of the time of day or what she was doing. She was wearing her green sheath dress when I found her back in the garden one evening, finally filling the herb box Conor had made. Her only concession to the grubbiness of the task was to put that old chequered shirt of Conor's on over her dress, and don a pair of gardening gloves. The herbs she'd bought in her first week with us were long dead, but she'd gone back to the garden centre that day and purchased more.

For a few minutes I watched her through the kitchen window. She picked up a stick and began measuring out how much space she'd need between each seedling. The action brought back another memory from Bendigo.

When Chrissy left home, I helped our mother clean out her bedroom, hoping she'd left some of her clothes behind but there wasn't much, only a couple of pilled jumpers, some old shoes, and a frumpish dress in floral cotton that Miss Marple might have worn. It took us no time at all to stuff these things into a couple of Council rubbish bags and dump them in the boot of Mum's car, ready for the nearest charity shop.

What remained was bizarre. Rulers. There were hundreds of them, tied in bundles of twenty or thirty and stuffed into every available space: the wardrobe, low cupboards on either side of the bed, and in the four deep drawers of Chrissy's old desk.

Once I'd recovered from the surprise of that insane find, I was faced with the startling knowledge that my big sister had plundered her way all through high school. Mum pulled in her bottom lip and bit down on it, something she always did when she was nursing mordant thoughts.

'Did you know?' I asked.

'I'm not a helicopter parent, as you know. What my children keep in their own rooms is their business.'

Mum went to find more bags for the rulers while I began piling them all into a heap on the bed. It was an impressive hoard. I picked up one of the bundles, untied the string around it and let the strips of wood and plastic fall on the floor at my feet and all over the bed. They were nearly all marked in some way, most with the initials of the real owner carved in the wood or inked on the plastic, and with doodles and drawings in dark blue or black ink. Some of the wooden ones sported Robbie's name, the letters roughly gouged. I began to imagine the stories that each ruler might tell and for about half a day considered the potential they offered for some sort of art project, not that I could do it at school or show it there. I envisaged a wall panel of some sort, rows of those rulers, each with its own story, arranged in flowing waves. It was tempting, but lying in bed that night I changed my mind; the sooner Mum got rid of those rulers the better.

The sound of the front door closing brought me back to Glebe. Conor came into the kitchen, took off his jacket and draped it over the back of a chair. He came up behind me and planted a kiss on my neck. I told him about the rulers.

He pushed back his hair – it was the one part of him he struggled to keep neat – and wrinkled his nose. 'Should I inspect the wine rack before she leaves?'

'No need to take the moral high ground,' I said, 'or have you forgotten the brass candlestick you lifted from that bistro in Canberra?'

'One teensy memento does not a criminal make. A few hundred is obsessive. I'm now beginning to think your sister may not be entirely normal.'

'Don't be unkind. It was yonks ago. She's probably doesn't even remember. And don't you dare say anything.'

Conor spread his arms and opened his hands to indicate compliance. I knew he didn't really mean what he said about Chrissy, and that if my sister did filch our wine, he wouldn't give it a second thought. Conor is a man who invariably sees the best in people.

He took a beer from the fridge, picked up his jacket, and left the room.

Why the hell rulers? What had Chrissy seen in them that she coveted? If it had been me casing classrooms like the Artful Dodger, I'd have snaffled pens or crayons, useful things, but I'm not Chrissy. For all I know she fantasised about giving some of the teachers a good whack with those rulers, or maybe inflicting an unexpected blow on the knuckles of a girl she didn't like. Maybe my sister subconsciously saw in them instruments of control. Don't they say that children in disturbed households develop an overbearing need to control? Not that I'm saying Chrissy and I came from a disturbed household, but isn't that what people say? That kids who are troubled in some way will shout and bite and cut if they must, to maintain control of the people around them, and their environment, without understanding of course, that they've failed miserably to gain control of themselves.

I've long forgotten what we did with the rulers, if I ever knew. Mum probably burned them in the garden incinerator, along with her rose clippings. We never referred to them again.

Through the window Chrissy was transplanting mint into a large clay pot, pressing in the dirt around the plant with her knuckles. She'd always liked gardening and she looked happy. I poured wine for us both and went out to join her.

'You must miss your garden at home,' I said.

She didn't immediately acknowledge my presence, instead looking around for a place to put the pot.

'It needs you,' I said.

'What are you talking about?' Chrissy placed the pot on a stack of old bricks under the kitchen window. She frowned and the happiness I'd glimpsed on her face, or thought I had, was gone.

'Your garden. I've seen it,' I said. Better I told her, rather than someone else. I might have been seen, by a neighbour for instance. 'I went up to your place, to see Peter. He wasn't there.'

'Why would you do that? I told you he was away.' Chrissy's voice, usually a pleasant alto, was like sand-paper, as if tar from all those cigarillos had finally accumulated to the point of impairing her vocal cords. She didn't look at me, intent instead on digging a hole at one end of the herb box and planting coriander in it.

'That conference in South America was finished ages ago. I googled it,' I said.

'What gives you the right to think this is any of your business?'

'Just want to help, that's all.'

She straightened up, took the wine I offered and perched on the rim of the herb box. She gave me a brief hard stare. 'He moved out, ages ago.'

'Why didn't you say? And he'll be back, won't he? You always patch things up.'

'Not this time.'

'What happened?'

'He met someone. Whatever.' Chrissy's attitude was cursory, as if to suggest my interest in her affairs was puerile, and this irritated me. She was the one being childish.

'What will you do?' I asked.

'Get a job I expect. I'm broke. Peter has cancelled our joint account.'

In retrospect, that was my opportunity to mention that I'd seen Peter's cheque book among her possessions. What do they say about zero tolerance? If you put a stop to the minor misdemeanours, the bigger ones are less likely to happen? But telling her I'd seen Peter's cheque book meant admitting I'd been prying in her room and god knows where that confession would lead; I hoped she'd never find out I'd actually broken into her house on my visit to Katoomba, and, worse, snooped through the rooms. Still, if I'd asked her about those cheques, or, more crucially, taken her to task over sleeping with my best friend's husband, things might not have escalated.

'You won't mind, will you, if I stay on a bit longer.' It wasn't a question, as it hadn't been a question the first time she asked. Chrissy took up another black plastic planter pot and squeezed it hard to loosen the seedling for planting.

15

Conor was getting antsy about the length of Chrissy's stay. We were preparing for bed and he was standing at the window, waiting for her to finish in the bathroom.

'It's becoming somewhat crowded here.'

'I can hardly chuck her out.' And there it was. Just as I'd earlier predicted, I was afflicted – this is the only word for it – by an infantile need to please both my sister and my husband, even when it should have been clear to me that this might well result in making all three of us unhappy.

'Why not? You don't owe her anything and whatever's going on with Pete, it's time she went home and sorted it out.'

'She's my sister.'

I'd been expecting this conversation and had resolved to discuss the matter calmly, to show Conor that I understood his point of view, because of course I did, but it was hard not to get defensive. Chrissy was my sister and any decisions about her staying or not staying in our house should be mine to make.

'What if she wasn't?' asked Conor.

'What's that supposed to mean?'

'Imagine you're not related. Would you still want her here?'

'You mean you don't.'

'Since you mention it, no, I don't.'

'You never said. I thought you liked Chrissy.'

'I do …' he began, 'but … you know. How long is this going to go on for? She's even got Sophie sending on her mail.' Conor put his arms around me but I shook him off. 'See what I mean?' he said. 'The longer she's here, the more uptight you get.'

I didn't answer.

'Lex, we haven't made love in weeks.'

He was right. Our joy in each other was dwindling and I didn't know how to revive it, and his words made me feel suddenly, desperately sad.

'Maybe you're too close to Chrissy to see what she's really like,' he said. 'Have you thought of that?'

'Are you suggesting I don't know my own sister? Do give me some credit.'

Bedtime is never a good time for difficult conversations. Conor was about to say something else, but I shook my head at him, expecting him to get the message that I didn't want to discuss it further. He didn't get the hint.

'At least she's up for it …'

'My god,' I interrupted, 'you fancy her. Is that what all this about?'

I could swear I saw my husband blush and it came to me why: his reason for wanting Chrissy to leave was to remove temptation. Could that be it? And would he give in to that temptation if she wasn't my sister? I banished these thoughts before I gave them oxygen, before I gave into any inclination myself, to voice them.

'It *is* possible to admire someone of the opposite sex without needing to fall into bed with them,' said Conor. 'Don't pretend you haven't felt the same way. Anyway, whatever my views about your sister might be, they have nothing to do with the effect she's having on you. On us.'

Point taken.

Chrissy finished in the bathroom and went to her room. She put some music on, Chris de Burgh singing *The Long and Winding Road*. I love that song but not when I want to go to bed and never so loud. I poked my head out the door and shouted at her to turn it down. I regretted loaning her my Bluetooth speaker.

'I'll talk to her. It's not easy talking to her these days, she's got so prickly. I have to find the right moment.' This in a murmur so low it was barely audible. It was all crackers; Conor and I were whispering in our own house while my sister didn't care how much racket she made.

'Good.' Conor went to the bathroom to clean his teeth. When he came back, I was already in bed and he snuggled against me. 'I want *us* back, the way we used to be.'

And so did I, more than anything. When he put his arms around me again, I turned and wrapped my legs around him and pulled him close. We kissed lightly, then gazed at one another as if we'd each forgotten what the other looked like, before kissing again, slowly this time, and deeply.

We made love and then lay side by side, relaxed and content. I moved my hand lazily back and forth across Conor's chest and savoured a lovely sense of peace, and the knowledge that I was in the right place.

16

The succeeding Saturday, Conor and I returned home from the markets to find Chrissy in the living room taking up the hem of a dress I'd been meaning for ages to shorten. It was an Ellery dress, burgundy crepe with bell-shaped sleeves, which I'd found in St Vinnies, practically new. I'd been really pleased with the find and had shown it off to Chrissy in the early days of her stay. I'd never got past the point of pinning up the hem.

Conor went out again immediately, to meet a mate, he said. As he left, he gave me a meaningful look, as if to say: now's your moment, make sure you take it.

All very well for him. Chrissy wasn't his sister. He'd have been surprised to know the extent of the emotional muddle I was in, and how unhappy I was that the sisterly feelings I'd once shared with Chrissy, or believed we did, were sliding away, into a bottomless, fathomless well. Day after day, I was doing my best to salvage some affection between us, even as our conversations became more and more acerbic.

Watching Chrissy sew made me think again of our mother who'd been an excellent seamstress. 'I still miss Mum,' I said.

'She didn't want you. You know that, don't you?'

Her words skidded across my consciousness, slithery as mercury and just as lethal.

'That's not true and you know it.'

Chrissy picked up a spool of dark red thread, snipped a length from it, then licked one end before easing it through the eye of her needle. 'You weren't an after-thought so much as an after-shock. She told me once that she never got over it.'

'Mum loved me.'

'Do you know how whiny that sounds?'

'I just don't know why you'd say such a vile thing.'

'Mum resented you and if you haven't figured it out by now, I can't help you.

'Why have you become so combative, Chrissy? We used to have good times together.'

'You're imagining things.'

'No, I'm not. Don't pretend you haven't changed.' In a vain attempt to lighten the mood I laughed but it sounded lame, even to me. 'Please would the old Chrissy come back.'

'Have you considered that it might be you who's changed?'

Conversation was pointless. I picked up the coffee mugs and went into the kitchen where I all but threw them into the sink. Part of me wanted them to break. Part of me was highly tempted to smash things up. I was pissed off with Chrissy and after washing the mugs and putting them away, I returned to the living room, determined to extract from her some fellow feeling, something at least halfway familial.

'If you can find it in yourself to be straight with me for just five minutes, tell me about Robbie at least. Did he stay in the army? You don't suppose he's still there?'

'Why do you keep bringing him up? Wherever Rob is, I neither know nor care.'

'Why don't you care? And why doesn't he want to know us?'

'He's persona non-grata and that's putting it mildly.'

'Why? What did he do?'

She removed the last pin from the dress, made a few final stitches and cut the cotton. I told her I was rapt that she'd done this for me, but she shook out the dress and handed it to me in a depressingly off-hand way, as if she regretted fixing it for me. The gap between her words and her actions was so discombobulating it made me shaky.

I was living on a see-saw, one minute up and the next down.

'Robbie. What did he do?' I couldn't let it go.

Chrissy gathered her sewing materials into an orderly bundle on the sofa beside her. 'I'd really rather not talk about this, but maybe you should know.' She turned away, but not before I caught an expression of what? Solicitude, or was it pity? When she faced me again, whatever that look had been, it was gone. 'Mum found him one night, standing at the foot of your bed, staring at you. This is when you were about four. She said Rob had a rum look on his face.'

'What did she mean?'

'A funny look, I think, as in creepy.' Chrissy got up and began to move around the room, straightening magazines on the coffee table, plumping up cushions on the sofa.

'I don't believe you,' I said.

'Suit yourself, but if you want the whole sordid story, big brother Robbie is a pervert. He was masturbating while he watched you sleep. Now are you satisfied?'

'You are so making this up.'

'He tried to rape me once too. He's probably still got the scar on his face where I scratched him.' Chrissy raised her hand and made a clawing motion, meowing like a cat. Then she gave a short laugh. 'Serve him right. When I told Mum and Dad, they chucked him out. Dad filled out forms for the army and made Rob sign up.'

'No way. Is this for real?'

Chrissy shrugged in that maddening way she had. 'You asked, Lexi, I've told you. End of story.'

That's how it was, our conversations becoming more and more

like quicksand. I was never sure which of us was in more danger. Sometimes Chrissy almost convinced me that she was the one sinking and I was duty-bound to hoist her out. At other times, actually it was most of the time, it was me being sucked under, while Chrissy watched, without showing the slightest inclination to rescue me. It was doing my head in.

17

Two days later I was walking down Martin Place during my lunch break and saw Chrissy in a café having coffee with Steve. My immediate impulse was to turn around and walk back the way I'd come, or cross to the other side of the road, and tell myself I hadn't seen what I saw. Then I noticed my blue Perri Cutten overcoat draped across the back of Chrissy's chair. My favourite winter coat, probably the best op shop find I'd ever made.

'She's wearing my coat!' I texted this to Conor, adding three furious-face emojis.

'CTN.'

What did he mean, he couldn't talk now? This was important. 'She's with Steve!!' I was practically bashing my phone with indignation.

'Rest my case. C U L8R.'

Back at work I tried not to think about what I'd seen, but it was no use. I couldn't concentrate. I wouldn't have minded loaning Chrissy my coat, if she'd only asked. It was her not asking that pissed me off. I was perfectly aware that my concern was less about the coat and more about the situation with Steve. I saved my work and switched off the Mac, tidied my desk and told Marley I had to finish early, but to tell Barry, if he turned up, that I'd be in super-early tomorrow.

Usually I walk home from work which takes me thirty or forty minutes, but that afternoon I caught a cab to Glebe. It was two-thirty and I was in a hurry to get home and have the place to myself for a while before Chrissy or Conor turned up.

At our gate I discovered I'd left my keys at work and Chrissy had the spare key we usually kept hidden near the house. Bugger the woman. I wanted to scream with frustration but there was nothing for it, I had to go back to the office. I managed to stop the taxi driver before he drove off again. He regarded me curiously in his rear-vision mirror and I realised I was noisily exhaling. I stopped, then started again. Blowing air out my mouth was the only way to relieve my stress.

On the way back to Mitchell Street, we got snarled up in traffic and it was getting on for three-thirty by the time I was home again. I hurried inside and went first to my bedroom and scanned the wardrobe to see if Chrissy had appropriated anything else of mine. As far as I could tell, she hadn't. I went into her room and searched her wardrobe again. This time I inspected it closely, every shelf and every drawer. I looked under the bed. I hauled her overnight bags down from the top of the wardrobe and rifled through those as well.

There was no sign of Peter's cheque book. Maybe he'd called her out on it. He must be looking at his accounts, online presumably, seeing the withdrawals. Maybe he was okay with it.

But there was other stuff, items I did not expect to find among my sister's things: on the desk among the jumble of Chrissy's toiletries was my Italian mosaic brooch I thought I'd mislaid a few weeks before, and Conor's bottle of Bulgari aftershave I'd given him for Christmas, and the ebony clothes brush he'd inherited from his grandfather. I put the aftershave back in the bathroom and the clothes brush on the shelf in Conor's side of our wardrobe.

Then, in a flash of intuition, or maybe suspicion about my sister was now becoming second nature to me, I looked through Conor's drawers where I found a lip balm which didn't belong to me, and a pair of sage green panties which weren't mine either. For almost a full minute I stared at them, unable to make sense of what I was seeing. I walked slowly around the bed and without consciously thinking what I was doing – it was as if some deific hand was guiding mine – ran my hand around under our mattress. On Conor's side I found the matching sage green bra.

For a minute or two I couldn't move. Medusa's stare pinned me down. My sister was all snake. These were *her* things I'd found. What was the message she was sending me? That she was sleeping with Conor? I sat on the edge of our bed and thought about what to do. I was miserable and to make matters worse my left breast began throbbing. I unbuttoned my blouse and examined it; my flesh was pink and angry. This scared me. The inflammation had come out of nowhere.

I went into the kitchen and drank a large glass of iced water. As I looked through the window, I noticed the bins in the back yard, and knew then what to do. I returned to the bedroom, gathered the panties, bra, and lip balm, took them out to the back yard and threw them into the one bin we owned that was made of metal. I added newspaper and set fire to it all. The burst of flame cheered me up a little.

I decided to say nothing, not even to Conor. What would be the point? He'd put it down to female bitchiness and tell me again to boot my sister out of the house.

Conor was right of course. It was time for Chrissy to go. She was a walking talking paper shredder and her behaviour was now driving me nuts. She was going to come home, flash me that mawkish smile of hers, and act as if nothing had happened.

I decided not to remind Conor of the texts I'd sent him either, earlier in the day. I decided to do nothing at all. If Chrissy wanted to trifle with us, let her. I wasn't going to give her the satisfaction of seeing how much it bothered me.

Sometimes I thought it was all in my head, that I was imagining demons where there were none, or that there was something *I* needed to do for Chrissy if she was to be her old self again. Sometimes I even lumpishly asked myself if what Chrissy was doing was somehow my fault.

I felt like Humpty Dumpty on his wall. One day I was going to fall off.

18

Instead of confronting Chrissy as I should have done, I avoided her. The tension in the house was affecting my health. The inflammation in my breast got worse and then I broke out in boils, first on the back of my neck, then on the side of my face. I prefer to tie my hair up for work, but until those boils healed, I was obliged to wear it loose, keeping them hidden until they healed a fortnight later.

No doubt anyone observing all this would think me a sissy for not standing up for what I needed, and in my own home, but looking back I can see why I responded to my sister the way I did. Calling her out on her behaviour would have made it real and once the words are out there you can't take them back. If I said nothing, there was a chance all this ghastliness would blow over and our old ease in each other's company would be restored, with no harsh words exchanged. Nothing would have been said that might preclude future rapport.

This is why I kept up the farcical pretence that nothing was amiss.

I hadn't, strictly speaking, grown up with Chrissy and I'd only ever spent short periods of time with her. Whether or not this excuses my naivety, I don't know. Just as I can't explain why it took me so long to comprehend my sister was not like me at all, and not at all the person I'd once believed her to be.

You think you know someone. You accept that because you are siblings, raised in the same house in the same town by the same parents, you share a common view of the world, live by an identical set of values. I'd always believed Chrissy and I were similar in character as well as appearance. This is what I wanted to believe. All my life I'd clung to the notion that somewhere in the world there was a woman just like me and that if every other person on the planet let me down, she wouldn't. As my sister, she'd be the one friend I could always count on.

This had become even more important to me after our parents died.

I cast my mind back to Mum's funeral. She'd died of cancer when I was still living in Melbourne. Chrissy gave the eulogy. She talked about Mum's love of gardening, her hobby as a horticulturist, and, after she'd retired, her contribution to the community, two days a week for Oxfam, and three as a Food Services driver. Chrissy had also read out a message from Robbie who was serving in Iraq at the time. I remember clearly what his email said. 'Wish I was with you today, and of course I should be,' he'd written. 'I'm proud to be an Aussie soldier, but I'm here only because of orders. From day one of my posting, it was blatantly obvious there is nothing and no-one here to hate. It's all bonkers. Muslim men are just like me and Dad, and Muslim women my sisters and you Mum: good people, decent, and kind. I want you all to know this. Mum, you will be in my heart always.'

I had wished Robbie home so much I was practically pining for him. In the weeks following Mum's burial, my grief slid into depression. I had a part-time job, waitressing, and after the funeral just stopped going into work, avoided going out anywhere at all. I even stopped eating for a while. I didn't say anything about this to Chrissy – I wasn't talking to anyone about anything – but she must have guessed because one day, about three weeks after the funeral, she emailed me tickets to Sydney and said she'd be waiting at the

81

airport. She took a week off work from the hospital and each day for five days, we went bush walking, not talking much, just letting the forest work its magic.

It was then I decided to move to Sydney and began looking for a job there.

My sister had been my remedy then. Now she was my Gordian knot.

19

Conor went to Canberra for a meeting. It was something to do with design proposals for a public building, a sports centre, I think, and the firm Conor worked for was pulling out all its stops to get the job. I wasn't surprised they sent him to woo the client. He was good at the cosy talk, knew when and how to say the right things that inspire confidence, and he was competitive enough to work the hours that would ensure a win. That was one of the things I first appreciated about my husband, his work ethic, and the way he could turn his hand to most things, whether it was drawing up plans for an apartment block or using old bits of timber he found under the house to build a potager box in the back yard for Chrissy's vegetables.

When I came into the bedroom after breakfast that morning, Conor was zipping up his overnight bag.

'If you win this job for them, will they make you a partner?'

'The top of the food chain draws near.'

'Step four on Maslow's hierarchy?'

'C'mon Lex, think big. Step five or bust, by the end of the year.'

'Montaigne said that once you get to the top, life becomes intolerably dull.'

'And Conor Devlin says once you get to the top, bigger house with sea view makes life tolerably first-rate.'

'Don't pretend you aspire to a Vaucluse mansion. You like it here too much.'

The sports gear he wore to play squash was still in the wardrobe. I took out shorts and t-shirt and tossed them across the bed at him. 'Won't you need these? Isn't that why you are staying over?'

'Thanks, almost forgot them.' Conor folded the clothes, unzipped his bag and placed them inside.

Conor's decision to stay overnight in Canberra, to catch up with friends and play a game of squash with one of them in the morning before driving home, was my chance to have that heart-to-heart with Chrissy. I'd suggested we go out for dinner, just the two of us. She agreed and said she'd book a table. I got home from work, had a shower and changed into some casual trousers and a clean blouse. By then it was after seven and no sign of Chrissy. I didn't know which restaurant she'd booked and sent her a text to find out. She didn't reply.

By eight I gave up and changed again, this time into my pyjamas. At half past eight, I made myself some cheese on toast and by nine was in bed with a book. I was reading Ann Patchett's *Bel Canto* but my mind kept drifting away from the story, and my whole body turned slowly rigid, my chest cavity filling with lead. I dared not move for fear of being crushed by my thoughts. Was Conor really in Canberra? Was the talk of a squash game in the morning real? He'd have left his sports gear behind if I hadn't reminded him. What if he was still in Sydney, with Chrissy? I picked up my phone to call him but thought better of it. Conor would never betray me. Sometimes I wondered if he even liked my sister because there were occasions, when she came into a room, that he'd leave it.

I tried again to give the novel my full attention and for a while succeeded. Immersing myself in the terrors of a fictional siege somewhere in the back-blocks of Latin America was better than imagining Conor succumbing to Chrissy's mojo in a Sydney hotel room.

She came in very late. It must have been after midnight, around one o'clock. I was still reading, sporadically, but as soon as I heard the front door close, I put the book away and turned off the light.

There was the tinkly shatter of glass breaking, followed by a muffled expletive. It took me a few minutes to realise Chrissy wasn't alone. She'd brought someone home with her. Steve? They crashed about in the kitchen for a while and then took ages getting to Chrissy's bedroom, one or other of them bumping against the wall, and making no attempt at all to curb their laughter. They were both pissed.

Once again, Chrissy sighed and shrieked her way through sex and I wanted to get up and bang on her door, tell the pair of them to bugger off. I wished I had more gumption, that I was less Labrador and more pit bull terrier, the savage sort. It wasn't only lack of fortitude that stopped me doing something about it; I also didn't want Chrissy to know much she bugged me.

I got up and searched in my wardrobe for an old travel kit where I knew I'd left some earplugs and wedged them in my ears. They were only marginally effective.

It was dawn, barely an hour after I'd finally got to sleep, when I was woken by the click of the front door closing. I got up and went to the window to see who was leaving. I wanted to know whether or not it was Steve and was reassured to learn it wasn't. The man who stepped through our gate was young, skinny, with tousled jet hair and a blue bomber jacket slung over his shoulder. He got into a red Ford Mustang and drove away. To his credit, he didn't rev the engine.

In the light of morning, my fears about Conor and Chrissy were ludicrous. I was relieved Conor was in Canberra. My husband's composure, not to mention his ability to sleep through a Mardi Gras, would only have made me feel even more miffed. When I staggered, exhausted, into the bathroom I felt like Zenobia being dragged in chains to Rome: defeated but righteous. My face in the mirror was pale, my eyes weepy from lack of sleep. The only good thing was that my breast was no longer sore.

The mere thought of food made me want to gag and I didn't want to run into Chrissy so I skipped breakfast and left the house early. I had no idea what to say to my sister and intended disdain for anything she had to say to me. She'd stood me up over our dinner date and any excuses she gave would be lies. I fluctuated between anger and depression, never quite sure which was which.

Right then, Chrissy was a pike with my blood on the point.

How was a person to sleep with her yelping like a bitch on heat every time she came? Surely, she was faking it half the time. It's not that I particularly cared whether or not my sister picked up men and bonked them. She was single again after all, or so she said, and what she did was her affair. But did she have to bring them home to Mitchell Street, be so damn thoughtless? Would it have been too much trouble for them to go to the guy's place?

Did I just use the word thoughtless? That was wrong. Chrissy was perverse and everything she did was thought out with military bloody precision. Having sex in that rowdy uninhibited manner was deliberate. She set out purposefully to goad me.

20

My sister's behaviour towards me could only mean one thing: she no longer cared to have a relationship with me. No, it was worse than that. My sister hated me and I decided then that I might as well accept it. If I could pinpoint this painful cognisance to a single hour, I'd say it was then, at seven-thirty on 8 July. This was the hour I woke up to the trouble with Chrissy and was able to name the problem: Chrissy was a bully and I was frightened of her.

And what she'd said about our brother couldn't be the end of the story. She'd spewed so much balderdash over the past few weeks, why not this? And even if Robbie had done the things she said, it was decades ago, when he was a kid. Who doesn't do witless things when they are young? Acts that needn't necessarily define them as adults.

I don't pretend to a saintly childhood myself. Like a lot of kids, I smoked pot behind the bike shed at intermediate school, I even took ecstasy once or twice on more adventurous occasions, and when I was thirteen, I joined a school mate in a few shop-lifting expeditions. I never stole anything of any value: a couple of lipsticks, a Kit Kat, my first pair of black stockings. I was always terrified of being caught and after those brief forays into the criminal world, I grew up. Most of us do.

I decided to track down Robbie and find out for myself what had happened to him. This was not without a twinge of compunction for not having done it years earlier. The fact that he was almost unknown to me, someone I hadn't seen since I was a little kid, was no excuse. It didn't occur to me to ask why he'd never made any effort to find me.

I went online and googled him. First, I keyed in Robert Madison but nothing came up. Then I tried Rob Madison and Robbie Madison, but still nothing. Even when I keyed in Robert Madison Australian Army, nothing came up. He must have changed his name. I didn't know where else to begin looking and was unwilling to ask Chrissy. It irked me that I knew nothing about my brother, what books and music he liked, places he'd visited, what his favourite sports were and whether or not he played them. Knowing these things would have given me some pointers, but instead, I had not a single clue to go on.

Around three in the morning, it occurred to me that if Dad had packed him off to the army against his will, Robbie might well have wanted to erase the connection with our father, but he might have used Mum's maiden name.

The next day I typed in Robbie Hardy, with a prayer to any deity listening that my guess was right. And it was. There he was, on LinkedIn. I choked back an involuntary sob. If that LinkedIn listing was current, I'd found my brother.

More than twenty years had passed since we'd last seen each other and I believed I had no memory of him. I'd always presumed that I wouldn't have recognised Robbie if we found ourselves sitting next to each other at an Al Anon meeting, but I did recognise him and seeing his face on my computer screen made me so intensely happy that I laughed out loud. Add a dozen years and I was looking at a male version of me. My brother had my high forehead, even the same slight crease between the eyebrows, the same intense blue eyes. He wore a beard, cut close, and his light brown hair was streaked with grey.

Out on the street, the sudden revving of a car's engine pulled my attention away from the computer. At the same time, and out of the blue, a wave of nausea came over me. I doubled over, gripping my thighs, at the same time thinking I needed to get to the bathroom before I puked. I breathed in deeply, counting to eight, and let the air out slowly, one, two, three until I reached twelve. The nausea passed as suddenly as it had arrived, leaving me only with uncomfortable questions: what had brought it on? Something I'd eaten? Morning sickness? I prayed not. I wasn't ready for pregnancy. Conor and I had talked about kids but only as a remote event, three years away at least, and not before we fixed up the house.

The photo of Robbie absorbed my attention completely. I leaned closer to the screen to scrutinise his face. He looked thoroughly decent, not at all like a man who would abuse anyone, let alone a child or a sister. A far as I could see, and admittedly the beard didn't make it easy to tell, there was no sign of a scar on my brother's face. Chrissy hadn't scratched him.

I didn't let on to Chrissy that I'd found Robbie on LinkedIn. For all I knew, she'd had his contact details all along and chosen not to tell me. Who's to say she wasn't equally to blame for what happened when they were young? I'd seen how flirty she was and, if my brother did once try to have it off with her, it wouldn't surprise me one little bit to learn it was because she'd been the one to seduce him.

We didn't talk about Rob again. I no longer wanted to talk with Chrissy about anything and whatever she had to say about anyone in the family – Mum, Dad, Robbie, me – I didn't want to hear it. My need for someone to call 'sister' had clouded my judgement, but not any more. And I was wary too, that whatever I said to Chrissy, no matter how sympathetically I said it, she'd put an ugly spin on it.

21

Janet phoned me about a protest she was joining and asked me to go along. I was in Vinnies, searching through the designer rack, hoping to swap one of my skirts for something more up to date.

'Here's your chance to take some action,' she said. 'I'll pick you up at five.'

The protest began outside her local supermarket in Paddington. There was a clamorous assembly of all ages and the leader, a tall sinewy guy called Mike Wallims, stood on the back of a grey Ford ute facing them. 'People Against Plastic' was printed on a decal in large green letters and stuck to the side of the vehicle. The slogan was also blazoned in white paint across the back of Mike's green overalls.

He began chanting: 'plastic kills, plastic kills', his voice increasingly vociferous as more of us joined in.

The weather was perfect, late afternoon sun in a cloudless sky, and not at all cold.

A couple of men in high-vis vests arrived and started talking to Mike. I saw Mike turn and take a squiz along the street, to where two paddy wagons were parked.

'Who are those guys talking to Mike?'

'Police liaison,' said Janet. 'They always show up, but only to make sure things stay calm. They tolerate our right to protest.'

'No truncheons then?'

'Never gets to that. Once the media turn up, we've made our point. Job done.'

Someone placed a banner in my hand and propelled me into the throng.

'They say there are groups like this outside supermarkets all over Sydney,' said Janet.

'Not before time,' I said. 'Let's hope this isn't the last.'

'It's not. There's a schedule for the next three months. They'll be happening right across the city.'

We swarmed noisily at the entrance to the supermarket, then lined up in orderly rows and marched across the car park, around the block, and back to the shop. At one point a car drove past and back-fired, sounding so much like gun-shots that a ripple of alarm ran through the crowd. Memories of the hostage crisis at the Lindt Café in Martin Place a few years before went through me like a tremor and I was pretty sure everyone else around me was remembering it as well. It took a couple of minutes for our panic to subside.

Mike Wallims kept up his firm impassioned chant which in an odd sort of way both steadied and rallied us.

It was rush hour so everyone was in a hurry. Only a few people coming and going from the supermarket paused to see what we were on about. Fewer still joined us. They didn't escape unscathed though. There were five women handing out cloth bags to onlookers and they targeted people who showed the least interest, especially anyone coming out of the supermarket carrying plastic bags.

The media arrived at the same time as another group of protesters turned up. This group had a different message: anti-bank and anti-corporate greed. Their placards were smarter than ours, professionally made, and they made even more of a din than we did, making the most of the occasion to get their message in front of the cameras.

It was all thrilling. I was a headlight on high beam, back in my student days, ranting outside the vice-chancellor's office for lower fees, and I felt the same virtuous surge of power. I was an activist again, with right on my side, shouting 'No more plastic, no more plastic'.

A pimply-faced radio journalist – he had to be a cadet – stuck a microphone in front of me. 'Can I talk to you? Ask why you're here?'

'Of course.' This was an opening I wasn't going to waste. 'You might tell your listeners to stop washing.' I was being deliberately provocative and succeeded in piquing his interest. We both stopped and while Janet walked on ahead, I gave the reporter my full attention, and my views.

'What is your shirt made of?' He was wearing a navy polo shirt in some sort of stretchy fabric. 'Not cotton is it? It's probably synthetic, from China, and every time you launder it, you're polluting our rivers.'

He patted the cloth of his shirt and grinned. Then he adjusted his equipment and moved the microphone closer to my face. 'Tell me more. Do you mind?'

'Most clothes today are full of micro-plastics. You can't see it, but just about everything today, and I do mean everything, is toxic with the stuff. Even our food.'

'What's the answer?' His face was uncomfortably close to mine, so close it was hard to ignore the spots of blood where he'd squeezed his zits, and he was intense, but I appreciated his zeal.

'It's not hard, is it? More social conscience, all of us, you, me, the government, and the manufacturers, especially them. We have to start caring enough to stop this madness. Buy something and what do you get? Plastic inside plastic inside plastic. It's insane.'

I started walking again, keen now to catch up with Janet. The journalist put his microphone away but strode along beside me. 'Thanks. Can I talk to you again, if ...?'

It may have been against my better judgement but I gave him

92

my number. When he asked, I gave him my name as well and where I worked although I was deliberately vague, revealing only that I worked for an advertising agency.

22

Barry called me into his office the next morning, before I'd even found a work station for the day. He had the morning newspaper spread across his desk and was drumming on it with all four fingers of his right hand. I hadn't seen the day's news until then. The lead article was about the demonstration, and in particular, the group I'd participated in. A photo of the protesters took up almost a third of the page and there was me, slap bang in the middle of it, swinging a banner that screamed: 'PLASTIC BAG? SHAME ON YOU.'

Barry held up the paper and glowered at me. 'And you were on the radio.'

'We're killing the oceans,' I said.

'Can you not see a conflict of interest here?'

'Not necessarily.'

'Lexi, we design packaging.'

'Exactly. It puts us in a position to change things.'

Barry waggled a forefinger at me, beckoning me to his side of the desk. He pummelled his keyboard until a YouTube video filled the screen like an arraignment. Me again, arm and arm with Janet, brandishing that banner and shouting along with Mike Wallims, so loudly it looked as if my lungs might burst. We'd gone viral. Far from feeling guilty, I experienced an unwavering sense of accomplishment. The message was getting out there. Protest against plastic was growing.

Barry gave me his flinty stare. 'If you want to continue working here, you'll need to keep your personal life separate.'

'Do you know how idiotic that sounds?' I wanted immediately to bite back the words. Barry was comparatively informal as managers go, but he was still my boss.

He scowled at me and I all but backed out of his office, although not without getting in the last word. 'Two supermarket chains have already said they'll stop using single-use bags, by this time next year.'

That evening I worked late, every other minute kicking myself for calling Barry an idiot. The last thing I needed was for him to regret my promotion or think he couldn't rely on me any more, or for Gray to feel I'd let him down. The agency was practically my home away from home and while the salary could have been better, I loved working there.

By the time I left the agency at eight-forty-five, I'd pruned the bulk of my workload, answered a week's worth of emails, and drawn up a work plan for the rest of the month. My inbox was pared back enough for me to focus on further developing a sustainable packaging strategy for Cleverly Holdings. I'd never done this strategic planning work before. My skill was graphic art and I'd only recently been elevated from drawing up someone else's designs to creating my own, but I'd been more than ready to learn something new and prove myself worthy of the title creative director; I didn't want to muck it up.

Marley's slogan was already being bandied around the agency and the Clever campaign was taking on a life of its own before I'd even finished fine-tuning it. Megan was the first to start; she brought in donuts one day and when she offered them to Marley, said 'for clever bags first', and bit into one before passing him the box. 'Clever clogs, you mean?' was the riposte from the other end of the work table. And another: 'If it was you, it'd be clever *old* bag.' Then, back and forth across the work stations: 'Yay, smart sack ...' Please, a deft valise ...' Oooh, clutch me baby.' They were all mad, in the best possible way. It was a party before the invites had even gone out and this was one of the things about working at Farras Leven that I most appreciated – everyone took an interest in every account; we were a team.

I was confident the Cleverly Holdings people would like my work. After all, they must have been aware that more and more consumers were demanding change. It was in the news nearly every day. Farras Leven could help them lead that change. It would be win-win all round.

First though, I needed to get the strategy done and by the end of the week if I was to placate Barry. I messed up on both counts. This wasn't because I wasn't trying. I just couldn't concentrate and would spend a whole hour staring at my computer screen without seeing what was on it, let alone keying in any words.

Barry rapped his knuckles against the desk in a disgruntled rattle. 'You've got until close of business tomorrow,' he said. Then, to punish me for not meeting the deadline, or maybe it was because I'd participated in that protest, he handed me two more projects: to write up a treatment for TV commercials for a finance company, and prepare a proposal for a real estate firm's ad campaign.

'By the end of next week ... if you'd be so kind.' His sarcasm hurt.

'I'll work on that strategy tonight, after everyone's gone home,' I promised.

'What, you don't like being with us any more?'

'It's not that. It's the constant chatter. Bit distracting.' This was a fib. There were times when I wished the office was quieter, but mostly I enjoyed the banter out there at the Macs. What I realised in that moment talking to Barry was that it was the jabbering in my own head that was driving me mad. There was no way I would tell Barry this, or reveal to him just how stressed I was.

'Don't start feeling sorry for yourself. If you're not up to this promotion, Lexi, just give me the word. I'll put Marley in charge.'

'Give me a break.' I may have made a small tutting noise, the best I could do to convey my reproachfulness without a full-on whinge, and left Barry's office in a huff. I felt his eyes fixed on my back like those red dots you see through a rifle's laser scope.

Marley must have noticed what was going on. He stayed on after hours that day as well and when everyone had left, arrived at my desk with two coffees and a plate of Anzac biscuits. He sat down at the Mac next to me, crossed his legs and pushed the biscuits my way. 'Barry's on your tail, I see,' he said.

'He'll come round.'

'As you know, Lexi, Barry's the agency's Mr Darcy. Once his good opinion is lost, it's lost forever.'

'He's always been on my side.'

'Only because you've been on his.'

'I don't care.'

'Yes, you do. C'mon. Show us where you're up to with this job and see if we can't nail it tonight.'

'Marley, you're an angel. I'm still waiting on data from the research guys, 'specially round the costs, but you know what they told me this morning? Plastic production has gone up twenty-fold since nineteen sixty-four, and only five per cent of it actually gets recycled. The rest ends up in a landfill somewhere, and, worse, in the ocean. I mean, check these out.'

I printed out the graphics I'd done so far and handed them to Marley. One showed an island of garbage floating off California. 'I want to scare them into taking this seriously. See that island? It's a bloody disgrace.'

'More than twice the size of France, I've read.'

'And growing! Doesn't that make you want to do something? I shudder to think what it's like on the ocean floor, and I just can't believe Barry thinks this has nothing to do with us.'

'Softly, softly, my dear. Our illustrious leader won't thank you for telling him what to do.'

'What you mean is, that any brilliant ideas around here have to be his.'

'All I'm saying is, ruffle Barry's feathers at your peril.'

I wasn't listening. 'There are manufacturers out there making packaging from plants, and plant waste, so we know it can be done. We should convince our clients to do the same, that there's no need to use petrochemicals any more. If I give you the data, will you write up some copy for me?'

'Consider it done.'

With Marley's help, my presentation was very nearly complete by ten o'clock. All I needed to do was add figures from the research team to show that using sustainable materials needn't threaten the client's profit margin.

Marley took a bottle of beer from the fridge in the kitchen, eased himself onto one of the leather sofas, and put his feet up on the coffee table. I got a beer as well and a bag of chips and joined him. I was whacked, and stretched out with relief on the other sofa. We drank our beers in silence for a couple of minutes. Then I sat up and pushed the chips across the table to Marley.

'Where did you get the name Marley from? Were your mum and dad fans?'

'I wish. Then they might have called me Bob. I'd have been okay with Bob.'

'But …?' I was intrigued now.

'Promise no Madison snort?'

'I don't snort.'

'Yes, you do.'

'Cross my heart then.'

'My folks saw fit to bless me with the name Melchior.'

Marley caught me suppressing a giggle. 'I knew you'd do that, though I will accept a laugh is more benign than derision.'

I covered my mouth. 'Not laughing … although it is pretty wild.'

Marley pressed his palms together and cast his eyes upward in an attitude of beatitude. 'Dear Mater, rest her soul, was High Anglican. Devout as a guru wasting in his cave. I don't think Dad got a word in when it came to my name. Melchior was one of the Three Wise Men, the one who gave Jesus the gold, and I can only presume Mum saw me as her little gift of gold.'

'Aw. That's so sweet.'

'Not,' snapped Marley, uncharacteristically touchy. 'Gave myself a soubriquet just as soon as I understood what a sad joke my name was. I think I was eight. Melchior. I ask you.' Marley curled his lip and snarled. 'Might have got away with it, just, if I'd wanted to be a funeral director, or a barrister maybe, but it's hardly the moniker for a creative bum like me.' Marley belched as if to prove his point.

'But don't you see, Marley? Melchior is perfect. I love it. Your mum must have known that one day you'd be a wise man handing out gold.' I was only half joking.

Marley flicked a potato chip at me, finished his beer and got up to fetch another. 'So, now I've shared my darkest secret, it's your turn. Tell me, Ms Madison, what's up with you these days. You're not on form.'

I picked up my beer to take another drink but the bottle was empty. I put it back on the table. 'Things are a bit crappy at home, that's all … it'll sort itself out.'

'If anyone is being tough on you, you know I'll beat them up for you.'

I looked at Marley. Of all my colleagues, working with him had given me the greatest sense of solidarity in the agency. He was a gem, but no one would call him fit. The buttons of his shirts were only just holding against his beer belly and if he had to walk further than two blocks he started wheezing. In a tackle with Conor I knew which man would end up with his face on the floor. As for Chrissy, she'd probably try to beguile him, but perhaps I was underestimating Marley. If my sister did attempt to exert her charm on him, I suspected he was savvy enough to recognise the termagant immediately and head for the nearest pub, alone.

'Word of advice? Don't let Barry see you under the weather. He can smell fair game a mile away and if he sees you struggling, he'll put the boot in.'

'Seems it's my year for bullies.' I jabbed at my forehead with my fist. 'Is there a sign here, a tattoo inviting people to kick me?'

Before I could even register surprise, Marley leaned over and planted a kiss on my forehead.

23

Conor was working late at his office every night. He said it was because he had a big project on and without his study to work in, couldn't bring the work home. I suspected the real reason was because he was waiting for me to get rid of Chrissy.

Whenever I got home from work, I went into Conor's and my bedroom and stayed there, going to bed earlier and earlier, frequently before Conor even got home. More and more often, Chrissy was out late too. I never asked where she went or what she was doing. I'd given up my attempts to find common ground.

Sometimes she and Conor arrived home at the same time, around nine or ten in the evening, and I would hear them in the kitchen, making something to eat or having a drink together. Chrissy would laugh, a low coquettish laugh which grated on me. Then there would be long periods of silence which did almost reduce me to shreds.

I knew she was flirting with Conor only to provoke me, and even though I knew he was humouring her out of politeness, I was getting more and more paranoid. Chrissy made me feel like an intruder in my own house.

Sometimes, instead of going home, I walked around the

neighbourhood. Sydney isn't very kind to pedestrians and I had to dodge busy roads while moving quickly from one green space to the next. From Hyde Park in the city I'd cut across to the Chinese Friendship Garden and sit there for a while, by the lake. From there I'd walk on to Wentworth Park, but never stayed long because it was my least favourite park, mainly because of the greyhound track in the middle of it which made me sad. I hated to think of those dogs being so harried, tricked into chasing madly after a mechanical hare, just to entertain people who have nothing better to do, and about as much good sense as the hare. Instead, I stepped up my pace and headed quickly for the Bridge Road end of the park, circling the sports fields until I got to a place where I could take in the view across Blackwattle Bay.

More often than not, I'd walk all the way up Glebe Point Road, through the shopping strip, until I reached Bicentennial Park at the end of the road and where I'd turn right into Rozelle Bay and wander along the foreshore until I arrived at Jubilee Park. There are more trees there and more space to roam.

By the time I got to the park, any children in the playground were long gone. There might be a jogger or two circling the oval and a few people walking their dogs, but usually I had the place to myself. Birds rattled in the trees as I passed beneath, feral cats bickered in the shrubbery before slinking off in different directions when I arrived, and sometimes a boat motored past, its wash a consoling slap-slap against the stone wall at the water's edge. I'd sit near that wall, with the trees at my back, and as dusk fell, watch the city fade like an old sepia photo. The musty aromas of salt and rotting kelp drifted up from the bay and for a while, my mind would be pleasantly stilled to monochrome.

There were times during those walks when I fancied myself in a John Brack painting, back in Melbourne and walking the entire length of Collins Street, lost among dour men in tobacco hats, or being driven in a car by a pointy-faced man, me sitting in the back, smiling like Barbie in anticipation of our destination.

Sydney smelled of pine and eucalypt, of diesel and bitumen, and of my disquiet. In my nocturnal wanderings I was trudging off my troubles when what I really wanted to do was talk them through with my friend Lauren, but I was avoiding her, worried I might inadvertently blurt out to her that my sister was having an affair with Steve.

I berated myself for being so woefully craven.

Conor was no help.

'You're never home any more,' I said.'

'What home?' he answered. 'We don't have a home so much as a boarding house.'

'That's not fair.'

'It's up to you, Lexi.'

24

In the end, asking Chrissy to leave was easy because our wrangling escalated to the point where she unwittingly made it a moral imperative for me to do so.

It happened a few days after the demonstration in Paddington. I came home to find my sister sitting on the sofa in the living room, staring into space. Her face in repose was forlorn, as if she'd suffered some painful loss at an early age and never quite recovered from it. It struck me then that maybe she had, and that my initial instinct, when she'd first phoned about coming to stay, had been right and that she was depressed.

That made two of us.

If we could just talk about what was happening, get things out in the open, I was sure she'd be her old self again. We'd both be our old selves again.

Looking back, my optimism was about as helpful as the Emperor's new clothes.

When she noticed I was there, she sat up straighter and I was pleased to see her expression soften. I thought she was going to confide in me at last, but then the shutters came down. I refused to be deterred. 'What's happened between you and Peter?'

'I told you, he cleared off.'

'You said he was at a conference.'

'I'm not his minder. We're not joined at the hip.'

Maybe it was because I was standing and she was sitting, or because I was still feeling cocky as a result of my recent activism, but this time I was undaunted by her opacity.

'For god's sake, Chrissy, I'm on your side so would you, please, put your belligerence aside for five minutes.'

She must have detected the shift in my attitude because she gave me a conciliatory smile and began to talk.

'You were only a kid at the time, so you wouldn't have known, but I was pregnant when Pete and I married. Up the duff. Gunshot wedding. You know ...' She gave a short laugh but there was no humour in it. 'Then I had a miscarriage. It took him a few years but Pete decided I'd tricked him into marrying me and once he got that half-witted notion in his head, it stuck. Nothing I could say would change his mind.'

'That doesn't sound like Peter.'

'First I'm combative, now I'm a liar.'

'No, I just meant ... I don't think he would hold that against you. It's not as if anyone is to blame, is it?'

'You don't have to be so goody-good about it. I'll cope.'

'There'll be someone else.'

'Don't be obtuse. Not like Peter. I miss him. And he owes me. I brought up his daughter for him, didn't I?' Chrissy's nostrils flared, and her cheeks flushed pink.

She was oleander in full toxic bloom but I suddenly felt sorry for her and would have given anything right then to end the antagonism between us. For her to be happy. I went into the kitchen, opened the fridge and took out a bottle of wine, and Chrissy's chartreuse. 'Let's hit the booze,' I called out. 'Chrissy? What do you say? Let's get thoroughly plastered. Like old times.'

I carried the bottles and two glasses into the living room.

'I've stopped drinking,' said Chrissy.

'Well, hallelujah. If I didn't already know you're not yourself, I know now.'

'Pete's given up,' said Chrissy. 'Improved his libido no end too. He's great in bed, but you know that.'

'You've lost me.'

Chrissy carried on as if I hadn't spoken. 'He told me the two of you played the *Tampopo* game.'

'What on earth are you on about?'

'You know, that Japanese film, the one where the lovers play a kissing game, passing a raw egg from mouth to mouth and making the kiss last until the yolk breaks. It always broke in my mouth, eventually, so, Pete always won.'

'That's gross.' I sipped my wine. 'Why would you think Peter and I have even kissed, let alone that?'

'You slept with him.'

'What?'

'When he spent the night in Sydney after that press dinner.' Chrissy flicked a speck of dust from her dress and inspected the spot where it had been. 'Maybe you've forgotten.'

If every wall around the house collapsed, leaving me and Chrissy exposed to the entire world, I could not have been more astounded. My surprise could have filled an ocean, the Pacific, or no, the Dead Sea, that heavy briny mass. There was a prolonged silence and, as I gaped dumbly at my sister, we were laid bare to one another and I understood at last the difference between us.

It took me a moment or two to gather my wits and reply. 'That is hardly something I'd forget.'

'Have it your way.'

'Chrissy, you are *so* wrong.' How could she not see that I was sincere? 'I have *never* slept with Peter. It would be like ...' I stumbled over the word. 'It would be like incest.'

'Don't be so precious. It's only sex.'

'You talk about sex like it's sport.'

Chrissy picked up the bottle of chartreuse, took a swig and then, without taking her eyes off me, sat back on the sofa and stretched out her legs.

'He's far too old, anyway.' I didn't wait to find out if Chrissy registered the insult in that remark, she and Peter were almost the same age after all. I grabbed the wine and my glass and retreated to my room.

Anyone observing me there, sitting placidly on the end of my bed, would have put me down as calm, a woman altogether in charge of her life, but inside I was an inferno. I put the wine aside. My brain felt fried as it was and I needed a clear head. It was time to think. I went over and over the conversation with Chrissy, trawling through the corridors of my confusion until a single logical point emerged: Maybe she *wanted* me to have slept with her husband because that would give her licence to sleep with mine.

The truth of this glared at me, sharp as surgical scissors, and what I had until then only intuited now manifested as a problem and I saw it clearly. I almost hooted with relief: problems have solutions.

I remembered that late night talk with Conor, when he'd all but admitted that he was attracted to Chrissy, enough to want to sleep with her.

Before breakfast the next day I told her to move out.

25

By the end of the week Chrissy was gone.

Living with her had been one long root canal and now it was over.

When I got home on Friday night and saw she'd left, I went immediately to Conor's study and stripped and folded away the sofa bed, bundled up the bed linen as if it were infected and deposited it in the washing machine. I reclaimed Conor's drawing tools and arranged them on his desk, then took down the print of Picasso's *Dream* and threw it in one of the bins in the yard. I needed the room back the way it was, exactly, but nothing in it that might remind me of Chrissy's occupancy. She would have lain in bed looking at that picture, fornicated with Steve under it; it had to go.

On Saturday morning Conor went shopping while I embarked on a manic cleaning spree. I opened all the windows, shook out every rug, cushion, and duvet. I vacuumed floors, scrubbed every inch of the bathroom and kitchen, and would have tackled the windows as well but since cleaning is not my pastime of choice, decided to draw the line there.

All that scouring was for myself rather than the house. Each time I filled the sink with hot soapy water I convinced myself that nothing would make me happier than to never see my sister again.

The longer I could remain furious with Chrissy, the longer I could keep at bay the yawning loneliness of a life without siblings.

While I cherished the knowledge of Robbie's whereabouts, I didn't try to contact him. I was afraid that if I did, he wouldn't be there, or if he was, he wouldn't reply.

I texted Conor, asking him to bring flowers home.

There was a text waiting on my phone, from a number I didn't recognise. It was someone wanting to make an appointment and if he was satisfied, would become a regular client. I deleted it. I was getting more and more wrong numbers lately and it was becoming tiresome. Half an hour later my phone pinged again and someone else was asking for an appointment. If the local medical practice or dentist or whoever had confused my number with theirs, I hoped they'd fix it soon.

Conor arrived home with five bunches of flowers and showed off by reciting some of their names: flannel flowers, hibiscus, leucospermum, a couple of birds of paradise, and some pale pink blooms that looked like poppies but might not have been.

'What's made you so smart?'

'The florist decided I needed to be edified. I was the only customer and presumably she was bored.'

We used our only vase for the leucospermum and arranged the rest of the flowers in jugs and old jars which we placed like totems throughout the house. At six o'clock we lit candles in the bathroom and lay in a hot bath together, drinking bubbly and eating toasted ravioli from a local delicatessen. Outside the window, ravens settled their last squabbles for the day and the evening warbled its way into night.

Conor dug his knuckles into the soles of my feet. 'Is everything okay now?'

'Like soft rain,' I said. 'Better than.'

'It was raining when we first met, remember?'

'Of course. The bookshop, what was it called? Pity it's not there any more.'

That ineffaceable Saturday afternoon, when one of Sydney's summer deluges arrived without warning, its thin start needling my face, then fat luxuriant drops soaking me until I dashed into a bookshop for shelter. I'd headed immediately for the back of the shop where there were books on art and architecture and that's where I met Conor. He was casually affecting an intention to buy when, like me, he was only whiling time away until the downpour passed. It took forty minutes and by then the chemistry between us was fizzing. Reluctant to part company, we went on to a café and then to dinner, and never looked back.

'Where have all the bookshops gone.' Conor sang the words to the Kingston Trio tune.

I joined in. 'Lost to Amazon, everyone. When will we ever learn?'

'When will we eeeever learn?' We finished together, drawing out each word and singing at the tops of our voices.

'You used to sing all the time,' said Conor. He leaned towards me, took my face in his hands and kissed me. 'We need more singing, songbird. Let's have a karaoke party.'

'Let's make a baby.' The words were out before I even realised what I was saying, as if my hormones had taken control of my mouth. 'I know we've always said we'd fix up the house first, but need we?'

'No, we need not and yes, ready when you are,' said Conor.

The water had cooled and I turned on the hot tap, paddling my hands through the water to distribute the heat across both ends of the bath.

'How come you and Marie didn't have kids?' Marie was Conor's ex, a primary school teacher from Dubbo, and they'd been married eight years.

'She didn't want any.'

'Did you?'

'It was up to her. I'd have been happy to have started a family although ... probably just as well we didn't.' Conor made a waggish

110

face, blowing out his lips and lifting his eyebrows. 'As it turned out, there was better breeding stock to be found.'

'Don't be cruel.'

'Sorry. Deem it redacted. Actually, Marie was good value . . . as you well know, our parting was amicable. No hard feelings at all. We outgrew each other, that's all.'

'As you do,' I said.

'We married too young. Who knows who they are at twenty?'

The ghost of Conor's first marriage hung over the bath like a vapour and for a couple of minutes neither of us spoke.

'Is it only up to me then?' I asked.

'Is what?'

'Whether or not we have babies. Will you be as committed as I am?'

'Are our pollies wallies? Of course, I'll be committed.' He picked up one of our bath toys, a small yellow duck, and paddled it round the bath, crooning gooey baby talk. 'Fatherly enough for you?'

I flicked water at him. He paddled the duck up the inside of my leg.

After the bath we made love, in the hallway, the living room, all through the house until we ended up in the bedroom where we made a glorious mess of the bed. We reclaimed our nest.

26

A few days later I found a note in our letter box, written in Chrissy's thick black handwriting on the back of a long envelope, one of those business ones with a window in it. She'd folded it and fixed the two ends with a staple. I opened it to find a curt request for Conor and I to redirect her mail. There was neither salutation nor thanks. I contemplated the address. Chrissy must have got things mixed up or made a mistake. Surely. The name of the street she'd written down was our street, Mitchell Street.

The truth hit me like a cattle prod. My obnoxious sister had moved just five houses away, on the other side of the road. She was practically next door and this unexpected proximity flummoxed me. What did it mean? At first, I was appalled but then, ever the Pollyanna, decided to put a positive spin on it. Hope flickered in me that Chrissy wanted to remain close, to leave the way open for us to patch up our differences. Now that we weren't under the same roof any more, perhaps that was possible.

On the ensuing Saturday morning I went to visit her. She had rented a flat in a terrace house like ours except that hers was two-storey, divided into apartments and recently renovated. Chrissy's place was downstairs. As I approached the front door, someone moved behind the curtains and I presumed it was my sister but when I knocked, she didn't answer. I knocked again and still she didn't come. From within the house, I heard a door slam, then another.

'Stop being daft, Chrissy. I know you're in there.'

After making me wait another couple of minutes, she opened the front door but didn't release the security chain.

'So here you are, Chrissy, still in the neighbourhood. I'm glad.' Even to me, those last two words sounded bogus which put me on the back foot immediately.

Chrissy released the security chain and opened the door. 'Come in. Wait there.' Her tone wasn't friendly.

Although there was still some small plaintive part of me that aspired to putting past misunderstandings behind us, my optimism was rapidly fading and, once again, her living so near to me and Conor was unnerving.

The apartment smelled of fresh paint and through the door into her living room I saw a room minimally but elegantly furnished in colours I like: cream covers on two long low sofas, ochre and pale gold cushions, arty coffee tables in distressed pine with curly metal legs. It was urban chic and what I could see of the place was magazine perfect; not yet scuffed and mellowed by living in the way that makes a home *gemütlich*. The rent would have been high.

I called out. 'Have you got a job, Chrissy?' She didn't answer.

Cups and saucers were arranged on a glass-topped side table, and plates with napkins, and what looked like a banana cake. If she were making afternoon tea for us, why ask me to wait in the hall? The answer was immediately and pitifully obvious: that tea party was not for me.

Seeing it laid out like that with no one around to eat it made me think of Miss Havisham's wedding breakfast. It looked as if it had been there all day and if it wasn't for me, who was it for? It crossed my mind then that if Chrissy had any friends, she'd never spoken of them and I'd never met them.

When she returned a few minutes later, my sister thrust a scrappy bit of paper at me. While I'd been waiting, feeling more and more like an errant pupil outside the principal's office, she'd scrawled in her boxy script a list of things she'd left at the house and now wanted back: a bottle of chartreuse in the freezer, a pot of face cream, a box of tissues – really? – and the DVD I'd believed was a birthday present for Conor – well, she could have that back.

'Pick them up whenever you like.'

'I need that cardigan back too,' she said, 'the one I loaned you.'

She meant the green cashmere cardigan she'd given me. That *had* been a gift.

'Since you're here,' she said, 'I've had an email from Rob. He says he doesn't want to be found.'

'You're lying. Show me the message. What's his address?'

'I deleted it.'

'You bitch.' Chrissy looked at me and I swear her eyes were glacial. It was as if she wasn't seeing me. *As if I didn't matter.* I experienced a stomach-churning mix of rage and dismay and uncertainty, the sort of uncertainty that made me doubt my own reason.

I scrunched up the paper with its dumb list and flung it at her, then fled from the house.

Outside in the street, I almost ran into a couple of joggers, reeling away from them so suddenly and clumsily that I veered into foliage growing over a neighbour's fence. I had to stop for a bit, to calm down, let my heartbeat return to normal.

At home I knocked back a glass of white wine, almost in a single gulp, poured another, but didn't drink it. I sagged at the kitchen table and for a while carped and snivelled until, feeling more and more sorry for myself, I cried noisily in loud convulsive sobs.

My face was hot and blotchy. In the bathroom I filled the basin with cold water and lowered my face into it, holding it there until I had to come up for air.

By the time Conor came home I'd recovered some sangfroid. I

didn't say anything to him about what had happened, other than to tell him Chrissy was living up the road, but I continued stewing over that barmy conversation, her words iterating in my brain, over and over, a lacerating sequence on a never-ending loop.

I castigated myself for letting them get to me. *Let it go, Lexi. Let it go.*

Sometime around three in the morning it occurred to me that I had never seen Chrissy cry.

While she lived with us, Chrissy had frequently put me down, monopolised Conor's attention, and pushed herself on our friends, casually and with all the cunning of a grandmaster. By the time she left, I had enough perspicacity to understand that she was turning our relationship into a contest, that for some puzzling reason, she saw me as her opponent.

I'd had rivals before, at school and at work, and I'm not going to argue with Hobbes' theory that humans are fundamentally competitive. The fittest do survive. And I'm a competitive person myself. What's the point of studying or of going to work each day if it isn't to do the best you possibly can, or for that matter, doing anything at all if it isn't to make your way successfully to the top of Maslow's hierarchy? And like Conor, I'm talking step five. My desire to be a successful painter is a background hum as persistent as tinnitus and I probably won't settle until I achieve it. And I want to win, who doesn't, but does the game need to played by crushing others along the way? I hold fast to the hope that people like Chrissy, who think they need to strong-arm their way ahead, will never actually get there. Or if they do, it's because, somewhere along the way, they experience some sort of Paul-on-the-road-to-Damascus moment and arrive at probity.

Having grown up more or less as a single child, I had no

experience of sibling rivalry. It was the fact of a sister, my *sister*, competing with me that caused me the greatest confusion and distress. I could never have conceived such a thing as animosity within a family and if someone had told me of it, I would have replied forcefully that it was unnatural and unlikely.

In the space of a few months I came to abhor Chrissy both for her repellent behaviour and for rubbing my nose in the glum reality of sibling discord, and to revile myself for my weakness in flailing under it.

There are patron saints of families – St Joseph is one, the animal-loving St Francis another – but they all let me down that year.

27

When Chrissy moved out at the end of July, I expected her to get on with her life and leave me to get on with mine and for almost two months that's what happened. Only now and then did I imagine my sister standing outside our house in Mitchell Street with a ravenous aspect, invoking djinns to harass us. I sent those thoughts back into the ether where they belonged. We heard nothing from her, I never saw her, and Conor and I settled happily back into our old agreeable routines.

In October we went to a party at John and Janet's place in Paddington. Their house was a brick California bungalow with stained-glass windows on either side of the front door and high-ceilinged rooms off a wide central corridor. I'd always liked it and even more when they ripped out walls to turn the whole back of the house into one large kitchen and living room. I was keen for Conor and I to do something similar at our place.

By the time we arrived at nine-thirty, the party was well underway.

The first person we bumped into was Steve. We hadn't seen each other since that Queen's Birthday weekend dinner at our place and I expected him to blush with shame or show some sort of chagrin at least for that faithless night in Chrissy's bed, not to mention going on seeing her, but he was all innocence.

'Where's Lauren?' I spat the question out and Conor gave me a disapproving look.

'Home with the kids.'

'You usually get a babysitter.'

'We left it too late to book.'

'Why is it,' I snapped, 'you get to come out and Lauren stays home?'

'Lex.' Conor gave me a tiny shake of his head, then exchanged a quizzical look with Steve, as if sharing with each other a mutual exasperation at the vagaries of women.

Sod off both of them, Steve for being rubbish and Conor for not calling him out.

'It's typical though isn't it?' I said. 'Someone has to stay home and it's always the mother.' The last two words came out more sarcastically than I intended, but I held Steve's eye, challenging him to show contrition.

Conor pulled me away. 'Let's find a drink.'

'You'd think he'd be embarrassed at least.'

'None of our business,' said Conor.

'You always say that. Lauren is my best friend.'

I was half relieved Lauren wasn't there. Every other day I wished she'd phone me yet was thankful she didn't. Our friendship was forever, I knew that, but right then it felt suspended in a holding pattern. Maybe she suspected Steve's infidelity with Chrissy and was shunning all of us.

We were heading towards the French windows and the deck along the back of the house when I saw Chrissy through the crowd. Instantly, my mood turned sour. What the hell was she doing there?

Chrissy saw me and waved. *As if we were the bloody Bobbsey twins.* She picked up a bottle and glass and headed our way.

'She's wearing my dress.' My voice became strident. I despise women who whine but couldn't stop myself. 'The bitch is wearing my dress.' It was the Ellery dress and Chrissy hadn't taken the hem up for me at all, she'd done it for herself. Why hadn't I noticed it was missing? It must have been in the ironing pile the day I hurried home from work to see whether or not Chrissy had helped herself to any more of my clothes.

'Don't make a scene,' said Conor.

Chrissy filled the glass and handed it to Conor.

I snatched the glass away, put it on the table and tried to wrest Conor away. 'Can't you see what she's doing? I want to leave.'

'We've only just got here.'

'She's spoiled it.'

'We're here now. Can't you just ignore her?'

'She contaminates everything.'

There was a buffet on the dining room table and lots of booze. I picked up a bottle of pinot gris, didn't bother with a glass, and went outside to drink and fume. There were other people out on the deck smoking and, even though I don't smoke, I cadged a cigarette. I knew it would make me feel ill, but it'd be worth it if it settled my spleen. It didn't so I was queasy as well as furious.

When I returned inside, Chrissy was holding court – the men, Conor and Steve among them, were hanging on her every word. This, I now fully grasped, was Chrissy's social style: disdain the women and entertain the men. The world is full of needy bitches who see other women – wives, girlfriends, sisters even, and daughters too – as competition for the attentions of men. I observed Chrissy's come-hither eyes, like some sort of femme fatale in a silent movie, except she wasn't silent. That night she regaled her audience with anecdotes from her days working in the Katoomba hospital and the men were mesmerised, indulging no doubt in collective schadenfreude. As I approached, she was saying more than she should about a young patient who'd come into the hospital to have a light bulb removed from his anus. When she saw me, Chrissy threw back her head and laughed.

To my disgust, Conor laughed with her.

I felt sick. *Conor is* my *husband and these are* our *friends, not yours.*

Conor didn't even notice when I stepped up beside him. 'Let's go,' I said.

He frowned and swallowed a mouthful of beer, and stayed put. Chrissy looked so smug I wanted to smack her. I picked up a bottle of beer and tipped it over her head. 'Why don't you just piss off back to Katoomba?' I wanted to smash the bottle, cut her face with it. I picked up a piece of cold pizza instead and crushed it in her face. She raised an eyebrow in that gallingly sardonic way she had but, other than that, didn't react.

Everyone in the group stared at me, agog at my behaviour. Janet came over. 'Lexi?'

'Don't you dare be nice to me,' I whispered to her. 'I don't want her to have the satisfaction of seeing me cry.'

Conor looked around for a cloth and handed it to Chrissy, then grabbed my arm. 'You're making a fool of yourself.'

'No Conor, it's her.' I couldn't bring myself to say my sister's name. 'She's the one making fools of us. Can't you see that?'

'You're over-reacting.'

'I want to go home.'

'Then go.'

'Come with me.'

'You've worked yourself into a fractious state, Lex. Go home. Go to bed.'

'Don't patronise me.'

He gave me a little push from behind and steered me towards the door. 'And now you're being vapid.'

That was enough to make me want to get away from him as well, forever. Janet followed me to the door. 'Are you okay? Is there anything I can do?'

If you value your marriage get her out of your house. That's what I wanted to say to Janet, but I couldn't. I couldn't say anything I

120

might regret, something she might later share with Lauren who was shrewd enough to join the dots, if she hadn't already.

I gave Janet a quick hug and hurried away. It was a relief to be outside, walking fast, into the night. At Ormond Street I turned left and shortly after that, right, into Oxford Street, then walked all the way to Oxford Square. The area was more subdued than it used to be, before they brought in the lockout laws, but it was Saturday night and there were still plenty of people about. An unruly clique of students crashed out of the Oxford Art Factory, brandishing magnums of champagne and raucously singing Beyoncé's *Crazy in Love*. I say they were students, but for all I know they were an out-of-work dance troupe.

At Hyde Park I turned left and headed for George Street and Broadway and home.

Broadway was an inky turbulent river and I had to fight hard against the current. I was dead tired and glad to be; exhaustion stopped me thinking. Neon signs and bright light spilled from cafés and gay bars. They drilled through me like Doctor Eckleburg's eyes. In the window of a strip club, set back from the road, a woman in flashy turquoise sequins gyrated languidly around a lucent pole. A tourist jostled me and I clutched my bag close to my chest. I didn't want to see or be seen by anyone. Someone grabbed my arm and an oily voice whispered in my ear: 'Whatcha on, luv? Wan' some more an' float higher?' I shook him off and walked faster, then ran.

At Liverpool Street I had the spooky feeling someone was shadowing me, maybe it was that lowlife with the oily voice, and at the intersection of Wattle street, even though Mitchell Street was only a few blocks away, I flagged down a cab.

When I got home, wide awake and on edge, I logged into LinkedIn and looked up Robbie again. This time I drafted an email: Blast from the past; it's your little sister Lexi, Alexandra … I deleted that and tried again: You probably don't remember me. I was only six, but … I deleted that too. I didn't know what to say, where to start.

121

The years since we'd last seen each other were almost as long as I'd been alive. And even if I did manage to write a half decent email, I lacked the mettle to send it. For all I knew, his LinkedIn page was years out of date. Even if it wasn't, Rob might not reply. He might not even want to be found. After the collapse of my relations with one sibling, I didn't think I could face being rebuffed by the other.

28

Conor didn't get home until nearly four am.

He slept in his study.

Over breakfast I was glum, but Conor, ever the optimist, ignored my mood. He put an arm across my shoulder and kissed the top of my head. I pushed him away.

'Love, it was just a party. You were the one who introduced her to our friends, we can hardly expect not to run into her again.' He started making coffee, a daily ritual in our kitchen I usually enjoyed but which that morning failed to comfort me.

'Did you have to talk to her? Be so damn genial?' The coffee machine started building up pressure and I had to talk loudly above its shrieking. 'And don't think I don't know how late it was when you came in.'

'Your unseemly departure did not go unnoticed. I was making up for it,' said Conor.

'Oh, very cute. Janet didn't mind my leaving.'

'I did.'

'Really? That's not what it looked like to me.'

Conor put a cappuccino on the table in front of me, but didn't say anything.

'You let me down.'

'Seems to me you managed that all on your own,' said Conor.

I took my coffee into the living room and sat with my back to the kitchen door. Conor followed. 'Well, I'd rather see your back than your cold shoulder,' he said.

His quips nearly always cheered me, but not this time. I was cross and scared. If Conor wouldn't share my anxiety about Chrissy, and stay away from her, I really wasn't sure I'd be able to stay with him.

The next day I went back to Robbie's LinkedIn page. Overnight his details had changed. He had updated his page and this made me jubilant. My brother was there, still in Newark, New Jersey and still in civil engineering, but now working for a different firm. Did he have some sort of sixth sense? Had he known I was checking his page? Whether or not this was the case, I saw the change as an augury, a good one, and, whether justified or not, it gave me certainty that he was as keen as I was for us to reconnect with each other. I didn't know what he preferred to be called, Rob or Robbie, or even Robert, and in the end stuck with Robbie. I re-wrote my message: 'Dear Robbie. Blast from the past. This is Lexi, your sister. I know it's been an insanely long time, too long, but I would love to hear from you. Love, Alexandra.'

At the bottom I put my email address and this time I hit send.

He must have been online as well because within two or three minutes he replied. As if he'd been waiting to hear from me. There was no Dear Lexi or anything like that, no sharing of regret or apology about how long apart we'd been. Instead he came straight to the point and issued an invitation to talk. 'Hey Lex. Do you want to talk? Are you on Skype, or FaceTime? Where do you live? What's your address?'

My hands were trembling with excitement and I kept hitting the wrong keys. By the time I'd fixed all the typos, and rearranged a few sentences, it was almost ten minutes before I emailed him back. I sent Robbie my Skype address, my home address, and my phone number. I told him I couldn't wait to talk to him, that I was ready just as soon as he was free.

Two weeks later, on the twenty-fifth of October, I turned twenty-nine. By then I'd more or less put that horrible party behind me and neither Conor nor I referred to it again. Conor suggested a night out. I reminded him we'd agreed not to make a big deal of our birthdays, but that Friday, we took a cab over to Potts Point and splashed out on dinner at Monopole, just the two of us, after which we went to the Marble Bar to listen to live music.

By the time we got to bed it was late. If I remember correctly, not that the exact time matters one way or another, it was two am and I'd just drifted off to sleep when I was woken by the dogs next door. Our neighbours, a couple of GPs who we never saw from one week to the next, had two ageing spaniels, one grey, one black. The dogs spent most of their time inside and we seldom heard them, so when they started barking excitedly, I knew something was up.

Conor and I got up and walked gingerly through the house, inspecting all the doors and windows until we heard the front gate slam shut. I yelled and we both sprinted outside and reached the pavement just in time to see someone scoot up the street and turn into Broughton Lane.

We thought we'd interrupted a burglar until I saw the flowers propped up beside the front door. They were peonies, one of my favourite flowers, pink and cream and lavish, and mingled with lots of greenery and wrapped in layers of thick cream paper and tied with green ribbon. There was no note and I presumed they were from Conor, but when he saw the bouquet, he shrugged and lifted his hands in the air, palms open, fingers splayed. 'Nothing to do with me.' He gave me a funny look then, as if he suspected I had an admirer, or a lover.

'Don't you go all Shakespearean on me,' I said. 'For all we know, they're for you.'

When I removed the cellophane wrapping and lifted the flowers to arrange them in a vase, I saw straight away that every flower head had been cut from its stem, then carefully re-attached with tailors' pins. I don't think I'd ever seen anything so loopy. Every single bloom was mutilated and would be dead by morning.

Conor grinned. 'Must be over then, if it *is* the other bloke,' he joked. Did I detect relief in his voice?

'It's not funny. This is so whacko it's downright unnatural. And we both know who is responsible.'

'Maybe. Actually, hard to tell, but it looked like a bloke to me.'

'It's dark. No way you could tell. And it's obvious anyway, who delivered these.'

'He was tall. Had shoulders. Looked as if he worked out.'

'Then Chrissy got someone to do it for her.' I didn't say anything more because it had just hit me like a thump on the back that my sister was mad. Certifiably lock-her-up-and-throw-away-the-key sort of mad.

I flung the bouquet into the waste bin, put the vase away in the cupboard and didn't even try to make sense of the madness.

Three brash peonies. One for each scabrous month of Chrissy's stay?

A couple of hours later I went back into the kitchen, grabbed the vase from the cupboard and slung that in the garbage as well.

29

I'd finished my work on the Cleverly Holdings brief, but the other projects Barry had assigned to me – those TV commercials and the ad campaign – were still languishing on my desk. When he asked me for an update on their progress, I had to confess that there wasn't any.

'Delegate to Megan,' said Barry curtly.

I turned around and scanned the bank of Macs. Megan was sitting at the far end, watching me. She was about twenty, with blue limpid eyes and changeable hair cropped short like a helmet. That day it was black, tipped at the ends with colour, one side pink and other green. It wasn't half bad; her hair was mental but she carried it off. Her wardrobe consisted almost entirely of Japanese street gear, which meant an eclectic mix of styles and colours that sometimes made you want to rest your eyes elsewhere. I liked Megan and appreciated her originality. That day she was wearing purply-yellow patterned stockings and a short baby-doll dress in Wedgwood blue. It suited her and I knew she'd found it an op shop. Whether or not her motives for buying pre-loved clothes were the same as mine, I felt an affinity with her because of them.

Megan was a junior and I have to admit to being taken aback that Barry should suggest to me that her skills were equal to mine.

'You've already spoken to her.'

'It came up.'

'So, I don't get a say on this?'

'You think you've earned that?'

'I don't mind working with Megan, you know that, but wouldn't Marley be better? We work well together.'

'Share the love, Lexi. Can't fathom why, but Megan seems to think highly of you. Be nice.'

I went back to my desk.

For the first time in a long time I thought about my days back at art school when I did whatever I wanted, whenever I wanted, and wished I was in my own big studio somewhere, throwing paint at a canvas, and rich and worldly enough to ignore phone calls from galleries falling over themselves to exhibit my work. A girl can dream, can't she?

Megan brought me back to the real world. She was gesturing towards one of the meeting rooms. Her enthusiasm was palpable and perhaps she could help me to re-ignite my own. I sighed heavily, picked up a notebook and pencils, and was about to go and join Megan when Craig arrived at my desk and dropped an artillery shell on my lap.

Craig Smithins worked in the IT department and other than seeking him out to fix a glitch in my computer, our paths rarely crossed. He was the agency dweeb, our very own Uriah Heep, always hovering at people's desks trying to engage in conversation and in denial about everyone doing what they could to avoid him. He was in his early thirties, rake-thin with sloping shoulders and a pasty complexion, probably because he spent his entire life in front of a computer screen; it's a lifestyle guaranteed to stunt anyone's growth.

'Hiya, Lexi.' He shifted his weight restively from one foot to the other. 'I was wondering …'

He was wearing a black t-shirt with a slogan in white across the front: 'Democracy is not a spectator sport.' Well, there was that to like about him, so I smiled and asked if he wanted me to do something for him.

'I was just wondering, Lexi, where you work from?' His voice was like a limp handshake.

'What sort of question is that? I work here.'

'I mean your other job.' He lowered his voice and practically talked out of the side of his mouth. 'The moonlighting one.' Craig winked at me then. I didn't think anyone did that any more. It was comical.

'This job keeps me busy enough without taking on another.' I was pushing my chair back, ready to get up and walk away, when he took out his wallet, removed a business card and showed it to me. 'This is you, isn't it?'

I examined the card. There was my name, Alexandra, and my cell phone number and the name of a company in curly Gabriola font: Elite Escorts. It was and it wasn't me.

My insides curdled. To cover my alarm, I adopted a peremptory tone I didn't feel. 'What is this? Where did you get it?'

'In a club. More a gaming lounge really. How much do you charge?'

Craig might just as well have been using a loud-hailer because by now everyone had tuned in to our conversation and I was aware of eight pairs of eyes on me. Their curiosity was demeaning and all that was needed to complete the bloodiness of the scene for me was for Barry to walk past. Fortunately, he was out somewhere with Gray.

'You really do need to get a life, Craig.' I handed the card back to him serenely even though I wanted to tear it into sharp little bits and throw them at him. 'You've got me mixed up with someone else. And just so you know, if it *was* me, you'd be so far out of your league, you'd be in Darwin.'

Marley was hot-desking next to me that day. He was the only one not watching me and Craig, but I knew he was listening. I could almost feel his ear drums vibrating. He stood up and began fussing with his chair, deliberately crowding Craig. I knew he was trying to break up the conversation but it only served to make Craig move closer to me.

The prat winked at me again. 'Mates' rates for a colleague?'

If this were someone else's story, I might have enjoyed the joke. But it wasn't. I knew exactly where that card came from. Chrissy was flinging mud at me and I felt it stick like tar; goose feathers were all that was missing to complete my mortification. My face must have betrayed my discomfort because that's when Marley intervened. 'What's up, Craig? You're looking clammy as a wet dream.'

Megan, watching from outside the meeting room, giggled.

Craig flushed, but wasn't put off. He waved the card at me and ogled me with avid eyes. 'Call you sometime, okey-doke?' Then, mercifully, he slunk back to his own office.

Without looking up, I picked up a couple of files from my desk and glanced at my watch as if I were running late and heading off to a meeting. I saw Megan out of the corner of my eye, waiting for me, but I ignored her, just as I would later have to ignore Barry's opprobrium. I needed to get out of the office, breathe in fresh air, compose myself.

Marley followed me out to the stairwell. 'What was all that about? Not that you have to tell me if you don't want to.'

'It was nothing, honestly. Just Craig being an eejit. He's such a crawler.'

'I'm heading out for a break. Want to catch a coffee with me?'

He was being kind, offering to talk, but that was the last thing I wanted right then, even with Marley. I shook my head and hurried away.

Halfway down King Street, I stopped, numb with consternation and zipping and unzipping my bag as if the zip were a string of worry beads. Those peculiar texts I'd been receiving and which I'd casually deleted now made chilling sense. I took my phone out, removed its chip and threw them both in the nearest rubbish bin. On the way home that day, I called in at Vodafone and bought a new mobile, with a new number.

Until that day it hadn't crossed my mind that I was a target. Now it did.

Everything, everywhere, my whole life, reeked of Chrissy's malice.

30

I wished Conor had said more, that night months before when we'd talked about my telling Chrissy to go. He might have suggested, for instance, that my regard for Chrissy had far less to do with her as a person, than it had with my respect for the *role* of older sister. Given he had more distance than I had, he should have seen that I'd fallen into the trap of attributing to Chrissy the ideal characteristics of a big sister without stopping to see whether or not she lived up to them.

This was the whirlpool of irony I had been flailing about in. To be fair to Conor, I'd been worn down by Chrissy's belligerence and probably wouldn't have been ready in those bruising days to accept his advice.

That night, still too upset by the phoney card Craig had shown me to tell Conor about it, and wanting the whole episode to just go away, I told him I wanted to move, to another house in some other town and, if he was up for it, that what I really, really wanted was for us to emigrate.

'You're not serious.'

'I am. We could go to Ireland, spend some time with your cousins. Why not?'

'I can't quit my job. They're going to make me a partner soon.'

'So will another firm, somewhere else. They'll soon see how good you are.'

'Lexi, get real, I'll be thirty-five next year. And I've just agreed to give lectures at the polytech. It's only one afternoon a week, but it'll be great for the business.'

'Nab the talent, you mean, before the competition gets a look-in?'

'Is that such a bad thing?'

'Not at all. I'd do the same. When did this happen, anyway? Why didn't you say?'

'Would you have heard? You haven't exactly been the attentive wife lately.'

'That is grossly unfair.'

Conor wouldn't hear of us moving. He'd lived in Sydney sixteen years, ever since he'd moved into Glebe as a student, and refused to even discuss the possibility of living anywhere else. I persisted anyway.

'They say time changes things, but that actually you have to change them yourself. I think it was Andy Warhol who said that.'

'His aphorisms were better than his art then.'

'I loathe being in the same town as her, let alone the same street.'

'This is my city. And there's really interesting stuff going on at work right now.' Conor's eyes flashed with enthusiasm; I hadn't seen him so animated in ages. 'We're angling to get in on the ground floor of this three-city project.'

'What project?'

'Turning Sydney into three separate but cohesive cities.'

'Spare me, please. That sounds too horribly like Canberra.'

Sydney had become my city as well and the two visits I'd made to Canberra confirmed my view of the place. It was altogether too *nice*. Too open. There were no murky cul-de-sacs and dingy alleyways that give a place atmosphere; no grimy buildings occupied by bats and squatters.

'Canberra's got no soul.' I said. 'It's boring.'

'Give it time,' said Conor. 'You know I love Sydney, but let's face it, the place is moribund. Downtown is a mausoleum in the weekends while the suburbs are deserted during the week. We've lost that old sense of community. The fix is to mix it up again, you know, jobs and people, people and jobs.'

'This is important to you, isn't it?'

'As important as sustainability is to you.'

'Fair enough, but honestly Conor, I like Sydney just the way it is, thanks. And it's an OE I'm suggesting, not a life sentence. Two years max.'

Conor refused to be drawn.

'Very well, then, one year. Twelve stimulating, career-enhancing months. Then we'll come back here.'

We were sitting on the sofa in our living room. It was long and deep enough to sleep on and I was at one end with my feet up and Conor was at the other. Somewhere in the neighbourhood an ambulance screamed its way to St Vincent's Hospital.

'Won't you even think about it?'

'My answer will be the same.'

I abandoned the subject of moving. 'Let's order in pizza. Margherita with extra olives and anchovies.'

Conor flicked through the playlist on his phone and suddenly Adele was in the room, singing *Someone Like You*. 'Not that one,' I shouted. 'Not that one.' Conor had just ripped the scab off my wound. Chrissy used to listen to Adele and any reminder of my sister, no matter how tenuous, made me recoil. Conor put Bryan Adams on instead: *Everything I Do*.

After he'd phoned for a pizza, I turned the music up. I loved that song. I couldn't help asking myself: did Conor live those lyrics for me, do everything for me, as I did for him?

He handed me a glass of pinot noir and poured a beer for himself before joining me back on the sofa. 'As for Chrissy,' he said, 'you've had a falling out, that's all. It will pass. Show me a family that doesn't have rows.'

'In case you haven't noticed, I'm not fighting. This isn't a row. It's a vendetta. Chrissy's not the mobster's moll, she's the entire fecking mob.'

Conor made a face, pulling down the sides of his mouth in an attitude of gloom. 'Ah, to be sure, she's a poor friendless Bonnie, searching for Clyde.'

'Not funny. It's wearing me down, Conor, and affecting my work.'

'She was lonely.'

'Who?'

'Bonnie Parker. She kept a diary.'

'For god's sake.' I was about to give up on the conversation and storm out in a pique, but Conor lifted my feet into his lap and began massaging them. We were quiet for a few minutes and I managed to put a lid on the stress that bubbled in me like an impending eruption every time I thought or spoke about my sister.

'It's easy for you to be cavalier. You're not the one being bullied.'

'Don't react and she'll soon lose interest,' said Conor.

'I need to know you're on my side.'

'I am, love, I am, but it won't help if we both behave like burnt offerings.'

He tickled my feet and I kicked him. Then I dragged out the cushions from behind me and threw them at him.

'Leaving town is still my preferred option.'

Conor didn't answer but he lobbed the cushions back.

There was a loud knock on the door. The pizza had arrived.

Over dinner we agreed to a holiday. Maybe, if we left town for long enough, Chrissy would take her rancorous preoccupations elsewhere. Conor went online and booked a hotel in New Caledonia, for two weeks. We would spend Christmas in Noumea, in a resort by the beach.

31

We were due to leave on the thirteenth of December. In the meantime, I tried and failed to put Chrissy out of my mind. She was a pustule seething on my consciousness and needed lancing. Lauren was the friend to help me with this and I sent her a text, suggesting we meet for coffee.

Lauren is a patent attorney and always busy. She couldn't get away until after one-thirty and we met for a late lunch in a café near her office. It was good just being in her company again. Lauren has a round, candid face with smooth olive skin and warm hazel eyes. Her brown hair is short and strong, and she has a stillness about her that inspires trust. I've sometimes envied her calmness and thought it must have something to do with her faith. She is utterly dependable.

'Why is she such a cow?' I wanted to say bitch or worse, like the C-word which while accurate was much too vulgar, even for me, and Lauren would wince at it. She never swears and sometimes makes me feel a bit improper when I do.

'Seems to me she's jealous of you,' Lauren said.

'She's got everything I've got and more.'

'Something must have happened to put that chip on her shoulder. Don't you know?'

'The weird thing is, I know very little about her life, and even less about when she was growing up.'

'Do you think she might have been abused once, you know, raped or something?'

'Possibly. She does have some half-baked story about our brother, but I don't buy it.'

'Maybe there isn't an explanation. Is she psycho ... you know, a sociopath?'

'That's a bit extreme.'

'Not necessarily. In the US one person in every twenty-five is a sociopath.'

'We're not America and thank god for that.'

'Still, I don't suppose it's any different here.'

'That's scary.' It took me a bit to absorb such a disquieting fact. 'I think my sister just needs to grow up.'

'If she's a sociopath, she won't,' said Lauren. 'There's nothing you can do about it. It's not an illness, it can't be cured.'

'How do you know this stuff?'

'Someone brought a book to Bible class a while ago, something about sociopaths living next door and devils being where you least expect them. They are around, you know, the devils. Might be one sitting at the next table.'

I scanned the restaurant. There was a family of four at the next table. Mum and Dad weren't talking much and the two teenagers, in his and hers school uniforms, were stuck zombie-like to their cell phones and about as diverting. All the other tables were occupied by office workers, most of whom were also scanning their cell phones. It made the place feel unnaturally quiet, apart from Classic FM playing softly in the background.

The food was Italian, it arrived promptly and was good.

'You just have to get away from them,' said Lauren. 'Sociopaths I mean.'

'Trust me, I'm working on it.'

When I referred to Chrissy as one of Satan's retainers, I expected Lauren to laugh but she didn't. She got all serious on me and quoted from the New Testament. 'It is by God's grace we are saved through faith. That's from the book of Ephesians. I know you'll want to mark it.' She beamed at me, knowing full well that I didn't even own a Bible. 'Our achievements are not the results of our efforts, but come from God's gift. That way, no one can boast.'

'Then would God please pass a little grace down Chrissy's way. Why doesn't he?'

'It's only given to those who accept it. That's what faith is. We are saved by faith, not by what we do.'

'Why don't you invite my sister to your church one day. She might get saved.' I was kidding of course.

'Would she come?'

'No.' An image of Chrissy, prostrate and penitent on the freezing stone flags in St Joseph's almost made me laugh.

'Anyway, it's up to God,' said Lauren.

'You know I don't believe in all that god and guru stuff. It just doesn't make any sense to me.'

Lauren's faith was unwavering. 'It's one of the great mysteries of religion, why some people are saved and others not.'

Can it be that simple? That all we have to do to recover from bad stuff is believe in God? Unlike Lauren, I'm not the evangelical type, but if I could have convinced myself then to believe in some supreme and benign being, I would have done so, anything to lift me out of the funk I was in. It was never going to happen. I've always appreciated Lauren's spiritual strength, but believing in some higher power, not to mention relying on it, is not for me. I like to think I have some control over my future.

Something Conor once said came back to me. He'd suggested I try to imagine that Chrissy and I were not related. If I only I could. I was as tormented by the need to understand Chrissy as I was by the need to file her away and forget all about her. I was tired of my parsing of her. Would believing in God mean accepting that she and I were one and the same, both of us the observer and the observed? I read somewhere once that when you accept the notion of unity in all things, you have arrived at some sacred understanding; you know without conscious thought that we are none of us separate, either from each other or from God. By then, too, you should be a better and more noble person.

I was never going to be a better person. The thought that I once believed Chrissy and I were alike, in any way at all, was as irritating to me as an onset of thrush and I refused point blank to accept that on some metaphysical level we were fundamentally the same living breathing being.

The subject of Steve hadn't come up during the conversation with Lauren. I'd kept to my resolve not to mention him, but that hadn't stopped me agonising over it. If it were me, and Conor who was unfaithful, I'd want to know. Wouldn't I? Maybe not. My uncertainty about this meant I went on saying nothing. If Lauren knew about Steve's infidelity, she was keeping mum about it and I'd swear an oath, anyway, that she would have absolved him.

32

I'd emailed Robbie a couple of times suggesting a Skype call. He hadn't replied to my first email, but came back on the second, briefly, saying only that he was busy and would get back to me. I tried again. He put me off another week, but agreed on a day and time to hook up. At last.

Our call was set for mid-week – ten am on Thursday morning in Sydney, eight pm on Wednesday in New Jersey – and it would make me late for work, but what the hell. This was my long-lost brother and I needed him.

I waited until after Conor left for work, then went into the bedroom and spent an inane amount of time deciding what to wear. I tried on a red dress, then my smartest black trousers and top, with pearl studs, then the red dress again. In the end I chose a pair of navy pants and a plain white shirt, no jewellery.

As I was setting up my laptop on the kitchen table, a cockatoo outside began screeching. I hoped it would shut up while Robbie and I spoke, at the same time thinking my brother might actually like to hear it and be reminded of home.

As things turned out, the parrot fell silent and we never got around to talking about birds, or Sydney, or my home in Glebe.

There were other more pressing subjects. I needed to know about what happened to him at home in Bendigo, and what it had been like with Chrissy in those early years.

'She was always jealous of you,' said Robbie. 'When you were a baby, she'd push you off Mum's lap. Ironic when you think about it. If it hadn't been for her moronic act, you'd never have been conceived in the first place'.

'Go on. What act?' I was listening intently. Every now and then I realised I'd been holding my breath.

'Mum wasn't supposed to have any more kids, the doctors advised against it. Chrissy and I overheard Mum and Dad talking about it. Chrissy found Mum's diaphragm – wouldn't surprise me if she went looking for it – anyway, she took a pin from Mum's sewing gear and pricked holes in it. She made sure I was watching too. It gave her a buzz.'

It was true then, what Chrissy had told me, that I was an after-thought, and unwanted.

'So, Mum didn't want me?'

'Oh no, you were a surprise at first I think, but once you arrived, Mum and Dad were both besotted. You were their favourite. We all knew that.'

'What happened with you? Chrissy said Dad threw you out.'

'Seems mundane now, but it wasn't at the time. When you turned up, Chris had to share her room and she didn't like that. Not one little bit. She was always the selfish one. She set her sights on my room and didn't care how she got it. First, she told Mum I was doing stuff, like perving on you. I'm not that sort of man, Lexi. Honestly. Just have to tell you that. Anyway, when that didn't work, she accused me of raping her, put on this massive performance, tears, screams, the works. It was quite a show.'

'Must have been awful for you.'

'Let's just say I was happy to leave. I didn't want to join the army, not at first, but it worked out well for me. I made friends, we're still good mates. And the army put me through uni, helped me get an engineering degree. I've no complaints.'

We were silent for two or three minutes, as if both of us needed time to digest the conversation so far.

'Let me show you where I am,' said Robbie. He picked up his tablet and panned its camera around his living room: pale grey walls, a charcoal sofa along one wall, big windows on another, a standard lamp with a yellow and grey floral-patterned shade in the corner. On a coffee table there were a few magazines, but I couldn't see their titles, only that one of them had a black and white photo of the Brooklyn Bridge on the cover. The room struck me as obsessively well ordered, and impersonal, almost like a hotel room. I supposed Robbie's family spent most of their time in another part of the house, probably where the kitchen was, just as Conor and I did in Mitchell Street.

Robbie held the camera close to a row of four small water-colours on the wall. They were landscapes: a beach scene, two woodland views, a bare yellowish hillside with a rusted red barn.

'My wife painted these. She's had a couple of exhibitions.' His voice was proud. 'She teaches art at the local primary school, part-time.'

I didn't say anything to my brother about my own aspirations to be a full-time artist. He'd left home years before I'd started art classes, when I was nine. But maybe, one day, I'd be able to talk art with his wife. For a minute or two, faith in my future as an artist warmed me like a bright flare.

'What's her name?'

There was a pause during which I wondered if we'd lost our connection. Then Robbie brought the tablet's camera back to himself. 'Rhonda. Her name is Rhonda.' I noticed then how much he blinked, an ocular stutter that was vaguely unsettling. 'Rhonda says she looks forward to meeting you one day. And the boys, they're really excited to learn about their Aunt Lexi in Australia.'

'You have kids?'

'Two boys. I've told them all about you.'

'Where are they now?'

'Having dinner with Rhonda's folks. It's a regular thing. I'll send you a photo, of the family.'

'Why did you change your name?'

'I wanted a quiet life.' Robbie cleared his throat and briefly closed his eyes. 'I regret falling out with Mum and Dad. They didn't deserve that. Chrissy's a liar but I suppose you know that?'

I nodded. 'She's a thief too, and … actually Robbie, let's face it, the woman is batty.' I told him about those decapitated flowers, and the Elite Escorts card.

A look of glee passed over my brother's face, almost as if he were elated by what I had to say, or gratified that I'd found out for myself our sister's true nature, and then he laughed, a short bark of a laugh. 'Sorry,' he said, 'don't suppose you find it funny, but that is just so typical of her.'

'She was nice to me when I was little, and later, after Mum died.'

'I should have kept in touch, but I'm here now for you, Lexi. Call me whenever you want.'

'Next time we meet, we'll talk about something else. I'd like to know about your job, what you guys do on the weekend, what it's like living in the States.' I didn't ask Robbie if he was eligible to vote and who he voted for, but I was fairly confident – no, I needed to *believe* that he'd support the Democrats if he did and if they could come up with someone worth voting for. 'Will you ever come home?'

'No. I'm settled here and this is where Rhonda grew up. Next time we hook up, I'll make sure she's home. You can meet her, and the boys.'

'I'd like that.'

We agreed to talk again, at the same time in the following week.

Within the hour he sent me an email, saying how much he enjoyed our talk and how much he looked forward to our next call. He'd attached photos of Rhonda and their sons. Rhonda had olive skin, brown eyes, and black hair. She looked as if she might be from the Caribbean, or maybe Mexico. The kids were teenagers, almost adults. They looked like your all-American family, all of them smiling, with perfect teeth and new perfect clothes.

33

Two days later, on my way home from work, I got a text from Janet. 'Protest happening. Pick you up in ten? Your place.'

I didn't have time to change before Janet met me in Glebe so I was still in my work clothes, my canvas work bag slung over my shoulder, when we drove out to Mascot, near the airport, where there are streets and streets of warehouses. The organisers of People Against Plastic were taking their protest to the source: manufacturers' storehouses rather than supermarkets.

There was hardly anyone around when we arrived, only four or five protesters milling about, and as far as I could see, the exercise was pointless. It was after hours and most of the warehouses were closed up already and the surrounding area seemed to be deserted.

'What's the point of this?'

'You'll see,' said Janet.

'Unless media turn up, I'll be the only one who does.'

I was hoping to see that young reporter again and suggest he talk to the CSIRO. If the scientists there weren't working on this, they'd know who was. I'd read some research somewhere that found the average person ingested five grams of plastic every week. I may just as well eat my Visa card. Eating all that plastic has to be having a deleterious on our brains and maybe that accounts for the growing anger and idiocy in the world.

Janet's voice broke through my reflections. She seemed edgy, looking around to see who was there, and who wasn't. 'The cops should be here first. Where are they?'

She grabbed my arm suddenly and jerked me back as a large curtain-sided truck came around the corner and parked alongside the entrance of one to the warehouses. Two men got out from the cabin and opened up the side of the lorry as the roller doors on the warehouse started going up. A storeman in a beige dustcoat came out from the warehouse and began helping the truckies load up. There were enough pallets of packaging plastic going into that lorry to float another island.

They'd filled about a third of the lorry when a squad of protesters – as many as fifty people, mostly adults but a decent number of school kids as well – marched around the corner and crowded around. It was the supermarket scene all over again. The same leader, Mike Wallims, was there, dressed in the same green overalls. They all carried the same banners and shouted the same war cry: 'plastic kills, plastic kills.' I sensed a greater urgency in the group this time. Everyone seemed more vehement.

We all watched and waited as the workers loaded the lorry. When they finished, the truckies lowered the curtain and began strapping it down. That's when I saw the name of Farras Leven's client, B K Cleverly Holdings Ltd – the firm for which I'd devised the sustainable packing strategy – in big black capital letters.

I grabbed Janet's arm. 'Let's get out of here.' I was half regretting my decision to join Janet, torn between keeping in good with Barry and wanting to stand up against companies that think it's their god-given right to pollute our planet.

'Wait. It's just starting.'

A police van with dark tinted windows arrived and a liaison officer stepped out and went over to talk to Mike. The cop was in civvies – jeans and polo shirt – but I recognised him as one of the two officers outside the supermarket in Paddington, except this time he wasn't wearing a high-vis vest. Three uniformed cops waited in the car.

'I should go,' I said. An image of my desk in the agency, without me there, floated across my consciousness. I saw Barry tearing more strips off me, and then Megan taking over all my projects.

'What do you want to do?' asked Janet.

I shook off the image of Megan glowing under Barry's praise.

'To hell with it. I'll stay. This is important.'

'Great. It'll be okay. The cops are here now so there's no risk of things getting out of hand.'

The liaison officer returned to his colleagues although he didn't get back in the car.

Mike bunched his fists and waved them in the air and shouted, 'Stop the truck.'

The squad crowded around the lorry to prevent it leaving. 'No more plastic, no more plastic,' everyone bawled. Except me. I was still in agony of indecision, torn between protecting my job and protecting the environment. The job won out. 'I think I better go,' I said again.

'If you're sure,' said Janet. 'I'll come with you, of course.'

We were turning to leave when a black Toyota van, also with darkened windows, screeched to a halt beside us. Seven men, or at least I presumed they were all male, wearing khaki combat pants and black hoodies spilled out, each wielding two spray cans. They ignored us and began covering the outside walls of the warehouse with fascist slogans: 'Unite the Right', and 'The Future is White'.

Then some imbecilic half-wit threw a bomb into the warehouse. I saw a thin arc of flame followed by a boom so loud and so terrifying that I dropped involuntarily to my knees. A wall of fire bulged at the entrance and smoke bowled towards us in a black acrid cloud. Fumes from smouldering plastic scraped my throat like a razor.

Sirens screamed.

Janet helped me to my feet.

It all happened so fast. What should have been another peaceful protest was so far out of control it became terrorism. The alt-righters dropped their cans, piled into their vehicle and squealed away. Three police cars arrived, one of which turned around immediately and chased the fascists. Less than a minute later media crews turned up. Protesters scattered, except Mike who stood on the tray of his ute and continued yelling: 'Say no to plastic, shout yes to life.'

Janet and I ran. An aeroplane roared its ascent from the airport nearby and I felt my insides implode with fear. I tripped and fell, landing heavily on my knees on the pavement. As I got up, I glanced behind me and saw police brutally hustling protesters into the back of the police van. I clutched my bag tightly against my chest and ran faster, and blindly. We were sprinting up O'Riordan Street when Janet tugged at my arm. 'Wrong way,' she said. 'Sorry, the car, it's the other way.' We turned back until we reached High Street when I had to stop and catch my breath. I bent over, hands on my thighs, and gulped in air.

Janet was out of breath as well. 'Lexi, I'm so sorry. None of that was supposed to happen. The Facebook page said it would be another peaceful demo.'

'Shouldn't be unexpected, I suppose. Advertise a demo on the net nowadays and it's a call to arms for every disaffected wanker in the city.'

I straightened up, stretched my back. My feet hurt. Fortunately, I'd put on low heels that day, but when I looked down, I saw one of the heels was loose. The other shoe squelched with dog shit. Thin trickles of blood dribbled down my legs. I'd skinned my knees when I tripped and they stung. I took my shoes off and put the clean one in my bag, and then wiped the blood off my leg with the back of my hand.

Janet looked equally shattered. 'That's the last time I join a protest,' she said.

'Me too.'

We grinned at each another and felt better. I don't think either of us meant what we said; there would always be issues you had to take a stand on and even though we'd had a scare, we were also exhilarated by the experience.

'Who the hell were those guys? Surely they weren't with Mike.'

'No, he'd never do that,' said Janet. 'Mike's a pacifist through and through. He wouldn't know one end of a pipe bomb from the other, let alone how to make one.'

We walked up High Street to where we'd parked Janet's car outside an old brick bungalow with a 'For Sale' sign at the gate. As we slowed down looking for it, I was annoyed to see Craig Smithins walking towards us, lugging two bags of groceries. He was wearing blue mirrored sunglasses which, as tossers go, define the breed. He was the last person I expected or wanted to see.

'What are *you* doing here?'

'This is my street,' said Craig. 'I live here.' To his credit he took his sunglasses off, then looked me up and down in his usual unctuous manner and smirked. 'What's that on your face, Lexi? Client get a little rough?'

When I touched my face, my hand came away with a smear of blood.

'Fuck off, Craig.'

If he wasn't such a jerk, I'd have complimented him on his shopping bags. They were made of a heavy unbleached fabric, hessian maybe, or jute.

On the news that night there was a brief item about the protest: firemen hosing out the warehouse and Mike Wallims being manhandled into the back of a police van, still shouting his catch phrase, but denying any knowledge of the bomb or of the guys with the spray cans.

Despite my involvement in the action, I couldn't at that minute muster up any interest in the outcome. A burned-out warehouse in Sydney was small beans next to news of eight teenage girls being dragged, dead, from the Mediterranean, along with four hundred other refugees, or of a gunman opening fire in a Baptist church in Texas and killing twenty-six people, or of smog in Delhi so thick schools had be closed and a state of emergency declared.

It was hard not to get depressed about the state of the world and my pathetic little rebellion against plastic seemed suddenly futile. Whatever I did amounted to diddly-squat; it wouldn't change a thing.

The only good news I could find that week was that Mattel had finally come out with a Barbie doll dressed in a hijab.

34

Mid-way through the ensuing week, I again lingered in the house after Conor had left for work, expecting to have another Skype call with Robbie, but he sent a text saying he was sorry as heck but had to take a rain check. He'd been called to a meeting in Chicago and couldn't get out of it. He'd get back to me just as soon as.

We never got around to that call because Conor and I left for New Caledonia. As the plane lifted from the tarmac at Kingsford Smith Airport, I felt my spirits rise with it. I'd made a point of leaving my phone and laptop at home. I needed to get off the grid, to not hear or see any news, or think about work, or … anything, anything at all. Even Robbie. By the end of the holiday, I promised myself, I'd be the old sanguine me again, a new old Lexi.

This didn't happen overnight and it was a measure of my stress that on the third day of our holiday, Conor and I had a silly row.

We'd spent the morning on the beach and were sleeping off the effects of too much sun.

Our hotel room was spacious with exactly the muted minimalist décor I particularly like. The floors were pale polished wood while nearly everything else was warm off-white: the walls, the bed linen, the curtains, and the cushions arranged on three fawn chairs and a dove-grey settee. The bed was indulgently wide with side tables of bleached wood in metal frames. There was a standard lamp with a rattan shade, and a long low sideboard in more bleached wood. And instead of the usual clutter of touristy magazines and brochures cajoling us into local shops and attractions, there were four anthologies of short stories. Full marks to the hotel management for that.

I was drifting in and out of sleep. Out in the corridor a door banged shut and through the window there was the distant whine of a strimmer. Conor slipped into bed beside me. It was hot, too hot for two bodies. I moved away. He moved closer. I felt the pressure of his long body against my side, and then he was on top of me. So heavy. I squeezed my eyes tight. There was a tightness in my throat, I had to gasp for air, I was being smothered. Conor's face was too close to mine, and his mouth ... his lips were parted, teeth bared. Animal teeth. I tried to call out but no sound came. I pushed him away, flailing with my arms until I struck something.

I woke with a start and covered in a sheen of sweat. The room was quiet. Conor, beside me, was nursing his jaw.

'Did I do that?'

'You had the sheet over your face,' he said.

'I was dreaming.'

'Sounded more like a nightmare. The bloke not letting you be on top, was that it?'

'Sorry.' I ignored what he said about my preferring to be on top although it was true; lying beneath a man, even if he was the love of my life, did sometimes make me claustrophobic. It's an irrational fear, I know, but there it is.

'Forget it.' Conor retreated to the bathroom where he got dressed. Then he went downstairs and spent a couple of hours at the bar. I knew he'd taken umbrage, but it was petty to behave as if I'd meant to hit him. What I did in my sleep was hardly my fault.

It was late afternoon, hot and sultry, and I took full advantage of time alone to indulge in a long cool bath. By the time he returned to the room, Conor had recovered his dignity and was in a better mood. No doubt alcohol had helped. He'd made friends with the barman who'd given him a tasting of the hotel's whisky collection. Conor announced that he'd decided to become a connoisseur and that our next trip would be to Scotland to visit some distilleries. This idea held zero appeal for me, but I didn't say anything; Conor's enthusiasm for it would probably wane anyway by the time we could afford another overseas trip.

That evening, to atone for offending Conor earlier in the day, I shouted us dinner at a restaurant run by nuns who, as we scraped out the last of our crème brûlée, emerged from the kitchen, removed their aprons and sang *Ave Maria*. It was a magical evening.

The next day, we took a boat out to the Amédée Lighthouse where we walked around the island, went snorkelling, ate fresh barbecued fish, and drank copious amounts of Beaujolais. When we got back to the hotel there was a local band playing in the foyer, something in French. We stopped to listen for a while. I had no idea what they were singing about – Conor did because he'd studied French – but I liked the tune and was still humming it when we got to our room. I was serenely happy.

'Come here, *mon petit oiseau chanteur*, my little scarlet robin,' said Conor and he pulled me towards the bed.

'You're talking daft,' I said and laughed, pleased with the endearment all the same. I couldn't remember when he'd last used his pet name for me. The first time, I thought it was because of a red waistcoat I used to wear, but it wasn't that at all. He named me for the songbird because I had a habit of singing around the house, nothing especially musical, just random snatches and snippets of tunes that came into my head.

I started unbuckling the belt on his shorts. He undid the buttons on my dress and slipped it off my shoulders. He bent and kissed my breasts. I unzipped the fly of his pants and slipped my hand inside. Conor groaned; he needed me as much as I needed him. He knelt and buried his face in my groin. We stripped and fell naked together on the bed and made love the way we used to, rolling over one another, Conor on top, briefly, then me, then Conor and because I was relaxed and happy and – it came to me in that instant, what the right word was: it was safe – I felt safe, so I let him stay there, on top of me, kissing, touching each other until neither of us could stand it any longer and I arched my back to meet Conor as he drove himself into me.

When we finished, Conor was very tender. He cradled me in his arms and I snuggled against him. After an hour or so we got up and while Conor phoned for room service, I gathered up the sheet, bed cover and pillows from the floor and remade the bed. A tray of club sandwiches arrived from the hotel kitchen, with fat slices of mango and papaya, along with a carafe of iced tea. As soon as the waiter left, we hung the do-not-disturb sign on our door and left it there until the following afternoon.

We'd hit the re-set button on our marriage and the rest of the holiday was idyllic.

I'd packed a sketch book and box of pastels and on a few afternoons when Conor went snorkelling, I reminded myself why I love to draw. My book slowly filled with scenes of kids playing in the surf, of their parents watching from under striped beach umbrellas, and of hawkers selling slabs of fresh pineapple. I made a few studies of Conor as well, when he wasn't looking, and was satisfied with the results. I hadn't lost my touch and resolved to do more when I got home, and to keep up the visits I used to make regularly to art galleries, to study technique and find inspiration. I'd forgotten how relaxing drawing is, how it takes me out of myself, completely, and it came home to me on that holiday what a distraction my job as a graphic designer had been; how far I'd strayed from my original intention to be a full-time artist.

Christmas lunch was a picnic on the balcony of our hotel room, of baguette with blue camembert, black olives, and a rocket salad, washed down with a bottle of pinot grigio. There seemed to be no one else in the hotel that day. Even the swimming pool had been abandoned. On any other day I would have leapt at having the pool to myself, but when Conor kicked off his sandals after lunch and lay down on the bed, I joined him and we dozed like sloths through the rest of the day.

I did not want to return home.

35

When we arrived back in Glebe and opened our front door, we were engulfed by a wave of warm damp air. There was a pungent earthy smell and the floors, from the hall at the front right through to the back of the house, were sopping wet.

'Shit, we've got a leak.' Conor removed his shoes.

I took mine off as well and my jacket. 'How come it's so hot in here?'

The climate in the house was tropical, as if we were still in New Caledonia. And there was no leak. Our garden hose had been extended and pushed through the cat flap in the back door from where it snaked through the house until it reached the living room where a slowly revolving sprinkler discharged a steady light smattering of water. The fan heater from our bathroom was on the coffee table and on high, blowing out hot air.

Conor and I were dumbfounded. Our old beige carpet was not only sodden, it was bright emerald green. The floor was covered in a layer of soil in which grass flourished, green, growing Kikuyu grass.

'What the hell … how …?'

'How the hell do you think?' I wailed. 'That bitch has been in here and planted a fucking lawn!'

We stared at the floor, then at each another, then the floor again as if gaping at the problem would make it go away. I turned the heater off. Conor went outside and turned off the garden tap. We sloshed through the rooms. Dead cockroaches floated in the sludge. There was a horrible smell of mould and decomposition.

'Do we know it's your sister?'

'Who else would it be? I suppose this is revenge for throwing her out.'

Conor nodded and, to my disgust, gave an approving smile. 'It's imaginative, I'll give her that.'

'Don't be absurd.' I dropped onto a chair, holding my feet above the sludge, and covered my face with my hands. 'She's never going to leave us alone.'

'It's not all bad, Lex. We could take up lawn bowls.'

'For god's sake, Conor.'

'You've got to admit it has a certain style. And she could have done worse, stuffed a few dead eels down the back of the sofa.'

Conor's flippancy was infuriating. Everyone who knows me knows I have a sense of humour and that I will almost always see the funny side of things, but there's nothing remotely comic about home invasion or vandalism or malice or spite or ... This was criminal.

'I'm going to call the police, have her arrested.' Conor had put his phone on the table. I picked it up and was about to make the call when he took it from me and dropped it back in his pocket.

'Best leave it, love. Getting the police involved will only make things worse. We've enough drama as it is. The insurance will cover it and probably wiser anyway to ignore Chrissy.'

'No way. You have to go and see her. Get our spare key back for a start. And tell her to piss off out of our lives.'

Conor went back to the front door, picked up our cases and squelched into the bedroom. 'You can finish the garden now,' he called out. 'The carpet will make terrific mulch.'

157

I rolled my eyes. 'If you're trying to make me feel better it's really not working.'

Conor phoned one of those companies that suck water out of carpets, then we went to spend the night in a hotel. Then we moved into a motel. For ten days. That's how we spent New Year that year, waiting for our house to dry out and for the stench to go away so that the place was passably habitable again.

Have I said that I'm a coward? I am. Not a scaredy-cat exactly, but I dislike conflict and will go out of my way to avoid confrontation.

At work I have no trouble standing up for myself because my role there is clear and the transaction unambiguous: my time and expertise in exchange for a salary.

When it comes to my personal life the picture is very different. There the boundaries blur like buildings in the Beijing smog. I'm frequently outmanoeuvred, too easily nonplussed by the strength of an opponent, or too ready to see their point of view before cottoning on to the fact that it unfairly imposes on mine. Only later, sometimes hours later, will I come up with the things I ought to have said, and I'll replay the conversation in my head, over and over, adding words I wished I'd said and editing out the ones I wished I hadn't. It's exhausting. I'd like to be stronger, a better advocate for myself.

36

My faint heart meant it had to be Conor who went to see Chrissy and extract an explanation if not an apology. I expected him back within half an hour but nearly three hours went by before he returned. I know how long it was because I was watching the clock and now and then pacing irritably up and down the pavement outside the motel.

When he finally turned up, he looked sheepish.

'You're late. What happened?'

'She brought out some whisky, Laphroaig. Single malt. Had to try it, and very nice it was too.'

'And that took three hours? Honestly, Conor, you were supposed to have it out with her. You were supposed to get some money out of her to pay for that mess, and scare the bejesus out her while you were at it.'

Conor was tipsy. He sashayed across the room towards the bathroom. 'Your big sis knows her usquebaugh.'

'And you're quite the grandiloquent.' It was hard not to be snide. If Conor was going to start throwing big words around, I'd lob them right back. 'Chrissy hates whisky.'

'That's not the impression she gave me.'

'She drinks only chartreuse, makes a thing of it, because she thinks it makes her intriguing. She was trying to impress you, that's all.'

Conor sat on the bed and swayed a little. He wore a doltish smirk which I'd never seen before.

'She said it wasn't her.'

'And you believe that?'

'As it happens, yes, I do.'

'I can't believe you'd take her word against mine.'

'Look, Lex, sweetie, has it occurred to you, you might have it all wrong? It really did seem to me that Chrissy was genuine. I mean, why would she do something so completely cretinous?'

'Because she hates me and because … because she wants you.' That last phrase, somewhere between a statement and a question, hung in the air between us, a miasma of my misgiving.

Conor shook his head as if he despaired of me, but I brushed aside the implication and carried on. 'C'mon, you know it as well as I do. She started flirting with you from the moment she arrived to stay with us. And slept with Steve, probably, now I think of it, to let *you* know she was available.'

'This is crazy talk, love. Any nutter could have broken in the house and done this ... some people do this sort of thing for kicks.'

'Where's the broken window then?' I had to stop talking for a minute, gather my thoughts a little so that I could persuade Conor of the truth. 'Can't you see what's she's doing? She's trying to drive a wedge between us.'

Conor pulled me down onto the bed beside him and wrapped his arms around me. 'That will never happen. You are my true and only love, my love.'

His inebriation debased the sincerity of this declaration and I pushed him away.

'But you like her, don't you? Please tell me you don't. I will sock you if you say yes.'

'Well, she's not boring, is she?'

160

I thwacked Conor across the side of his head, not hard, just enough to make me feel justice had been meted. He smelled of perfume, Burberry, Chrissy's perfume. I shoved him away and sat up. 'You stink of her.'

Conor got off the bed and straightened his clothes. 'There's no need for you to get so het up, it was nothing. When I left, she kissed me, that's all, one of those fatuous air kisses, but close enough I suppose.'

'I don't believe you. I'm going to bed.' I picked up his dressing gown and slung it over an armchair in the corner of the room. 'You can sleep there.'

'What about dinner?'

'I don't want any.'

'Why do you always have to over-react?'

I went into the bathroom, slamming the door behind me. The smell of my sister's perfume on Conor made me bilious. He stank too, of those revolting cigarillos she smoked, but what repulsed me most was the whisky on his breath.

I felt my past and my present collide.

37

Dad was an alcoholic, what they call a functioning alcoholic so that he went cheerfully to work each day, held down a responsible job, and enjoyed the company of his friends. He did as well as anyone I know to fulfil his obligations as a dependable and caring father and I'd loved him.

Every other Sunday he put on a blue and white striped apron, and fried steak and onions on the barbecue in our back yard, and sometimes after lunch drove us all to Myrong Beach where we had a picnic for tea.

It was only when he locked himself in our garden shed for three days at a time, with four or five bottles of Johnnie Walker, that the illness manifested itself. It didn't happen often, maybe once or twice a year at most, and he was always sorry afterwards. Mum said he wasn't a drunk, or weak in the head, but that these binges were just his way of picking the scab off his psychic wound. I was at high school when she explained that Dad's mother had abandoned him when he was a baby, given him away for adoption. Whisky helped him forget something his DNA never would.

Dad didn't return to the house until he was sober and I never actually saw him drunk. Mum always told me to stay out of the back yard when he was in the shed, but sometimes I heard him crying there, or shouting angrily. Mum left meals for him at the door and when he came back inside the house again, she'd run a bath for him, coddle him, and say nothing.

When Conor told me in Noumea that he'd decided to become a whisky connoisseur, I remembered my childhood anxiety during Dad's bouts of drinking. Whisky made me nervous and I made Conor promise me that he'd never to have more than one glass of the stuff at a time.

He'd clearly put away a lot more than that at Chrissy's place. The next morning, he was hung-over and I was crotchety and we were tetchy as hell with each another.

'Grown-ups make mistakes,' said Conor. 'Like forget to do their homework, or stay out after curfew.' He was rummaging through his toiletries bag looking for Panadol.

'Don't be so patronising.'

'You put me in an awkward position. I haven't exactly relished playing go-between.'

'Is that what you call it?'

'She told me she's depressed.'

'If you believed that, why did you get her tanked up on whisky? Not helpful for someone suffering mental illness I would have thought.'

'Now who's being patronising.'

'People who are depressed don't go around destroying other people's houses. They cut themselves if they're of a cutting mind. They don't go slashing out at others.'

'We don't know it was her and anyway, I don't recall seeing any slash marks last night.'

'Do you know what you just said?'

'Give it a rest, Lex. Haven't we enough provocation without you adding paranoia to the list? Chrissy wasn't wearing a burka. We talked. We drank. That is all.'

'You went to pick up our key.'

Conor had found his packet of Panadol. He swallowed two tablets and went into the bathroom to shave. As far as I was concerned that ended the conversation.

The décor in the motel room was dirty beige and maroon and the breakfast bar offered only instant coffee and tiny boxes of unappealing cereal; fake food. The cardboard boxes probably contained more nutrients. I needed to escape the room, soak up the sky, and find a coffee worthy of the name.

Conor poked his head around the bathroom door. 'What is she so frightened of?'

'Your point being …?'

'You know, love or fear. The two motivations. Obviously, if we accept that Chrissy did it, and I'm not saying she did, Lex, planting a lawn in our living room isn't an act of love. Ergo, Chrissy acted out of fear. Some deep anxiety. I'm just wondering what caused that.'

'You're talking like a self-help book.'

'I'm talking like someone interested in being helpful.'

'Helpful to who?'

'Whom.'

'Jesus. Must you be so pompous? Anyway, anxiety's not the right word. Insecurity would be more accurate.'

'Now there's a more caring approach. Do I detect a little détente in the Madison camp?'

'Not for a nanosecond. I really am quite over giving a shit about what does or doesn't drive Chrissy.'

I pondered briefly on how Dad's drinking had affected my siblings. Maybe it was during one of those drunken episodes that Dad and Robbie fell out. Maybe Chrissy had inherited Dad's pain gene and that's why she lived her life behind a veil of treacherous charm.

And what about me? For the first time it occurred to me to ask what impact those pitiable episodes in the back yard might have had on my own my life. This first question led me to an uncomfortable second: Had my need for Chrissy to like me, and Conor too for that matter, anyone in fact, been excessive, unhealthy even? What's the word people use to describe that sort of thing? Co-dependency? But that was for people suffering some sort of psychological disorder. Not me.

Conor emerged from the bathroom towelling his hair dry.

'We have to find some way to move on from all this,' he said.

'Let's just both say sorry, then, and forget it.'

'Good idea. Let's both be grown-up.'

'Your facetiousness is really aggravating, you know that?'

'Enough. I'm going out for coffee and fried eggs. Come or don't come.'

'Nice of you to give me the choice.'

Conor grinned, whether or not he meant the pun, and the tension between us melted away. It was like that with Conor and me; we never let our disagreements fester.

'I'm sorry.'

'Me too,' I said. 'I should never have let her stay so long.'

'You weren't to know. What's done is done.'

'Did you get the key back?'

'She said she left it in the usual place.'

'And you believe that of course.'

'Enough. Please, Lexi, let's agree not to talk about this any more.'

Chrissy became a taboo subject. I hoped my reasons for this concurred with Conor's, but there were times when I wasn't entirely sure.

38

We were back in Mitchell Street by January seventh, but it was late April before we were happy with the state of the house.

The carpets were stained and putrid so we ripped them up, only to find the boards underneath were rotten. When we put in a claim for insurance, we didn't say the damage was deliberate, or that it was the work of a relative, and fortunately no one asked us any leading questions. We made the most of the payment, and the need for some repairs, to go all the way and give the house the revamp we'd talked about since we began living together. At the back of the house we demolished every wall that wasn't load-bearing to create one large airy room in which we would cook, eat, relax, and entertain. We opened it up to the back yard with French doors.

We installed bamboo flooring through most of the house, dedicated an entire wall of the living room to books, hid the television behind sliding cupboard doors, and replaced our old claw-footed tub with a bath long and wide enough for two.

After the work inside was finished, Conor carried on outside. He built a deck, then paved an area for a barbecue. After that, he tackled the garden and, at my insistence, dug up the apple tree that Chrissy planted and which I later replaced with native frangipani.

While he was working outside, I was busy inside, spending every spare hour I had on a *trompe l'oeil* along the hall. We'd painted the walls there in Spanish White, hoping that would make the hall feel wider, but it was boring. I suggested decorating the entire length of the passage with a scene of jacaranda trees. Our wedding photos were taken beneath jacarandas and I like their symbolism; jacarandas denote wealth and good fortune, especially if they drop their flowers on your head, or so the legend goes. But Conor wanted something more architectural. After hunting through our library of art and architecture books for ideas, we settled on a cloister of pillars and arches through which you see a manicured garden with a row of green European hornbeam trees in the distance. I used acrylics, the medium I'm most comfortable with, and we were both thrilled with the result.

I wanted to refurbish the study and bedroom as well and buy new furniture, but we ran out of money. We were still paying off the holiday in New Caledonia and over the course of the rebuild had maxed out all our credit cards. We combined the debts into one and Conor re-mortgaged the house, and we chopped up three of our five credit cards, leaving Conor's AMEX and my Visa. Replacing the old sofa-bed would have to wait.

We talked about our real estate aspirations. I wanted to share the mortgage with Conor but only if my name went on the title. He assured me that he regarded the Mitchell Street house as half mine and suggested I buy my own house instead, or an apartment, and rent it out. That way, he rationalised, we'd move faster up the property ladder. It seemed like a good plan to me, and I wasn't above putting my daily intake of espressos and café lunches on hold for a year or so if it meant saving for a deposit on my own slice of real estate.

Working on the Glebe house together was good for us. The gap that had been threatening between us closed. We rekindled our shared goals and celebrated each time we reached a milestone in the renovation.

At the end of April, we had a house re-warming party. It was Miss Havisham's again, only this time it was at our place and the wedding went ahead.

We kept the catering super simple – a dozen large gourmet pizzas delivered at eight – and the music disco-loud. As well as our friends, Conor invited some of his colleagues who spent much of the evening discussing Palladian architecture and the merits of symmetry. I'd invited Marley and he took it upon himself to play DJ. He was a Bryan Adams fan which immediately endeared him to Conor. We almost had to shout over *Tracks of My Years* to be heard, but no one minded. By nine o'clock we were all tipsy, except Lauren who drank sparkling grape juice, and the repartee darted back and forth across the table so fast it was hard to keep up with who said what.

'What's the difference between being in love with someone and loving them?'

'Love is warts and all. In-love is not seeing the warts.'

'Unless they're your own …'

'*Especially* if they're you're own.'

'Much better to talk about sex, love being such a slippery subject …'

'So's sex if you do it right.' Conor lightly pinched my backside.

'Funny ha ha,' I said.

'Hashtag Me Too,' said Janet.

'Oh, don't start.'

'You don't think it's all gone a bit far, all this PC Me Too palaver?'

'Well I never minded a wolf-whistle, or if a guy flirted with me. It boosted my self-esteem.'

'Does it need boosting?'

'Every day.'

'I'm all for the Harvey Weinsteins of the world getting their comeuppance, but does it really matter if a guy pinches a woman's bum in passing? Only to signal appreciation of course.'

'Oh, it so matters,' said Lauren.

'The Italians do it all the time and who doesn't like an Italian?'

'The French?'

'The thing is, women haven't exactly been respected in the workplace, have they? This whole Me Too issue is lifting the lid on wage inequality as well, and how women are treated generally, so I say bring it on.'

'Barry Leven is bit of a shit,' I said.

'Your boss?'

'Chief bully and office bogey.'

'Not getting defensive, are we?'

'And there you have it. A woman calls a man a shit and she's either defensive or aggressive. A man calls someone a shit and he's management material.'

'We are but beasts in the field,' said Conor.

'Beam me up, Scotty,' cried Marley. 'Party's turning weighty.' He blew me a kiss, picked up a bottle of ale and left.

'Sometimes, I want to spit in Barry's coffee, honestly.'

John inspected his glass, as if I might have spat in his wine, but the glass was empty. We were all wilting. It was late, nearly one o'clock, and everyone who hadn't already left made moves to go. That's when, out of nowhere, Steve asked after Chrissy.

'Where's that luscious sister of yours?'

Shut your mouth, Steve.

'Shut up, Steve,' said Lauren.

'Why? I thought we were talking about sex.' His words slurred into one another.

'You're drunk.'

'S'right. Far too drunk for you to drive, dear wife. Hand me the keys.'

'It is *so* time we weren't here.' Lauren gave me a look of apology and took Steve's arm. He leaned drunkenly against her. Conor and I helped her get him outside and into their car.

As we all emerged onto the pavement, a man stepped out from

the shadows across the road and strolled away. I had an eerie sense I'd seen him before, my impression compounded, although god knows why, by the fact that he was walking towards Chrissy's place. I pulled on Conor's sleeve. 'That man, haven't we seen him around here before?'

Conor was still preoccupied with getting Steve into the car. When he looked up, the guy had disappeared. I wished Conor had seen him because it came back to me what he'd said the night someone sent me those sinister peonies, that he believed it was a bloke who delivered them. Was it the same person? I shook my head to dispel the idea. I was probably imagining things. It was late and I'd drunk too much. No doubt, Steve bringing up the subject of Chrissy had resurrected my paranoia.

When everyone had gone, Conor put *Please Forgive Me* on, turning the music down low, and we did a slow shuffly sort of waltz around the room until I almost trod on an empty wine bottle and deflated onto the sofa, too tired to do any more.

I wished Steve hadn't mentioned Chrissy, but when he did, I realised whole weeks had gone by during which I hadn't once thought of her. It was reassuring to know that time does heal. Those two weeks would grow into two months, I thought. Two years. Five. Forever.

39

Conor said Chrissy had done us a service and maybe he was right. Because of her we'd finally fixed up our house, and I'd found Robbie. The idea of reinstating my sister as fairy godmother amused me, briefly. Despite the perverse intent, her tricks had indeed created a couple of happy outcomes. But I wasn't as generous as Conor and couldn't imagine ever regarding my sister again with anything other than antipathy.

'You used to see the best in people,' said Conor.

'I've acquired discernment.'

After that stunt with the grass, I decided to never again refer to her as Chrissy. If I could help it, I wouldn't give her a name at all but, when I had to, it was her given name I'd use: Christine. This was a name I'd never particularly liked and by then had come to detest.

It was autumn. The weather cooled, the cicadas slowed their mad chirruping, and the streets grew quieter, as if summer had been one long exuberant festival which was now over. And then, a week or so after our party, Medusa turned her evil eye on me again, as if she'd been waiting for all our hard work on the house to be done before letting the vipers loose.

I hadn't been well.

The agency had been engaged on branding for a new food product – fish-shaped fish-fingers for kids – and I was assigned to attend its launch in Melbourne, just to make sure our designs on the signage looked the way they were supposed to look. This wasn't the same firm as Cleverly Holdings. That project seemed to have fallen by the wayside. Back in December, just before I went on leave, Barry had taken it on himself to present my strategy, without involving me, and I hadn't heard any more. Cutting me out of that meeting had stung, so much so that I didn't even ask Barry how it went and given how much time had passed, I assumed Cleverly had gone to another agency.

I flew down to Melbourne the day before the launch, so that I could have dinner with an old school friend. His name is Dion Lewes. At Bendigo Secondary we'd both been members of the school debating club and played together in the senior volleyball team. At uni in Melbourne, we'd hung out with the same crowd, lived in the same group house for a year, then kept in touch after I scored the job with Farras Leven and left for Sydney.

Dion finished uni with a PhD in history and he'd wanted to stay on in the faculty as a lecturer, but there were no openings at the time. He tried to find work with the state parliament, but no one there would give him a job either. For a while he lived in a squat at the squalid end of Footscray and eventually got work as a barista in a wine bar. After a couple of years of this he went back to uni and re-trained as an accountant.

We met at seven, at Cecconi's in Flinders Lane, and caught up with each other's news.

'On your own again?' I asked.

'Oh, you know …' Dion fidgeted with his table napkin. When he looked up, he grinned at me. Dion's eyes are grey and clever, and he has a sweet smile, and I'd forgotten how nice he looked. 'Still waiting for the right woman,' he said. 'You got a sister or a cousin who might be interested in a lonely accountant?'

'No one good enough for you.' Hearing the word 'sister' threw me for a minute. It was as if a southerly wind blew suddenly through the room. It crossed my mind, briefly, to confide in Dion, but just saying Christine's name would sully the evening for me and I didn't want that. I'd always appreciated a rectitude about my friendship with Dion and wanted it to stay that way.

Two waiters arrived and while one uncorked a bottle of pinot gris the other put plates of seafood linguine in front of us. We'd ordered the same dish. That used to happen a lot and was always a joke among our friends. While the sommelier fiddled with the water jug, topping up our glasses, I changed the subject. 'Tell me about the job. What's it like working for one of the big four?'

'Straight up? I'm not cut out for it. The corporate world is just a little too self-important for me. And it's all about the money, Lexi. There doesn't seem to be much room for benevolence. I hope that doesn't sound too precious. Anyway, it doesn't really matter any more. I've decided to strike out on my own.'

'Good for you. When?'

'Next year, if all goes well. I'm working on the business plan now, and talking to the bank next week. But what about you? Will you stay with Farras Leven?'

'Yes … maybe no. I like everyone there, most of them anyway, but it's starting to feel a bit same old, same old.' I thought about Barry's increasing disrespect, and of Craig and what a relief it would be never to see him again and be reminded of those detestable Elite Escort cards.

'My boss can be difficult,' I said. 'Getting out from under his roost would be a relief I must say. I admire you starting up your own business.'

'Hold the applause until the first clients come knocking.'

'And then?'

'And then, watch this space. I feel optimistic about it, but we'll see what happens.'

173

We stopped talking and the silence between us settled and stretched into minutes and we were both fine with that.

After dinner Dion walked me back to Carlton where I'd booked a room on Airbnb. I was reminded of the walks we used to share, going to and from the university together when we were students and our lecture times coincided.

Dion wears hipster gear, narrow pants and casual jackets, which suit him. He's lean, a head taller than me, with thick dark brown hair combed back to reveal a widow's peak. And he's one of those men who look as good with a beard as without; he'd frequently grow one, wear it a few months, then shave it off. That night it was somewhere in between.

He suggested another coffee, but my landlady probably wouldn't have appreciated late night visitors, and anyway, I had a big day in front of me. We each swore, hands on hearts, that we wouldn't let so much time pass before getting together again.

The launch of those fish-fingers was held in a restored brewery on Southbank, by the Yarra River, and in between speeches that were too long, and a tedious exchange of clichés and congratulations, I picked at a smorgasbord of food. There was almost something inevitable about it, but something was off, if not the fish-fingers then the prawns, or the salmon pâté. By the time I was on the plane home that afternoon I felt like limp spinach and it was all I could do to stagger through Sydney airport and collapse into a taxi. In my haste to get through our front door, throw up twice in the bathroom sink, and collapse into bed, I didn't empty the letter box so it wasn't until the following evening that Conor brought in the mail.

And that's when Medusa shook out her nasty coils again.

Among the usual bills and advertising bumpf was an invoice from the local rag, for an ad to be published the following week in its Public Notices column. I assumed they had the wrong address and tossed it into the rubbish bin. Conor retrieved it.

'Lex, this is your name and our address. They can hardly have got both things wrong.'

'S'ppose.' I was still a bit jaded.

'Don't you think you should find out what the ad is going to say?' He handed me the invoice but I didn't look at it.

'Surely, she wouldn't,' I mumbled. 'Surely, she would bloody not.'

'Who? Wouldn't what?'

At the time, I hadn't told Conor about the card Craig taunted me with: Alexandra's Elite Escorts. Elite-effing-frigging-whores. I could put a positive spin on the matter and say it had been family honour – utterly misplaced I know – that had stopped me telling Conor about those cards, but the fact is that I'd been so embarrassed that I hadn't want to talk about them, instead I just longed for the whole thing to disappear. That day I told him everything.

'Maybe she's placed an advertisement for my escort service.'

He picked up the phone. 'We can stop it. They want payment before they run the ad. Do you want to know what it says?'

'I'd rather gnaw my right arm off.' I'd almost recovered from my bout of food poisoning but right then I was ready to puke again.

Conor phoned the newspaper and cancelled the advertisement. He didn't ask them for any details about the notice, just quoted the job number on the invoice and left it at that. I set light to the invoice in the kitchen sink. 'Whoever said blood is thicker than water got it so wrong.'

'Actually, it's not about family at all,' said Conor. 'It refers to the bond between soldiers, the blood they shed together in battle.'

'There you are then.' I was umpty as hell. It was all just too much. After weeks of Christine lying fallow, her resurgence on my patch had stress digging its claws into me all over again.

Conor put the kettle on and brewed coffee. 'You need to talk to her.'

'The woman is bloody certifiable. I've absolutely nothing to say to her.'

If I saw Christine walking along the footpath towards me, I'd cross to the other side of the road to avoid her. Yet Conor was right, something had to be done. And it was up to me to do it. I made up my mind, that as soon as I could manage it, I'd make another visit to Katoomba.

40

The next day was a Saturday and Conor and I were lingering over the remains of a late breakfast when there was a loud and peremptory knock on the door. Conor went to answer it and returned with a policeman, a solid, middle-aged man with thick fleshy jowls, blue gimlet eyes, and a pallor which suggested a regular diet of cheap take-aways. He took a wallet from his pocket and showed us proof of his constabulary status. It wasn't necessary. The uniform had been enough.

'Sergeant Doug Harvey, Ma'am. And you are?'

'Lexi. Alexandra Madison.'

He produced a photo of Peter's silver Volvo. The car looked more battered than I remembered it.

'We're trying to track down the owner of this vehicle?'

'That's Peter's car.'

'We understand you might be able to help us locate Mr Everson.'

'You need to talk to his wife, my sister.'

'We've spoken with Mrs Everson. She says you are the last person to have been with her husband.'

'That's not right. She's lying. I haven't seen Peter since ...' I turned to Conor. 'When was the last time we saw Peter?'

'Ages ago. Easter, wasn't it? A couple of years ago.'

Sergeant Harvey gave Conor a cursory once-over, then turned on me a hard stare. 'What is your relationship with Mr Everson?'

'He's my brother-in-law.'

'Nothing more?'

'What more could there be? He's married to my sister. And as far as I know he's working overseas somewhere. Have you spoken with his daughter, Sophie?'

This conversation took place in our living room, the three of us standing rather awkwardly around the dining table. A group of kids over the back fence were racing one another around on their bikes. A parent yelled at them from somewhere to come inside for lunch. It was bizarre to think of people out there going about their normal weekendy-happy lives while mine was descending rapidly into a Jacobean tragedy. I wondered if Sergeant Harvey had driven to our place in a paddy wagon and what the neighbours would think of us being visited by the cops. To find myself the subject of others' morbid curiosity would be excruciating. I had bitter thoughts of Christine, five houses away, stirring her cauldron.

The policeman tucked the photo away in a pocket inside his jacket. He was exasperatingly inscrutable, but then, to be fair, I was doing my utmost to follow suit.

'How are things between you and your sister?'

'Sisterly,' I said, leaving the cop to interpret that as he liked.

He regarded me with a jaundiced air, as if he wasn't quite sure whether or not I was being cute and didn't particularly care. I didn't know what I was being either. He let it pass, and scanned the room, slowly, as if looking for something, or perhaps he wanted us to offer him a cup of tea. My civility wasn't going to extend that far. I wanted him gone.

'Mrs Everson alleges you assaulted her.'

The duplicity of this accusation very nearly buckled me. My response was visceral, as if something inside me shrivelled and I had to steel myself to answer slowly and calmly. 'I've already told you;

my sister is a liar. She's not to be trusted.'

Sergeant Harvey took out a notebook and flipped through it. He paused as if waiting to be sure of our full attention and then read his notes in a court-room monotone. He sounded stagey and what he said was ludicrous. 'We understand the alleged offence occurred last October, at a party in Paddington. You poured beer over Mrs Everson, then hit in her the face'.

My mouth turned dry as papyrus. 'It was nothing.'

'We understand there were witnesses.'

'Who? There was nothing to see.' I knew most of the people at that party; they were my friends and none of them would have any truck with this fuckery, and certainly not when it was directed against a mate.

'Have you always had these aggressive tendencies, Mrs Madison?'

'It's Ms ... Look, this is ridiculous. Conor, tell him. It was nothing, a family spat.'

'She's right, Sergeant. It hardly warrants taking up police time.'

Sergeant Harvey slapped his notebook shut. 'We may need to speak with you again.'

41

Conor showed the policeman out while I slumped like Spenser's shrunken man on the sofa.

'That was pretty surreal,' I said when Conor returned.

'You need a whisky.'

'Are you being funny?'

'No. You need a strong drink. We both do.'

'She wants to spoil our new house, the jealous cow.'

Conor knocked back a measure of whisky and put the cap back on the bottle. 'A good bonking would sort her out.'

'Oh, and you'd be the one to give it to her I suppose.'

'Does Alexandra's Escort Service cater to women, do you think?'

'Now you *are* being funny. This is serious, Conor. She's sicked the law on to me. On to us.' I put heavy emphasis on the 'us', needing Conor to share ownership of my dilemma, lighten my load, but he didn't. He set fire to it instead.

'Cards on the table time,' he said. 'If we're to sort this situation we need everything out in the open.'

'What are you talking about?'

'She said you spent a night with Peter.'

For a minute I didn't know what to say. The atmosphere became frosty, as if we were both trapped inside a snow globe. 'When did she say that? Have you been seeing her?'

'No, why would I? This was months ago, when I went to get the key back.'

'And you've been nursing that little ice pick all this time.' Someone just shook the snow globe. 'Well, she's lying, I did not.'

'Come on love, you're a crappy liar.'

I'd taken a sip of the whisky Conor had handed me, but I really can't stand hard liquor. 'I need a cup of tea.' I went to the kitchen and put the kettle on, then returned to the sofa where I burst into tears.

'Lex. I'm not holding it against you.'

'There is nothing to hold … look, this is what happened. We went out for dinner, got munted, and he stayed over. And yes, we shared the bed, but that was all. Hadrian's bloody wall might as well have run through the middle of that bed for all the contact there was between us. Peter is Chrissy's husband, he's like a brother and I couldn't, I wouldn't.'

'I believe you, but can't you see how it would make Chrissy feel? She was offended.'

'So, you're on her side now, is that it?'

'I'm just trying to see things from her point of view.'

'How bloody sanctimonious of you.'

'No need to be snarky. Why has everything suddenly become bloody this and bloody that with you? It's exhausting.'

'And you never swear of course.'

'Now that you mention it, not very often.'

'Well, bitch bloody buggery good for you.'

That night, if our house had a clock that chimed, I would have heard it proclaim every caustic hour.

When I wasn't dwelling on Christine, I was cogitating on Peter Everson.

The last time I'd seen him, he'd just returned from a six-week assignment in Jordan and we were all out at Katoomba, sharing a Sunday lunch. My sister had cooked calzones with ricotta and spinach, and we were drinking a chilled rosé. Peter was expounding the troubles Jordan was having with its influx of refugees from the civil war across the border. He deplored al-Assad's brutality which was driving so many of his own citizens from their homes. He talked about giving up reporting and taking up aid work instead.

Where was Peter now?

After that dreadful visit from the police, I needed more urgently than ever to see my brother-in-law, find out his side of the situation with Christine, but more importantly, talk to him about us, that night we spent together and what he'd told Christine about it. Surely, he hadn't made it into a bigger deal than it was. I didn't think for a minute he had; that simply wasn't his style.

Twice during the previous months I'd sent him emails but received no reply.

Perhaps I should have just left things alone. Christine was under the misapprehension that I'd wronged her, well so be it. Let her steal my dress – there were more where that came from – and let her flirt with Conor; I could take all that, let it go, and move on. But this wasn't punishment, it was persecution, and Christine's vengefulness was now causing me grievous trouble, Silverwater Correctional sort of trouble. Was that the endgame? Me locked away in striped sodding pyjamas?

The sooner I got back to Katoomba the better, try to discover once and for all whether or not my earlier instincts about Peter were bats or if they were correct and something untoward had indeed happened to him. I was too scared of what the truth might be to let my imagination go any further than that.

I'm told, and I'm coming around to accept this, that intuition is more than just an innate sixth sense. That it's actually a skill we can develop, and that if we learn to pay attention to what our gut tells us, we are more likely to make good decisions. My stomach complained vociferously in a state of total stupefaction, as if I'd followed a plate of broccoli with a bag of Caramello Koalas. On one hand, my gut was mute as a doorstop. On the other, it was telling me forcefully that something in the Everson household was seriously amiss.

42

I felt so wrecked on Monday that I didn't go into work, emailing Barry to tell him I had food poisoning. On Tuesday he called me into his office and closed the door behind us. He didn't even wait until he sat down before laying into me.

'How many days off have you had this year? Annual leave is one thing,' he grumbled, 'and a bit of sick leave, fair enough, but you've taken leave without pay, not to mention absenteeism without notice.'

'I told you yesterday I was crook and you know perfectly well that it was because of that launch in Melbourne. I was *working*.'

'Guess I'll just have to take your word for that.'

'And I have never been absent without notice.'

One of the finance guys knocked on the door and opened it but Barry waved him away and sat down behind his desk. He didn't invite me to sit but I did anyway.

'I've done work at home,' I said. This was half true. I had roughed out a few vague notes on how the creative team might work more efficiently together, really nothing more than throwing some words at a Venn diagram, but Barry didn't need to know that. 'And, by the way, I got stuff done in twice the time I can out there in Grand Central.' This time it wasn't a fib. I meant it. Day by day, I was finding it harder to concentrate in the open plan office.

'I don't hear anyone else complaining.'

'Maybe that's because you're not interested in hearing what any of us has to say.'

Barry put his hands up, palms facing me in that habitual blocking gesture of his that never failed to irritate the hell out of me and I suspect he knew it. 'Enough with the bleating,' he'd said. 'You've been working at those hot-desks, how long? Oh, no, I forgot. You haven't been here.'

Barry's implacable tone took me aback, and the sub-text was loud and clear: pull my socks up or be demoted, or worse, be sent back to work among the juniors where I'd have to prove myself all over again.

He paused so long I thought the conversation was over and almost got up to leave but Barry wasn't finished. 'You've always done great work, Lexi, but lately … well, it's just not up to par is it? What's going on?'

'Nothing. Well, a lot actually, stuff I won't bore you with, but … there's a few things at home I need to sort out.'

'Can I depend on you?'

'You know you can. What is this?'

Barry scratched at his lower jaw as if there were ink spots there he was trying to erase. 'And what about after hours?'

'What about after hours?' For a wobbly moment I thought he might have seen one of those Elite Escort cards. Had Craig bandied it about the office behind my back?

Barry was giving me his iron ore stare. 'Can I depend on you to not behave like a delinquent teenager?'

'I don't know what you're talking about.'

He pointed both forefingers at me. I hate it when people do that.

'Don't shit me, Lexi. You were seen. God, woman, you and your little cohort of guerrillas blew up a building. One of our client's trucks was outside.'

'That was more than four months ago, Barry. Are you going to bring it up every time you feel like taking a pot shot at me? And they weren't … *aren't* my cohort. What happened had nothing to do with me and I wouldn't have gone if I'd known.'

'But there you were, all the same.' He pushed his chair back and swung his feet up onto the desk. He inspected his fingernails. As if he cared about them. 'You know what puzzles me most about all this right now?'

I didn't respond, waiting instead for his next affront.

'What the fuck you're going to do to redeem yourself.'

'I ….'

'Spare us the soliloquy. You've got work to do.'

He dropped his feet back to the floor, swivelled his chair around and pushed a couple of briefs across his desk. I flipped them open. One was to design a four-page sales leaflet for a supplier of bathroom fittings and the other instructions for a local pet shop on how to take care of your ageing cat.

'A junior could do these.'

'Indeed, he could.'

'You're cross with me.'

'Indeed, I am.'

Barry put his feet back up on the desk, plucked up a trouser leg and scratched his shin. I ignored the provocation.

'Are you penalising me for taking a day off? You don't think that's just a bit, well, petty?'

'Bad for morale when the seniors are conspicuous only by their absence. The underlings start asking if you've gone into rehab.'

I rolled my eyes, not caring if Barry noticed, in fact, hoping he would.

He pushed a sheet of paper across the desk. It was a letter, very formal, on Farras Leven letterhead, from me to them, under-taking not to participate in activity that might compromise the reputation of the agency, or in any way injure its relations with clients, bla bla bla.

I placed the letter face down on his desk and propelled it slowly back towards him. 'What I do in my own time is my business.'

'We've trod this ground already.' Barry turned the letter over, slapped a biro down on top of it and told me to sign it.

I refused. 'You wouldn't try this on if I belonged to a union.' I turned my back on Barry and left his office.

On my way back to the work stations I stuck my head through the door of the IT office. Craig was in there with our other propeller-head, Marty Harper. Marty had folded back the sleeves of his navy shirt, exposing a new black tattoo on his left forearm. It was a small picture of an echidna. Cute. The tattoo must have been done only a few days before because Marty was scratching it, as if the healing process was just beginning. I could see the skin was flaking, adding more grunge to the general grottiness of the room.

Craig and Marty were playing a computer game together and clicked out of it as soon as they heard the door open. I kept it open and spoke loudly enough for anyone nearby to hear.

'God, it pongs in here.'

We were discouraged from eating food at our work stations, but in the IT office there was nearly always a fuggy smell of old hamburger wrappings and half-empty sushi boxes. It stank too of soiled clothes. Craig was sweating and his shirt showed damp patches at the armpits.

'And you stink, Craig. You're an offence against decency, you know that? A bloody public menace.'

Being caught out at that demo in Paddington and having my mug published in the paper had already blotted my copybook, enough for Barry to take the packaging account off me, and come up with that insulting letter, but I was damn sure Craig had stuck his odious oar in and told Barry he'd seen me at Mascot.

Before leaving the IT office I switched the fan on. 'You need air. May as well have one thing in here that isn't foul.'

My colleagues in the main room were watching me curiously

187

and at any other time I would happily have filled them in what was happening, but not that day. I didn't even acknowledge them as I sat down at my Mac and attempted to knuckle down to some work. I was working on a series of advertising leaflets, matching photos with captions, deciding where on the page they'd best fit and what fricking font to use where. The work was way beneath my pay grade and about as diverting as counting the tiles in a public urinal.

Stress was making me trembly. I went out for a brisk walk around the block, twice, and this time it wasn't inspiration I was looking for but composure. There was no going back to the office that day until I'd calmed down and got myself under control.

I'd told Barry he could depend on me, then refused point blank to sign that devious letter. I was distracted by the havoc in my personal life, demoralised by that visit from the police, and more desperate than ever now to return to Katoomba and sort everything out, once and for all.

43

Sergeant Harvey turned up at the house again, this time accompanied by a colleague, a shrewd-looking detective in a spruce navy suit. It looked tailored, like him. He was impeccably groomed, clean-shaven, with chiselled features and smooth black hair. His brown eyes were keen. He wasn't much older than me.

It was Saturday. Conor had gone to a footy match with John. Had the police been watching the house, choosing a time when they knew I'd be alone? Paranoia floated like scum to the top of my consciousness.

'My name is Moretti, Ma'am, Tony Moretti. If you don't mind, we'd like a few minutes of your time.'

'Why? What's happened? Is Conor …?'

'Nothing has happened, Ma'am. If we could just come inside and talk.'

They stepped briskly into the house, as if concerned I might try to stop them, as if I could, and the two men filled the hallway. I felt myself shrink a little, like Alice, except this wasn't Wonderland. And I needed mushrooms that guaranteed a great deal more transcendence than the ones Alice got from Caterpillar.

'You seem anxious, Mrs Devlin, but there's no need. We're not accusing you of anything.'

'My name is Madison. Devlin is my husband's name. Why are you here?'

'Mrs Everson claims you have her husband's cheque book.'

'Then I *am* being accused.'

'Not by us, Ma'am. But if you don't mind, we'd like to take a look around. If that wouldn't be an inconvenience.'

'Go ahead, but you're wasting your time. There's nothing here that doesn't belong to me and my husband.'

'Best we investigate anyway, just to be sure. You know, dot the Is and cross the Ts.' His voice was Olay smooth, as if to soften the sharp edge of his purpose, but there was no need. Once I'd recovered from the initial shock of their arrival, I was untroubled. Pleased to see them, in fact. When Christine's allegation was found to be false, she would be exposed at last as a trouble-maker.

Both policemen donned thin plastic gloves, like surgeons preparing to make an incision. I followed them around the house as they went into every room, looked around, turned over a few things, and moved on. They obviously hadn't taken Christine very seriously because as far as I could tell, and despite those clinical gloves, their search wasn't assiduous.

'What about the car? Peter's Volvo. Have you found him …?'

'That investigation is still ongoing, Ma'am,' said Sergeant Harvey.

By now we were in the bedroom. It galled me to watch them open drawers and poke about among my underwear. My serenity subsided into trepidation. The detective ran his hands around under the mattress, exactly as I had done myself, months earlier. I'd found Christine's lingerie then, maybe there'd be more there now. I realised I was holding my breath, but they found nothing.

We all trooped into Conor's study where Sergeant Harvey found the cheque book. It was at the back of a drawer in the desk, underneath Conor's slide rule. The policeman held the cheque book up triumphantly, dangling it between thumb and forefinger as if it were a gun.

Mr Moretti gave me a sorrowful look, as if he were disappointed in me.

'That has absolutely nothing to do with me.' I had to steel myself to refrain from shouting. 'And nothing to do with Conor either. My sister put that cheque book there. What's the word you use? Planted. She planted it there.'

'I'm afraid you'll have to come with us, Mrs Devlin.'

'Madison,' I snapped. 'My name is Mad-i-son.' My jaw had been clamped so tight it ached. 'You don't know my sister. She's done this.'

They peeled off their gloves and stowed them away in pockets. Neither man answered me, nor did they pay any attention to what I said.

'I need to phone my husband,'

'You can do that from the station,' said Mr Moretti. 'If you'll just come with us, Ma'am. I don't imagine it will take long to clear this up.'

Out on the pavement I saw Robbie. I could have sworn it was him. I didn't see his face fully, just a side view, but there was the beard and his hair; they were the right colour and cut, and who else would be waiting at my gate to help me if it wasn't my brother? Just when I needed him. I called out: 'Robbie?' He turned away as I came down the path with the policemen and I was about to run after him when Mr Moretti restrained me. I shook him off. 'That's my brother.'

I stepped out onto the road. 'Rob? Robbie? Is that you?' Two cars drove past and my shout was lost in the noise of their tyres on the tarmac. By the time they passed, Robbie was gone.

Mr Moretti came up beside me. 'Shall we carry on, Ms Madison?'

I gazed up the street in the direction Robbie had taken. If it was him. I simply couldn't be sure. If it was my brother, he wouldn't have walked away. I wasn't blind to the fact that my need for Robbie's

191

presence in my life was probably making a brother of every brown-bearded man I saw.

Mr Moretti's hand on my arm brought me back to why I was out on the street.

When I got into the back of the police car I was shaking with apprehension. I had handled Peter's cheque book, thumbed through its butts; my fingerprints were all over it and it was going to be my word against Christine's.

44

They took me to the police station in Surry Hills. It was a concrete monster of a building, as if the architect's sole intent had been to prepare visitors for incarceration, whether or not they were subsequently found guilty and convicted. How many times had I walked or driven past it, never dreaming that I'd one day be inside it, and involuntarily?

No one locked me up, but nor did I feel free to get up and leave, and the three hours I spent there were among the most wretched of my life.

There's something about boot-faced officials in bulky uniforms, vaunting their police badges, that makes you feel guilty even when you're not. I had visions of large dogs, barely restrained on tight leashes, snapping at me with their big white teeth.

Under the sceptical eye of a stolid constable, I emptied the contents of my bag. Everything spilled across the reception counter: my phone, hairbrush, lipstick and a stick of Nivea lip balm, a pack of tissues, and another of tampons, and a small spiral-bound notebook in which I'd jotted random thoughts and made small rough sketches for future development. I always have one of these notebooks with me. This one fell open at a pencil drawing I'd done of Conor, naked and full frontal on the bed in our Noumea hotel room. The cop kept a straight face as he picked it up, but I sensed him stifling a grin and would have snatched the notebook from him if he hadn't first, with deliberation, closed it and put it down.

I also had to show the constable that I had nothing in my pockets, then lift my shirt to prove I wasn't wearing a belt, and finally show him that my shoes did not have laces. Did he really believe I might try to throttle myself with them?

After all that ignominy, I was led to an interview room and told to wait. It wasn't a cell, yet being there made me feel like a criminal, the way you feel when you go through customs, mentally repacking your suitcase to probe it for bags of cocaine or wads of hash and even though you've never smoked the stuff, you feel in some small part of your gut that you wouldn't be unduly surprised if they found drugs hidden beneath your sundresses.

It occurred to me I might need a lawyer and that I should probably park my current disapproval of Steve and phone him. Have I talked about Steve, apart from the prickly matter of his adulterous liaison with Christine? He's a law clerk and works for a hot-shot firm that regularly wins acclaim, or censure depending on your point of view, for keeping known crims at arm's length from Corrective Services. He's studying part-time to be a lawyer himself which accounts for Lauren still having to live in a rented house in Blacktown, near the university. Course fees are crippling and I don't know how they manage, given they have children.

Steve's got close-cut gingery hair, slightly protuberant pale eyes and a washed-out complexion which burns easily in summer. He reminds me of that actor who played Ron Weasley in the *Harry Potter* movies. Steve works hard and Lauren says he's smart and I trust her judgement. I could have done with his counsel that afternoon.

The possibility that Steve might prefer to lend his time and advice to Christine, instead of me, his wife's best friend, never crossed my mind.

For the first two hours at the station, I was alone in the interview room. Every now and then, like a customs official frisking a suspect, I scanned my emotional state for lesions, to be sure my sanity remained inviolate. I thought of the cashmere cardigan Christine had given me. It occurred to me then that she'd probably nicked those cardigans from a shop, which is why, when I first saw them, they'd appeared brand-new and unworn. And if she hadn't stolen them, they would have been paid for by Peter's money. Could that somehow be used against me? I didn't know.

I thought about Robbie too, and the more I thought about him the more convinced I was that I'd seen him. Was he in town, and if he was, why was he just hanging around, avoiding me instead of getting together? Had he spoken with Christine? Maybe he was staying with her and they were they ganging up on me? After all, they were of an age; they'd been kids together, played together, probably cooked up some kooky games which they were now playing again. At my expense.

This was all rubbish and I needed to pull myself together before any of the cops came back. I was suffering a persecution complex, that's all. I stood up, rubbed my arms briskly up and down, wrapped them tightly across my chest and did a few circuits of the room.

When Mr Moretti returned, we repeated the entire conversation we'd had in Mitchell Street, as if he thought the change of venue might change my story.

'There really is nothing more I can add,' I said.

'Now's the time to say if you do.'

'Do I need a lawyer?'

Mr Moretti gave me a congenial half-smile. 'That would be premature.' He escorted me from the station. 'There will be a court hearing. In the meantime, I'd advise you to stay away from Mrs Everson.'

As always happened with me when I was put under pressure, hours passed before I realised what I could and should have said in my defence. When the realisation did come to me, I phoned Moretti straight away and told him all about the things Christine had taken from our bedroom: my Italian brooch, Conor's clothes brush, his aftershave. These would have her fingerprints on them just as much as my prints were on that blasted cheque book.

I insisted the detective come back to Mitchell Street with his finger-printing kit and check them out. He asked me instead to bag them up – those were the words he used, as if my home were a crime scene and we were actors in a whodunnit on the BBC – and deliver them to the station.

He turned up at reception almost as soon as I arrived.

I dumped the bag on the counter, confident that this would quash Christine's accusation, and mortified at how asinine, not to mention time-wasting for them, our sibling tit-for-tat carry-on must seem.

'My husband and I will both sign affidavits swearing that these things belong to us and that we are the only people with any right to handle them. You might like to ask Mrs Everson to explain why her fingerprints are on them.'

What more could I do?

45

The events of that weekend left me feeling so shattered that it wasn't until after lunch on Tuesday that I was able to face going into work, and this time, I was absent without notice for days rather than an hour or two. I didn't phone in or send an email, so it probably shouldn't have been a surprise to turn up and find the crumbling remains of my career fall into smouldering rubble.

Everyone looked up as I entered the main room, then looked away when I sat down at the only available hot desk. Megan just had time to warn me before Barry arrived, snarling, at my chair. 'Look everyone, there *is* a Lexi Madison on the payroll after all.'

Megan gave me a supportive smile, and Marley shook his head reprovingly at Barry.

'What's that Mr Staines? You think we have an imposter in our midst?'

'Give it away, Barry.'

I didn't want Marley defending me, especially in front of everyone, so I got up and walked into Barry's office. He followed and when he didn't close the door, I did.

'If you've got something to say, Barry, say it.'

'Happy to. Clearly, I made a mistake, letting you lead accounts.'

His voice was measured and precise as a Swiss Army knife, a sure sign he was fed up with me.

'I'm good at this.'

'Not disputing the quality of your work, Lexi, when you see fit to produce any. It's your attitude that's off.'

My face flamed and I couldn't think of a single thing to say in my defence.

It wasn't as if I hadn't seen this reprimand coming. For weeks I'd been fudging it, day after day passing without applying myself to the job. It wasn't that I didn't want to, or that I was lazy. It was just that …

'Look,' he said, 'I know you've been having a rough time at home.'

'That's all over now. We've ….' I blinked back tears. I would not, *would not* show weakness, or give Barry any reason to feel sorry for me. There was no danger of that; Barry was unmoved in the way a six-storey parking building is unmoved.

He put a hand up, his palm in my face, to fend me off. He wore a narrow gold ring with an inset of onyx on the little finger of his right hand. It must have been new because I hadn't noticed it before. It sat oddly with his donnish dishevelment. 'Spare me the unhappy details,' he said.

'I'll be on deck from now on, I promise.'

Barry sighed, in the manner of parent dealing with a recalcitrant child. 'We've been through this before. This is a business, Lexi, not an art class for five-year-olds.'

I started to speak, but that hand went up again, blocking my reply. 'I know, I know, life intervenes and I'm supposed to be magnanimous, follow the health and safety manual and all that. I'm not inhuman, Lexi, but enough is enough.'

Until then I'd been standing. Now I took one of the two visitor's chairs facing Barry's desk. It was newish black leather and creaked whenever I moved. Barry closed his laptop. Apart from a framed photo of his wife and daughter, arm in arm and smiling on the deck of a ketch in Sydney Harbour, that laptop was the only thing on his desk.

'There's always a line,' he said.

'And I've crossed it. Okay, I get that.'

'You've made yourself obsolete.'

'Are you asking me to resign?'

'Would you rather I fired you?'

'No.' My back was to the glass wall that separated Barry's office from the agency's main work room, but I knew my colleagues were watching. I could feel their collective eyes on me like two rows of halogen lamps. I hoped they were gunning for me. I'd never been fired before and I know my face was more and more flushed at this public humiliation.

'This is because I wouldn't sign that dopey letter, isn't it?'

'Let's just call it an incompatibility of viewpoint and leave it at that. No hard feelings.'

'You'll give me a reference then?' It was a long shot, but he'd said there was nothing wrong with my work.

'You're making a fairly crap job of minding your own reputation, why would you think I'd entrust you with mine?'

'Because you owe it to me. And you said no hard feelings.'

He waved me away. 'I might send you an email.' He put heavy emphasis on the world 'might'.

He flapped his paw at me again and I got up and left his office, turning towards my desk. Over the next four weeks, before I left, I'd do such brilliant work that Barry would plead with me to stay. Barry called out, his voice padding after me like a cougar. 'Where are you going? The door's that way.'

I stopped and went back into his office. 'I'm happy to work out my notice.'

Barry ran his hands through his hair, turned on me a pitying look, and beckoned his PA who went and got my bag and deposited it at Barry's door.

'Why do you people never read the fine print? There's no notice. When your time's up here, you walk. And don't think you're special. It would be the same for me.'

'Hardly. You own the place.'

'Just being empathetic.' Barry picked up some papers on his desk and began reading them.

'Can't I even say goodbye?'

'Don't push it, Lexi. What did you expect, a drinks party?'

'Does Gray know? I want to talk to him.'

'He's out.' Barry was wearing one of his habitual corduroy jackets that day, the navy one, and a shirt so white and crisp it had to be on its first outing. He leaned back in his chair and laced his hands together across his chest. 'Now there's a coincidence, you being out as well. Only difference is that Gray will be back.'

Barry's scorn turned the air in his office rank and I suppressed the urge to howl. 'I don't see why you have to be so snide, Barry. I've worked for you for five years.'

'You'll know how stale you are then.'

'You know, something like this would put the agency in a very bad light, if it got out.'

'That does you no credit. Get outa here.' He didn't look up and I did as I was told, walking out of the agency, feeling sick, but stubborn too. To hell with the lot of them and especially Barry. I was proud of myself for sticking up for my principles.

I was also nauseous with concern for my future.

46

Out on the pavement in George Street, a hoary busker was tunelessly singing *Irish Blessing* at the top of his voice. 'Until we meet again, may God keep you in the palm of His hand.' I grimaced. What could God possibly do for me now?

I stepped out into the street, drawing back in fright as three buses thundered past in a convoy, belching diesel. I found I couldn't move, and didn't know where to go if I did. In every direction, my life was a dead-end street.

Marley appeared at my side and took firm hold of my arm. 'Let me buy you a drink. A strong pick-me-up, I believe, is what is now required.'

He steered me along King Street and then down Clarence Street to the Baxter Inn. The pub was dim to the point of darkness and, apart from a couple of tourists drinking at the bar, it was empty. Bluesy jazz was playing softly on the sound system. Preisner's *Requiem for My Friend* would have suited my mood better. We headed to a table in the far corner where I threw myself on the banquette while Marley ordered drinks at the bar. When he came back to the table, he put a margarita in front of me.

'I'm not really into spirits.'

'Wine doesn't have the same anaesthetic quality. Drink up.'

I took a sip, then another, and was braced by the salt and alcohol.

Marley had bought stout for himself and two bags of potato chips. He pushed one of them my way. 'Clever you?'

'Don't.' I didn't want to be reminded of those reusable bags I'd designed.

'Made you smile, though, didn't it?'

It had, and the cocktail was already restoring my equanimity. I leaned back against the upholstery and de-stressed a little.

'Marley, do you think my work is stale?'

'Not a bit of it. You caught Barry on a bad day, that's all.'

'You're being generous. I did see this coming, sort of.'

'Well, you know how it is with Barry. Once you rub him up the wrong way, his bristles have a surly tendency to stay rampant.'

'You warned me. Wish I'd listened.'

'You could sue for unfair dismissal. It'd be hard, but you'd win.'

I shook my head. 'I don't want to work where I'm not wanted.'

Marley nodded and I knew he'd feel the same way.

We both finished our drinks. I declined a second and waited while Marley went up to the bar and bought himself another beer. As I watched him, I thought what a terrific friend and colleague he was and felt so thankful and so miserable that I had to fight hard to hold back tears. When he came back to the booth, Marley took one of those little packs of tissues out of a pocket, opened it and handed me one.

'There's no need,' I mumbled and briefly jammed my knuckles against my eyes.

'I know that.' He left the tissues on the table anyway. 'Don't sweat it too much, Lexi. It's not worth it and you'll see the upside in no time. Might even be the making of you.'

'Then why do I feel like the wheel on a roulette table?'

'All things pass, my dear.' Marley's mouth was full of potato chips. 'He'll give you that reference, you know. For what it's worth, so will I, if you ask nicely.'

'Consider me asking, with a capital N.'

'In the meantime …'

'I'm sort of hoping there won't be a meantime.'

'An old mate of mine, his name's Jackson, works in the media in Melbourne. I'll put a word in for you if you like, if you ever think of heading south. Isn't that where you're from?'

Marley opened his tablet, extracted a pen and crumpled notebook from a pocket in his jeans, and from the screen copied down a name and number. He ripped out the page and handed it to me. 'I'm pretty sure they've got an office in Sydney as well. If you're stuck for work. Might help.'

'I meant to put a folio together.' We weren't supposed to take files out of the agency, but everyone did, surreptitiously copying their best work onto personal flash drives. Unless you can produce a portfolio of your work, no other agency will give you a look-in. I thought about the times when I'd done a bit of work from home and how much I'd enjoyed that. Could I go free-lance? Tout for my own clients? Maybe even start up my own agency? I thought about my friend in Melbourne, Dion Lewes, going out on his own. Was I ballsy enough to do the same? I was sure, if I asked him, Dion would help me put together a business plan.

Marley read my thoughts. 'You could of course strike out on your own.'

I took one of the tissues and blew my nose. 'That's a possibility. Will you send me some files, if I tell you which projects?'

'Presumably you want that sustainable packaging sensation. The Cleverly lot were totally wowed by the way. Did Barry say?'

'No. He did not. No surprise there I suppose … God, what a bastard.'

'I should have told you.'

'I thought the project had died, that Cleverly didn't like what we'd done.'

'They sat on it for ages, probably waiting to see if the competition came up with anything better. Sorry you got left out.'

'Don't be. Barry's boorishness isn't your fault.'

More people came into the bar. I looked at my watch, it was six-fifteen. The after-work crowd had begun flowing in. I went up to the bar and ordered more drinks, returned to the corner with a lime and soda for me and another bottle of stout for Marley.

'What would I have done without you, Marley?'

'And whatever will you do without me now?'

'Your email address is my most valued possession.'

Marley patted my hand. This was out of character. I wondered if he was about to kiss me again, on the forehead as he'd once done when we'd worked late together. Marley rarely revealed his feelings and was almost never demonstrative. I put my other hand over his and held it there.

'One day,' he said, 'this will be no more than a wrinkle in your otherwise brilliant career. Want my advice? Move on and don't look back.'

47

It was Sunday before I got around to telling Conor that I'd lost my job. Given he left for work before I did, and got home later, he hadn't noticed that for three days I'd been home, which suited me because I hadn't been ready to talk about it.

On Saturday we went out to lunch with John and Janet and had a great afternoon. It felt like a long time since we'd done anything as carefree and normal as spending an afternoon with friends and, putting aside the mess my career was in, I was happy.

The convivial lunch and the warmth of the day relaxed both Conor and me and we were amorous. As soon as we got home and closed the front door, we began kissing and went on kissing, until we reached the bathroom. I ran the bath while Conor rummaged in the cupboard looking for our old bath toys.

We took off our clothes and got into the bath, lying quietly for a while to luxuriate in the hot water. Then I picked up the sponge to give Conor a back massage. It wouldn't go. 'The battery's flat.'

Conor got up and wrapped a towel around his waist. He kissed me and put a finger to my lips. 'We can do better than that, love. Wait here.'

'Where are you going?'

'It's a surprise.' He came back with his hands behind his back and got into the bath.

'What are you hiding?' I lifted my eyebrows in anticipation, expecting a treat.

'Ta-daa,' intoned Conor who, with a flourish, waved an egg in the air. An egg! He was very pleased with himself, grinning widely like Alice's friend, the Cheshire cat. As far as I was concerned, he might just as well have been the Queen of Hearts sentencing me to a grisly death, and I leapt up so abruptly that water sloshed in waves over the rim of the bath and across the floor.

'What's got into you? It's an egg, not a thumb screw.'

'You slept with her. You slept with the bitch. You've played that ridiculous egg-kissing game together. How else would you know about it?'

Conor sighed. 'Lex, settle down. She told me about that movie, that's all. What's it called? *Tampopo*? Chrissy said you liked it.'

'Well, she would, wouldn't she? I've never even seen the dumb film.'

I wrapped a towel tightly around myself. Conor would never see me naked again, never touch me again. 'Of all people, Conor, of all people, it had to be my sister.'

God, what a cliché. Man sleeps with wife's sister. If I hadn't felt so gutted, I might almost have laughed. Instead I yelled at Conor. 'Do you know what an utter prat that makes you? What an arsehole?'

'Can you hear yourself? You need to calm down.'

'No, I won't effing calm down.' I blundered into the bedroom, slammed the door shut and sat on the edge of the bed, immobile apart from slow hot tears. It's possible an entire hour went by before I moved again. By then I was cold and more miserable than ever. I crawled into bed, dragging the duvet around me and piling all four pillows over my head.

Conor left me alone until the evening when he came into the room with a pot of tea on a tray, with my favourite Maxwell &

Williams cup, and a plate of cheese and salty biscuits.

'Can we talk about this? It was just the once, months ago, and, honestly, Lexi love, it's over, I swear. You might say it never really started.'

He poured the tea and held out the cup and when I didn't take it put it down on the bedside table next to me. I ignored his offer of food as well.

'It's because I spent that night with Peter, isn't it? You had to even the score. Even though there was nothing in it. We did *not* sleep together. How many times do I have to tell you?'

'I know you didn't. This thing with Chrissy, it happened before you told me about all that. Look, this doesn't even warrant an explanation. I mean, there's nothing to say. That's how insignificant it was. Bit like you and Peter.'

'I don't want you in here tonight.'

Conor retreated. I called out after him. 'Take this crap with you.'

He came back in and took away the tea and the snacks. I heard him banging about in the kitchen for a bit and then listened to him set up the sofa-bed in his study. I wished he'd gone into the living room instead. I didn't like him sleeping in the room Christine had used.

That night I felt pinned like an entomologist's specimen to the bed, a moth in a bell jar. Death was an attractive proposition. For hours I lay staring at the ceiling, making a blank black canvas of my mind to keep away all thoughts of Conor and Christine.

I listed all the things I didn't like about Conor: he was a hoarder, never threw anything out; he was never going to use that old bike again. He always left it to me to make the bed and clean the house and for all his tidiness elsewhere, in the kitchen he had a pathological inability to replace lids, on jars of pesto, or Vegemite, or raspberry jam. He'd abandon them on the kitchen bench, with spoons or knives still in them. These are trifling complaints, I know. There was his growing taste for whisky. That wasn't trivial. Nor was his reluctance to take my side when I needed him to. I despise disloyalty.

At the back of my mind I couldn't help remembering the things I liked, loved about my husband: his cleverness, how he made me laugh, the way he looked, dressed, the way he made love. The way he called me, during our most tender moments, his little songbird, his scarlet robin. That's when I began bawling and couldn't stop. I cried until my ribs ached and the bones in my face ached. Conor had broken my heart and I was devastated. Almost from the day we'd met, I'd admired and cherished him. We were mates. We'd built a history together, accumulated shared memories, established a social circle. I'd believed we would grow old together. What would my life be like if I left him? Divorce was anathema to me and I didn't think I had the energy or appetite to start over with someone else.

Loneliness crept over me like rust.

I thought of Lauren and her big generous heart. She probably wouldn't say it in so many words, but I knew she'd expect me to forgive Conor.

Maybe I could. Maybe having it off with Christine one day had just been something he had to do, a male-ego thing perhaps, to take back the power in our relationship? Why would he even think he'd lost it? And did he really expect to have more power than I had in our marriage? We were equal partners, weren't we?

I got up and went into the kitchen to make myself a mug of warm milk, with honey and nutmeg. I combed through our pantry cupboard until I found an old bottle of St John's wort, swallowed two tablets, wishing they were lithium, or better still, propofol, then wandered through the house, thinking of all the work we'd done together to make it lovely. For a few minutes I stood at the door to Conor's study, watching him sleep. His feet stuck out the end of the sofa-bed. His hair on the pillow was tousled. When his eyes were closed, you saw how long and black and adorable his eye-lashes were.

I went back to bed.

All couples have crises and get over them. Isn't that the explanation for a long marriage, that the couple stayed together? They got through.

Around two am, Conor came in the bedroom and slipped into his side of the bed. He put an arm around me and we lay cuddled together like spoons and I got warm at last and finally drifted into sleep.

At six, the magpies started up their fluty call, and Conor left. He returned an hour later with orange juice, coffee, and French toast, arranged on a tray with a white cloth and napkins, and a single flashy bird of paradise poised precariously in the stem of a tall champagne glass. He must have gone out while I was asleep, down to the shops, to find that flower.

He sat down on the bed beside me. 'Sorry, Lex.'

'Let's forget it.'

He held out the orange juice. That's when I told him I'd lost my job. I made light of it, as if it were no big deal and people in the industry moved around all the time, that in fact I'd been at Farras Leven so long it was probably bad for my career.

'What are you going to do?'

'Find another job, I suppose.' Then, with more energy: 'I thought I could sell some paintings.'

'You have to paint them first.'

'Thanks for your confidence.'

'We have to be pragmatic, and anyway, even if it were practicable, where would you paint?'

'You hardly ever use the study.'

'That doesn't change the fact it's mine.'

There were times, becoming more frequent lately, when I wondered if Conor and I were on the same side.

'You haven't asked me what happened. Why I was fired.'

'You said it was no big deal.'

My being blasé about losing my job did not mean Conor had to be blasé about it as well. I didn't say anything more because what would be the point, but I asked myself if all those weeks ago, when that florist in Glebe gave him a lesson on the names of flowers, whether or not she'd also told him what those flowers symbolise. Did he know that birds of paradise symbolise joy, and anticipation?

And did he know about blue irises? They symbolise faith and hope.

48

I stewed over the state of my marriage, and realised I'd forgotten Conor's birthday. This wasn't entirely a surprise to me. I was guiltily aware that I'd given in to a subconscious wish not to remember his last birthday, when my sister put on that gross TV show and made sick overtures to Conor, sitting there showing him her pubic area; it was an evening that, looking back, seemed to presage the awfulness of the year that followed.

I considered how I might make it up to Conor and then admitted to myself how little I cared. He'd been turned on by Christine that night, and subsequently, I was sure of it. And his indifference to my professional life hurt, as did his lack of support for my artistic aspirations. And then there was his story about being and not being with Christine. Exasperation with them both, and a growing disaffection with everything and everyone, fuelled my trip back to Katoomba.

This time I'd intended to make no stops along the way, even though I'd left home without breakfast and craved coffee and toast, but something unpleasant happened and I was still half an hour from Katoomba when I pulled over to the side of the road. Ever since I'd left Sydney, I'd been made disturbingly aware of the same car behind me. It was a grey Mazda, one of those low sporty ones, and the driver was wearing dark glasses and a cap pulled low over his forehead. I thought he must be drunk or on drugs because he drove dangerously close to my rear bumper. At one point I tapped my foot on the brake pedal, to signal my disapproval. He took no notice, instead coming so close I was sure he was going to hit me.

It scared me. I detest people who don't respect a safe driving distance. I contemplated phoning the cops, and taking a picture of his car, to record its registration number, but my phone was in my bag on the back seat, and I couldn't take my hands off the wheel, or look away from the road. The need to drive defensively demanded all my concentration.

It crossed my mind that the loony-driver might be someone I knew, that dork Craig Smithins, for instance; he was wearing the same mirrored sunglasses that Craig wore. Whoever it was, he creeped me out. I looked in the rear-vision mirror. Was that him? Why would he be tailing me? Craig was gauche but he wasn't nasty. That driver behind me surely was, and when he suddenly revved his engine, I pulled over. He accelerated and I watched with relief as the car speed past. It was an old RX-7. I remained sitting in the car for a few minutes, regretting I hadn't had the presence of mind to at least note the Mazda's registration number.

After that, there were no more rude drivers and I carried on without further incident to the Eversons' place.

Once again, I did a circuit of the house. Everything was more or less the same as I'd seen it during my last visit except the water in the pool was even more fetid, and this time there was laundry on the line: a pair of jeans, two blouses, still damp. I supposed they were Sophie's although there was no sign of her or her car. I was relieved she was out. There was something I had to do to put to rest, once and for all, my uneasy imaginings.

Behind the garage was a narrow lean-to shed where Peter kept his tools. It was locked, but I knew he kept the key on a nail tucked into the elbow of a eucalypt, just behind the shed. I couldn't reach it. I found an old metal bucket and stood on that. It still wasn't quite high enough for me to see the key and I had to fumble around until my fingers landed on it.

Inside the shed I found a crowbar which would have been perfect for the job but was too heavy for me to manage. I took a mattock instead, and a small gardening fork, and walked through the trees, past the swimming pool to the area where those new trees had been planted. The spade was still there where I'd left it after my last visit. Two more of the saplings had died. The earth around them all was still clumped in mounds, but had turned hard and compacted. Was one of the mounds longer and higher than the others? A grave? I attacked it with the mattock.

It was bitterly cold. Autumn in Sydney is mid-winter in the Blue Mountains. In the distance, the trees in the national park were a brooding watchful congregation while overhead, the sky hung low and grey like a seam of iron.

Somewhere nearby a dog barked. Then something rustled in the trees behind me and I froze, momentarily convinced that someone was watching me. My nerves got the better of me and my bowels loosened. I had to rush around behind the shed, near the safety of the house, and relieve myself. I felt better after that. I took some deep slow breaths and told myself to stop being so jumpy. Conjuring up shadows and menace where there were none wasn't going to get the job done.

I worked quickly, one minute righteously resolute, and the next, guilty as a little kid caught stealing lollies. I hoped Sophie wouldn't come home and find me grubbing about in her dad's garden. I was so absorbed in the task that I didn't hear the car arrive at the house or the sound of a car door closing. It wasn't until I heard footsteps along the side of the pool that I realised I was no longer alone. I kept digging, fiercely determined now to find out if there was anything there.

While I'd half expected it to be Sophie arrived home, I wasn't surprised to see it was Christine. She must have driven up to Katoomba behind me. Had she been watching our house in Mitchell Street, followed me? Whatever she was up to, I was past caring.

'What are you doing?' She looked more amused than nettled by my incursion into her home.

'What do you think I'm doing? I want to see what's buried here, because something bloody well is.' My grip on the mattock tightened.

Christine wandered off towards the swimming pool and returned a few moments later with a chair on which she sat down to watch. She was wearing a long tartan skirt I hadn't seen before, with brown ankle boots and a short jacket in russet wool. She crossed her legs, as if we were at the City Recital Hall and she was settling down to enjoy a performance of Handel's *Messiah*.

I glanced up at her and she waved a hand airily at me. 'Do carry on. Don't stop on my account.'

Her self-possession demoralised me. Maybe I had it all entirely wrong. Or maybe she'd set all this up as part of some depraved plan to manipulate me into making a complete dick of myself.

The mattock hit something hard. Bone? I experienced a panicky rush of adrenaline and for a moment doubted my ability to carry on. Then I registered Christine's wry expression which made me more furious and more determined than ever. I got down on my hands and knees and scooped out dirt. There *was* a body and something soft. Fur. I scraped away more dirt until I'd exposed a dog with a long filthy coat that was once creamy yellow. It was Peter's dog. Not Peter. I kept my head down to hide my relief. For an abject moment I thought I was going to cry.

Christine gave me a pitying look. 'What did you think you'd find? Peter? My step-daughter?'

I gazed at the dog. Its name was Bix, a friendly Labrador, super affectionate, and Peter had loved him. 'He wasn't very old.'

214

'He was eleven, and arthritic.' Christine picked up the mattock and handed it to me. 'Keep digging, why don't you? You might find Sophie's cat.'

'There's no need to be sarcastic.'

Bix hadn't been in the ground very long, maybe a few weeks.

I stood up and brushed myself down, then confronted my sister. 'What happened to him? Did you …?'

'Honestly Lexi, you have so lost the plot. He was an old dog. He died.'

I picked up the spade and began shovelling dirt back over the grave. Then I knelt and with my hands, flattened it like a pall across the grave. 'I don't know what to think any more. You've been so weird and secretive. I mean, where's Peter? Why won't you tell me what's going on between you? Would that be so hard?'

Christine shrugged and got up to leave. She picked up the chair and went back to the paved area by the pool. I followed. When I reached the pool, I realised I was carrying the garden tools. I dropped the spade and mattock and put the fork on the table.

'Christine, Chrissy, please.' Calling her Christine was suddenly an effort not worth making and I gave up. 'What am I supposed to think?' There were no phone calls when you were staying at our place, you and Peter used to talk every day, and you lied about him being in South America, and … and you had his cheque book, you were using it. You've been forging his signature.'

'That's between me and Peter. It is absolutely none of your business.'

'Bloody hell. Listen to yourself. It's my business when you plant the thing in our house and accuse me of theft.' The horror of that day when the police came to the house tugged at me like a rip current. 'You went to the cops. They came to my house,' My voice was getting louder with each sentence and by the end I couldn't keep rage and hurt out of it, and was shouting at her. 'I was treated like a criminal.'

My sister took a long time to answer. As I studied her face, her habitual carapace of condescension briefly softened. It took years off her and I caught a glimpse of the girl she used to be. I said nothing, wanting more than anything for that old Chrissy to reveal herself fully to me, and to remain. When she did reply, she lifted her hands, palms open towards me in a gesture of surrender.

'So, I called the police. But only because I lost the damn thing and assumed you or Conor had taken it.'

'I'm not even going to reply to that. As for that stupid list, wanting those things back. Tissues, for heaven's sake. And you didn't want them, you never came to get them.'

'Look, I admit it, I was mean, but I was pissed off with you.'

'That doesn't even begin to cover how I felt.'

What would she have done if I'd stormed into her apartment and attacked her with a machete? 'I get it. You wanted me to have taken that cheque book, give you something to be mad at.'

Chrissy was lost in her own thoughts. 'Ah, I know what happened,' she said at last, 'or at least who …'

I wasn't listening to her either, ruminating instead over her thoughtless treatment of me. 'I'm your sister.'

Until then we'd both been standing. I sat down at the table and rested my hands in my lap. I was hoping Chrissy would take a seat as well, but she leaned against the table instead and folded her arms, and waited for whatever I had to say next. It was then that I noticed she was still wearing her wedding ring. Had she taken it off while she was staying with us? I couldn't remember, but was glad to see it now; I didn't believe she'd have it on if Peter really had found another partner.

'You said Mum never wanted me. Why say such a hateful thing?'

'It was sort of true. She didn't plan on getting pregnant.'

I cast my mind back to my childhood in Bendigo, me drawing at the kitchen table and Mum pausing in her preparations for dinner to comment on my work and plant a kiss on the top of my head, or rising from her weeding in the garden to spontaneously wrap her arms around me before sliding the stems of pansies through the hair bands of my plaits.

'She loved me.'

'Yes, she did.'

'I'm your sister,' I reiterated.

'I withdrew the complaint.' Chrissy's hand-bag, made from the same faux ocelot-like leather as the shoes she owned, was on the table and she pulled it towards her and unclipped it. She took out a bar of chocolate, unwrapped it and broke it into pieces, then offered me some.

If this was her attempt at appeasement, I was ready to accept it although I would have preferred an apology, to hear her tell me unequivocally that she was sorry, and know she meant it.

I tried to picture Mum there, the three of us conversing companionably by the Eversons' swimming pool, but the picture resisted definition. Try as I might, I just couldn't place our mother there. In my mind, she was locked safely in the past, the precious fulcrum of my early, carefree life in Bendigo.

49

Chrissy lifted one of the wicker chairs away from the table, just far enough to create a little distance between us, and sat down as well. For at least a minute we each looked the other way. This time I waited for her to speak, wanting her to begin, but minutes went by and in the end, it was me who broke the silence. If we were ever going to have it out with one another, it was now or never. I put my piece of chocolate down, uneaten, on the table.

'What happened to you?'

Chrissy frowned. 'I never pretended to be the perfect sister. That was your illusion, not mine.'

There was nothing I could say to that. She was right. I leaned forward in my chair, pressing my palms together between my knees, and let her continue.

'It was watching you and Conor, your oh-so-perfect lives. It got to me and ... I guess I was bored with myself really, or my whole vapid life ... take your pick. Everything just seemed to turn to custard last year.'

Had a crap year myself, all thanks to you. My eyes welled with hot tears and I blinked them away. 'But why take it out on me? You were so abrasive, and mean-spirited ... god, those antics.'

'I do wish you'd stop banging on about all that.' Chrissy exhaled loudly with impatience. 'How many times do you have to hear it? I did not plant that lawn in your house. You really think I don't have better things to do? Although, I admit, when Conor told me about it, I had to applaud the ingenuity.'

'It wasn't clever.'

'No, I don't suppose it was.' Chrissy tried and failed to hide her amusement.

'Not funny either.'

My sister got up and paced along the edge of the pool, as if pondering what to say next, and how. I noticed the smoker's lines on her upper lip were more pronounced than they had been. Her face sagged a little and I saw how tired she looked. I had to remind myself how much older than me she was, and how little I knew of her life since she'd left Bendigo.

She came back and sat down, resting her eyes on me. When she spoke again, her tone was unexpectedly placatory, something I'd thought gone forever from her repertoire of feeling. 'What makes you think you were the only target?'

'What do you mean?'

'Hot Phone Sex with *my* number on the card, that's what I mean.' She gave me a bleak stare. 'And it was you who brought him here.'

'I don't understand.'

'Rob. You gave him your address, your phone number, so he knew where to come, how to find us'.

'Chrissy, I haven't a clue what you are on about. Why shouldn't Robbie find us? I was looking for him. I want to see him again.'

'Don't you get it yet? He's a nut job. He planted the lawn in your house. He's behind those idiotic call-girl cards.

'How would he get your number?'

'He's been inside your house and it's a dead cert he went through all your stuff. And unless you ripped out the offending page, my mobile number is in your phone book, where you wrote it. And haven't you noticed someone stalking you? It's Rob. For all I know he's watching us right now.'

We both involuntarily turned around as if we had indeed heard someone behind us.

The trees trembled, a long dark patch moving against the sky. The sun broke briefly through the clouds and the sudden light was almost too harsh. For a moment we were illuminated in dappled light and a semblance of warmth. The clouds closed over again and Chrissy pulled her jacket tight while I pulled myself together.

'This can't be right. Robbie lives in New York. He's married to an American. They've got kids. We've got nephews. I saw the photos.'

'Anyone can find happy family pics on the web.'

'She's an artist. Her name is Rhonda.'

'Oh dear, oh dear. Poor little Lexi. You so want it to be true, don't you? The wife is a figment of Rob's demented imagination.'

'I don't believe you.' And yet, what Chrissy was suggesting wasn't entirely unexpected to me. As she spoke, thoughts and memories tugged at my mind which, although I couldn't quite catch, resonated. When we'd had that Skype call, I'd been aware of something out of kilter, and, later, that things about my brother just didn't add up.

And then it came to me, what I hadn't been able to put my finger on. When we'd spoken with each other online, it had been night time in New York, yet his apartment had been lit not by lamps but by daylight. I was sure of it. Chrissy was right, Robbie wasn't in the US at all.

'He really conned you, didn't he?' Chrissy spoke in a soft voice. 'Our dear brother Robert lives in Perth, in some sort of halfway house last I heard. He went to prison once. Probably became a regular inhabitant.'

'How come I didn't know?'

'It was in the papers.'

Chrissy lifted her skirt to expose a long ugly scar high on her leg. 'See this? That's Rob's handiwork. Proof enough for you? I'm telling you, Lexi, our brother is certifiable.'

The very word I'd used only months earlier to describe her.

I didn't know what or who to believe. For months, Chrissy had been godawful and now she was telling me it had been our brother all along. I couldn't take my eyes off the scar on her leg. The flesh across the top of her right thigh was mottled, the skin in some patches stretched white and shiny, and in others, grotesquely puckered into dark salmon-coloured ridges.

'You did that. Mum told me. She said you stood too close to the heater and your PJs caught fire.'

'That's what she wanted people to think.' A vein throbbed in Chrissy's forehead. 'Rather me be careless than her only son a psycho.'

So many conflicting stories. My head was spinning. Yet now I understood why she hadn't joined us in the pool during barbecues at her place, why she never wore shorts.

Chrissy picked up the garden fork and began fiddling with it, tapping her fingertips one by one against the tines.

Suddenly I am four years old, or maybe I'm five, hiding in the hedge at the bottom of our back yard in Bendigo. I am watching my big brother. He has used Mum's trowel to scrape clear a patch of dirt in the vegetable garden and is building a fire there, feeding it with twigs and sticks and dried eucalypt leaves. While the fire burns down to hot coals, he whittles the end of a thin hard branch, chewing his bottom lip in concentration. He puts one end of the stick into the fire, gets up and goes around to the front of Dad's shed where the rabbit hutch is, and returns to the fire, fondling a rabbit, murmuring to it. The rabbit is grey and soft with big floppy ears and I want to come out of my hiding place, join Robbie at the fire, cuddle the pet, but something holds me back. Alarm. It is alarm that holds me back, and the sickening knowledge that I have seen this before. Robbie lifts his wood from the fire and holding the rabbit tightly on the ground with one hand, picks up his fiery stick with the other and pokes the rabbit's back with it. The animal squeals and

221

wriggles madly to escape, but Robbie holds it tight. He presses the still smouldering stick into the rabbit again. I push my hand into my mouth to stop myself crying out. The smell of scorching fur and flesh makes me gag and I'm about to run away when Chrissy comes sprinting out from the house. She slaps Robbie hard against the side of his head and wrests the rabbit from him. 'You vile, heinous boy,' she yells. 'This time I'm telling Dad.' She turns to leave, but Robbie grabs her ankle and she stumbles and falls. He scoops hot coals from the fire with the trowel and throws them against her leg. They sear through her denims, shrivelling the cloth, and stick to her skin. She screams.

' … thought Rob would grow out of it.'

Chrissy's voice brought me back to the present and her own garden in Katoomba.

'You told me you were the one who injured him, that you scratched his face.'

'I was trying to put you off looking for him. Have you been listening, Lexi? You do not want our brother here. He's seriously unhinged.'

'So, it was true, what you said, about him trying to rape you?'

Chrissy let out an exasperated sigh. 'He more than tried, he succeeded. And I told you, he tried it on with you. When are you going to believe me?'

'And that message you read at Mum's funeral, the one from Robbie? Was that real?'

'Of course not. There was no message. He was never in Iraq. I was only doing what Mum would have wanted, keeping the skeleton tucked safely away in the closet … where she and Dad put it, not me.'

All this was doing my head in. I kneaded my forehead, trying to collect my thoughts, to remember …

I felt a constriction in my throat. That appalling feeling again of being smothered. A deep shudder went through my body.

That's when Robbie arrived.

50

My brother stepped through the trees. I knew him immediately. He'd shaved off his beard, but was wearing the same tan leather bomber jacket he'd worn when we Skyped each other, and blue jeans crisply ironed as if he'd never let go dress habits acquired in the army. In the flesh he was taller than he'd appeared on the screen, and more muscular.

How long had he been there, watching us?

And how long in Sydney, watching me? I was now in no doubt that it had been Robbie outside my house that day I was taken to the police station. And on the night of the party. Why hadn't he spoken to me?

Chrissy and I both stood up. I felt her stiffen beside me and wanted to tell her she could relax because now was our chance at last to get everything out in the open. Lauren would talk about forgiveness; I just wanted us all to move on, as a family.

'Robbie?' My mouth was dry and the word came out in a hoarse whisper.

He strode up to me and wrapped me in a big bear hug. How I had yearned for this moment. He smelled of soap and something musky. Aftershave. We separated, but Robbie kept his hands on my shoulders, and stared at me and for so long it became embarrassing. He was, after all, practically a stranger.

'Lexi girl,' he said. 'How long has it been?' He let me go and turned to Chrissy. 'What bullshit have you been feeding our baby sis about me?'

He didn't wait for an answer, instead he addressed me again, giving me a sly snigger, as if he and I shared a secret. He rotated his right index finger against the side of his head. 'You know she's doolally, don't you?'

Chrissy had recovered from her start at his arrival. She adopted a languid air. 'You're not welcome here, Rob,' she said, and bent down to adjust the zip on one of her boots, as if to announce an end to the matter and that there was nothing more to be said.

'C'mon, Chris, give me a break.'

'You forfeited your right to that a long time ago.'

'I'm not a brainless kid any more. I went back to school, I'm an engineer now, got my own firm.' He was doing that blinking thing I'd noticed when we'd spoken online, and for all his bravado, I couldn't help thinking he was nervous. He pressed his right hand against his heart and bent forward from the waist in a mock bow, only slightly, but low enough for me to see he was losing his hair.

Chrissy gave a loud sniff of derision. 'You always were a liar.'

'Ever the cynic. But *you* know, don't you, Lexi girl, about my life in the States.'

I wished he wouldn't call me that, Lexi girl. The "girl" really grated.

He cleared his throat as if about to say more, but instead removed a packet of cigarettes from a pocket inside his jacket and in an unhurried way went through the motions of tapping out a cigarette, searching his other pockets for a lighter.

The three of us stood around like some sort of triptych-noir except there was nothing holding us together.

Robbie turned to face me full on, his hands raised and open, cigarette between the fingers of one hand, lighter in the other. 'A man can change and I really do want to make it up to you, you know, be your big brother.'

Had he changed? He smiled at me, but much as I wanted to, I couldn't see any warmth in his eyes.

'It's your decision, Lex … steady bro or catty sis … deal or snow deal.' He chuckled at his own joke.

'This isn't a game,' said Chrissy. She sat down, crossed her legs and with studied indifference, swung her right foot back and forth while I watched our brother, weirdly fascinated by him.

'How right you are,' he said. 'Always the wise one, our Chris. We must give the situation its due weight. I suggest a name to mark the occasion.' He tapped his fingers against his bottom lip and hummed to himself. 'Hmm … I know, we'll call it the Madison Divertissement. No, we can do better.' He continued muttering to himself and then suddenly looked up and all but shouted at us. 'The Madison Diversion. How bleeding apt is that?'

'You got the mad bit right anyway,' remarked Chrissy.

It popped into my head then that 'diversion' was the very word Chrissy once used to describe her weekend visits to Sydney.

Robbie regarded her for a long cool moment before whipping back and forth between us, jabbing a finger first at me, then Chrissy, then me again. 'Your start, Lexi. After all, this game is all about you, isn't it? So then, who's it be?'

He lit the cigarette and as the tip flared, memories of his cruelty crackled in me like static.

'I remember the rabbit,' I said.

Robbie took a long deliberate drag on his cigarette, then exhaled just as purposefully, squinting at me through a billow of smoke.

Without thinking, I took a small step back and regretted it. I didn't want him to think I was afraid because I wasn't. 'You broke into our house.'

Conor had been right all along; Chrissy *had* returned our key and it would have been child's play for Robbie to find it beneath that fake drain cap. What a dumb hiding place. How careless we were. 'It's been you all along, hasn't it?'

'Is that what she told you? She's lying. I *saw* her in your house, you know, planting that lawn. I was watching.' He pivoted back to Chrissy. 'With admiration, I might add. Didn't know you had it in you, Chris. It was inspired, first-rate.'

Sarcasm, the ultimate weapon of the bully. Must be a family trait, I thought.

'If that's true, why didn't you stop her?' I recalled that flash of triumph on his face, when I'd told him on Skype about Chrissy's antics, or what I'd believed at the time were hers. His glee had struck me as inappropriate at the time, but now it made perfect sense.

I noticed Chrissy watching me, observing my changing expression as the facts of the past year's pranks became more and more clear to me. Our eyes met. She gave a tiny nod, then confronted Robbie.

'You've had your say, Rob, now bugger off.' Chrissy's air of nonchalance was gone and she was toey, tracking our brother's every move with guarded eyes.

'Be fair. I've only just got here.' He grasped my hand again. 'C'mon, Lexi girl.'

'Please stop calling me that.'

His palm was hard as a batsman's glove, as if he'd spent years at some form of manual labour. 'We've such a lot of catching up to do.'

'You've been stalking me.' I tried to shake free of him but that only made him grip my hand even harder.

'Let her go.' Chrissy's face flushed red and her mood was suddenly incandescent. She reached out to prise me away from Robbie.

'It's okay, Chrissy. I want us to talk, Robbie, I really do, but let me go, please.' He released my hand. I suppressed the impulse to walk away.

'Just tell me why,' I said. 'I want to understand.' I still held on to the dim hope that if we were all willing, now was our opportunity at last to heal the rift between us, close that painful gap.

'Because he's a mad fucker,' Chrissy retorted.

Robbie's eyes narrowed with antipathy and he gave up trying to disguise his truculence. 'You always were a superior bitch.' For just a second, he seemed to droop a little and I saw raw self-pity cross his face. 'That's how it was at home, everyone always ready to put yours truly in the wrong.'

I thought of Chrissy's behaviour towards me over the past year and, for a fleeting moment, was almost inclined to sympathise with him.

'I was only little. I didn't even know you.'

'You can know me now. Let's go somewhere more hospitable than this dump, and talk, just you and me. What do you say?'

'Piss off Rob, I mean it,' said Chrissy. 'Find yourself a life somewhere. Just make it somewhere else.'

There was a long pause during which Robbie's bearing hardened. His whole face became clenched with hate. I'd seen it before, only then he'd been a teenager, lying on top of me, yanking up my nightie, his forearm rammed hard against my windpipe.

The truth buzzed in my head like an electric knife.

'You tried to rape me. You're my brother and you … you abused me.'

Chrissy groaned loudly. 'I so hoped this day would never happen.'

Robbie dropped his cigarette and ground the stub against the pavers with the toe of his shoe. He tilted his chin at me. 'But look at you now, Lexi girl, all growed up and ever so purdy.' The phoney American accent jarred and I was relieved that when he spoke next, he dropped it. 'You're all right though, aren't you, Lex?' he asked rhetorically. 'No harm done.'

'Are you out of your mind?'

'I did say.' Chrissy sat down heavily by the side of the pool and put her head in her hands, but not before I saw her pained expression.

'You really had better go, Robbie,' I said and placed a hand lightly on his sleeve, only to withdraw it swiftly when I saw his face.

The man was livid as a tumour. He balled his hands into tight fists and made an ugly little grunting sound, then lifted a hand to strike me. I put an arm up to protect myself. Chrissy leapt to her feet and stepped between us.

'You so much as touch her Robert Madison and I swear to god I'll call the cops.'

'How like our dear mother you are.' The words came out in a baleful hiss and I saw a flash of metal, a knife? and the next thing Chrissy was bent double. She staggered a bit, then toppled forward. There was a sick-making crunch as her head hit the edge of the swimming pool.

I dropped to the ground beside Chrissy. Her face had turned deathly white. She was moaning and I couldn't tell whether or not she was conscious.

'What have you done?' I glared at my brother. 'Who *are* you?'

I got up and sort of lurched across to the table where I'd left my bag. 'We need an ambulance.'

Robbie was behind me, so close I could feel his breath on my neck. I batted him away. As I struck his forearm, the knife fell from his hand and skittered across the concrete pavers. We both watched it fall. I thought he was going to go and pick it up which would give me time to reach my phone, but Robbie left the knife where it fell. He grabbed hold of my bag instead and for a risible minute we were both manhandling it. I held on until my knuckles turned white and, in the end, it was Robbie who gave in. He let go of the bag so suddenly I lost my balance and teetered, grasping hold of the table to right myself. Not soon enough. Robbie slapped me hard against the side of my head. I reeled and tripped over the mattock and for the second time almost pitched forward, but managed to save myself. I tried again to reach my phone.

Chrissy had stopped moaning. Her stillness scared me.

228

'I'm calling the police.'

Robbie picked up the spade and swung it at me. I saw its leaden blade out of the corner of my eye, too late to duck or dodge. There was a rushing noise in my ears and searing pain in my head. I crumpled to my knees and keeled over, face first and hard onto the pavers. The impact made my teeth rattle and my mouth filled with spit. No, not that. Not saliva. The taste of old iron was unmistakable.

The last thing I heard was someone yelling. 'Stop it, stop it.' And then the monitory wail of sirens.

Everything turned black and spongy like peat after rain and I sank into the dark.

51

Katoomba's district hospital is a low red brick building on the Great Western Highway. I'd passed it a couple of times with Conor when we went to Leura, after visiting the Eversons, but I never expected to see the inside of it, least of all find myself checked in as a patient.

But that's where I came fully to, after a short drive during which I drifted in and out of consciousness. At one point I'd touched the side of my head and my hand came away sticky and slick with blood. My blood. I heard someone groaning and shut up when I realised it was me.

I was only vaguely aware of a doctor assessing me, peeling back my eyelids, fixing a bright light on my face, and asking me questions to which I mumbled semi-coherent replies. When I opened my eyes, I closed them again immediately. St Paul's sixteen-ton bell was tolling inside my head. It felt like Armageddon.

'What happened?' I asked. My tongue hurt. I'd bitten it and that accounted for the blood in my mouth when I was knocked out.

'Thank goodness,' said Sophie.

A nurse took my pulse, asked me my name, date of birth and where I lived. I was nothing more than a faint echo of myself and my voice sounded as if it belonged to someone else.

'Desperately thirsty,' I whispered. The nurse gave me a glass of water and two painkillers. When I lifted my head to drink the water, the clapper in my skull belted me again. I swallowed the painkillers. 'Can I have more of those?' I asked. 'Five might do it.'

The nurse smiled and finished a dressing on the side of my head. 'Doctor Chatwal says you'll live, but he needs to confirm there's no concussion. We'll keep you in overnight, just to be sure.' She bustled away then, into the corridor where she vanished into the medical machine.

Sophie lifted her chair and brought it closer to the bed. 'I called the police. And an ambulance. You were . . . Chrissy was . . .' Her voice trailed off and she chewed her lip. She looked as if she was as far down the rabbit hole as I was.

'What happened?'

'I don't know. I turned up and heard shouting, and there was this guy.'

It all came back to me in a gut-churning rush. Robbie. Chrissy. The knife. 'My sister, where is she? Is she all right?'

'Chrissy's fine. She's in a room down the corridor. She needed five stitches, and she's badly concussed, but the doctor says she'll mend.' Sophie wrung her hands. 'If only I'd got home sooner.'

'Just as well you didn't or he might have hit you as well. It was very lucky for us you turned up when you did.'

Sophie nodded. My step-niece was in her early twenties, with her father's blue eyes and her mother's dark hair which she wore tied back in a careless chignon. A youthful version of Madeleine. Sophie favoured new-age gear and that day was wearing a long paisley skirt in green, grey, and orange, with a loose mustard-coloured jersey. She looked thinner than I remembered, and even though summer was over, still had a residual tan and a friendly scattering of freckles across the bridge of her nose.

I sat up. The painkillers were kicking in.

Sophie adjusted the pillows behind me. 'I brought your bag.' She put it on the bed, within my reach. 'How do you feel?'

'Like a cane toad on a bad trip, crossed with Jeff Fenech on a losing streak.'

Sophie grinned. 'That's sort of what you look like. Sorry. Don't mean to be rude.' She tucked away a few strands of stray hair at her neck and then fussed a little with the bed sheet. 'It's such a long time since I've seen you, Aunt Lexi.'

'My fault entirely.'

'Who was that man? Do you know?'

'My brother ...' That was more than I wanted to say. Rob would be a sort of uncle to Sophie which was a horrible thought; better she didn't know about him.

Gingerly, I put my hand up against the side of my head. It was tender and there was a bump on my forehead the size of an emu's egg. 'I need to see. Is there a mirror anywhere here?'

'Sure you want to do that? You'll get a shock.'

'You don't think I haven't had one already?'

Sophie went out and returned with a hand mirror and reluctantly gave it to me.

'No point putting it off, is there?' I took a deep breath and looked in the mirror. It was indeed a helluva whammy. Under that enormous bump on my head, the entire top half of my face was swollen and marbled blue, shiraz red, and black. The bruising began in my eyes, spread around both sockets and leaked down past my cheek bones. I dropped the mirror on the bed.

Sophie picked it up and put it on the other bed. 'You can't say I didn't warn you,' she said and peered at my face. 'At least it's still you. And I'll be back to see you tomorrow. Have to go now and see how Chrissy is.'

'Sophie, wait. Did Robbie, that man, did he have a car?

'Yes, the police took it away.'

'What make was it, do you know?'

'No. I'm not good at cars. It was grey, and small. Sporty.'

So, it had been Robbie tailing me to Katoomba, frightening me with his reckless driving. I pulled the bed sheet up to my chin. Sophie turned to go but I had one more question.

'Where's your father?'

'In the Middle East, doing some work with Al Jazeera, and research for a book. The book is why he went. It's taken longer than he thought. Didn't Chrissy tell you?'

'She said he'd gone off with someone, found a new partner.'

'That's rubbish. When he realised how long he'd be there, he pleaded with Chrissy to join him, even if only for a few weeks.'

'I wish I'd known. I emailed Peter, weeks ago.'

'He probably hasn't seen it. You know Dad, textbook Luddite. He's got two addresses and the one for work is the only one he ever checks. He doesn't even turn on his private phone. Used to frustrate the hell of me, but I'm used to it now.'

'The police came to the house, about his car.'

'Oh, that. Sorry, it was my fault. I over-reacted. He loaned it to his mate Ethan. And then a couple of hoons nicked it. Happens all the time out here. I reported it.' Sophie pushed her hair off her face and kneaded her forehead. 'What an idiot. I should have phoned you.'

She got up to leave. 'Conor will be here soon. I found his number in your mobile. Called him.'

'Thanks.'

At the door she paused, 'I see you found Bix. I didn't do a very good job of burying him. Did some other dog dig him up?'

'No, I ...' My voice trailed away to nothing. I was too embarrassed to tell Sophie about what I'd done or about the suspicions that had led me to digging up Bix, how shamefully mistrustful I'd been.

For an hour or so I slept, until a woman from patient services brought me lunch: a rubbery omelette, two slices of thick white bread, and some tinned pear sliced into quarters. I picked at the egg, but wasn't hungry and left the food on the tray. I drank a cup of milky tea.

A nurse came and asked me to say my name again, and repeat my date of birth and where I lived. If I gave any wrong answers she didn't say.

52

When I woke, it was the middle of the night and Conor was sitting by the side of the bed.

He leaned down to kiss me but thought better of it and stood back. 'How do you feel? You look rather grim.'

'Nice of you to say, but yes, I'm fine. Looks worse than it is.'

'I got the nine pm train. Sorry I wasn't here earlier. I worked late, left my phone at home. I didn't get Sophie's message until I got back.'

'It doesn't matter. You're here now.'

Conor rearranged the pillows behind me and I pulled myself up into a sitting position.

'I forgot your birthday.'

'You weren't yourself.' Conor ginned. 'Plenty of time to make up for it.'

'What did you have in mind? No, don't tell me . . . makes my head sore just thinking about having to do anything.'

'This will help. I've got some good news. That Detective Moretti phoned. They've dropped all that business over the cheque book.'

'I know, Chrissy told me. All that's okay now, we sorted it.'

'She looks ever more battered than you do.'

'You've seen her?' How could he know what Chrissy looks like?

Did he visit her before he came to see me?

'You were asleep.'

I hauled myself up. 'I need to see her.'

'In the morning.' Conor put his hands on my shoulders and eased me gently back against the pillows. 'You're not going anywhere. Sophie told me what happened. My god, your brother . . .'

I nodded weakly. 'Where is he?'

'In a cell, no doubt. Sophie said the police carted him off and none too gently either.'

'Poor man. I feel sorry for him.'

'Will you go see him do you think?'

'What would you do?'

'Up to you, love. He's your brother, your problem really.'

I sagged further into the pillows and closed my eyes. 'I can't think about all that right now.' My head churned with pain. When would *my* problems become *our* problems? Wasn't that what marriage was supposed to be about? Sharing our burdens?

In the morning Conor returned with flat whites for us each, an answer to my prayer for decent coffee, and Sophie who carried a bag of gear for Chrissy. Coffee had never tasted so good. It cleared my head and just in time because five minutes later a policewoman arrived.

Sophie left to see how Chrissy was and Conor sat on one side of my bed while the policewoman stood on the other. She loomed and I was glad when Conor got up and found her a seat. She took it, but warily, as if sitting while questioning wasn't in the police manual.

As I relayed everything I could remember of the fight at Chrissy's house, she wrote it all down, now and then casting me a professionally encouraging glance. When I'd finished, she stood up and returned the seat to the side of the other bed which, mercifully, had remained unoccupied since I'd arrived.

'Where is he, my brother?'

'Mr Madison, or Hardy, is known to us.' I waited for her say more, like how they knew Robbie, since when, and why, but the policewoman didn't continue.

'What will happen to him?'

Is it police policy not to give anything away, even to a relative? The cop put her notebook away in a pocket and remained frustratingly enigmatic. 'It will be in the hands of the courts now, I expect,' she said.

'Do I need to do anything?'

'When you're up to it, come into the station and sign a statement.' She headed for the door and was gone before I could ask which station.

My window was open a little and I could smell the eucalypt, see the blue haze of it across the mountains. A tea trolley clacked past my room. The woman pushing it was humming quietly to herself.

Sophie returned just as I was asking Conor where he'd stayed the night before.

'I put him up at ours,' she said. 'It's only me there, and Chrissy will be there too, of course, when she's better. Plenty of room for you both.'

'Thanks, Sophie, but we'll manage.' I wasn't sure I could face going back to that house.

I'd finished my coffee and resisted the urge to ask for another; my adrenal glands were suffering enough. Conor took the cup and rinsed it out in the basin and put it on the table while I watched, noting that whatever business had sold him the coffee was smart enough to use eco-cups.

'Spoke to your doc on the way in. He says you can probably leave this afternoon, but has to give you the all clear first.'

'I'm not going anywhere before I see Chrissy.'

'She's feeling better,' said Sophie. 'Says she wants to see you. And now it's time I wasn't here. I skipped the morning off work.' Sophie taught yoga and aerobics in a local gym. 'The manager covered my classes for me, but she'll be expecting me back.'

Conor and Sophie left together and I filled in the time flicking through a few women's magazines – not that I was the slightest bit interested in what Kate Middleton wore to the British Film Awards, or whether or not Angelina Jolie managed to save her celebrity marriage – until the lunch time flurry and the arrival of a room-mate. She was rake-thin, with messy grey hair, and as soon as she was out of the wheelchair and settled in her bed, turned on the television. We each had one, suspended from the ceiling at the end of our beds, but I didn't want to hear or see either of them. The volume went up and I groaned with disapproval, loud enough for her to hear and, bless the woman, she muted it immediately.

Having to share the room made me restive to leave. What I most needed were things hospitals can't provide: peace and quiet, and decent food.

Two hours passed before the doctor arrived, at the same time as Conor.

I expected an Indian accent but Doctor Chatwal's vowels were Oxbridge and mellifluous. 'No serious harm done, Miss Madison, but don't take this lightly. You have a moderate head injury and until that bump goes down, and the bruising has healed, you need to take things slowly.'

'How long?'

He surveyed my ruined face. I admired his which was a great deal lovelier than mine, with smooth unblemished skin like honey, and eyes so melty brown they were almost black. Beneath his white coat he wore a light blue collarless shirt, the top button undone. His bedside manner was exemplary, fifty per cent professional authority and the other half avuncular concern. 'I'd say it'll be a good month before you're ready to go to the ball.'

I rewarded his quip with a smile. 'Please tell me about my sister. How is she?'

The doctor gave me a blank look. I persisted. 'Chrissy, Christine Everson. You must know her, she used to work here.'

'Ah yes. She's not my patient.'

My look of reproach was not wasted on him. 'I'll find out for you,' he said.

'Thank you.'

'How do you feel about driving back to Sydney? There's no concussion, but you may be woozy for a while. Is there somewhere you can stay locally for a day or two?'

Did he know how grateful I was to hear that? Conor would be twitchy about getting back to Sydney and work, but even if I was ready to get home to Glebe, the thought of ninety minutes on a highway full of peevish drivers made me jittery. As it was, I wasn't going anywhere until I'd visited Chrissy, seen for myself that she really was all right, and cleared up some loose ends.

Doctor Chatwal looked steadily at Conor as if he expected immediate compliance.

'She may not feel like returning to the scene of the crime,' said Conor.

I sighed heavily and Conor looked sheepish. 'Sorry. Bad joke. There's a motel in Leura we've used before,' he said. 'We'll go there.'

'It's not that,' I said even though it was. I thought of Chrissy; she may need me to stay. 'I don't mind going to the Eversons'. In fact, I want to.'

53

When I went to see Chrissy, she was toying with some fruit Sophie had brought in, without actually eating any. Nor did I when she pushed a small bag of mandarins towards me.

'The police told me they already know about Robbie.'

'Didn't I say? They've known him since he was twelve.'

'Tell me. No more secrets, please. I need to hear it all.'

'He smashed all the windows in the science block. Spent a year doing community service, something to do with rubbish collection I think.'

'Was he ever in the army?'

'Yes, and he should have stayed there, but he blew it. They chucked him out after a year. One weekend on leave, he commandeered a Merc from outside the Perth City Council and drove it into a lake somewhere. Bibra. That was the name of the lake.'

'That message from Iraq, or non-message, why did you write it? Wouldn't it have been better to say nothing?'

'I told you, Mum would have wanted it. It's true, I probably said more than I needed to, but it seemed an opportunity too good to miss to say something about the idiocy of that senseless war.'

I shook my head as if to shake off my pique at being left,

deliberately, for so long in the dark. It hurt to move my head. 'How come I was never told any of this?'

'You were just a kid. Whenever anyone asked, Mum and Dad told people Rob was still in the army, that he was serving overseas. For a while, they kept in touch with him, until he sort of drifted off the radar. No one was sorry to see the back of him.'

'Mum and Dad must have been sorry.'

'There's no rule says you have to like your kids.'

An elderly man dawdled past the door, wheeling his drug supply with him. He paused at our door and bobbed his head at us before moving on.

'If you had your way, we'd all be neutered at birth.'

Chrissy laughed weakly. 'That was dinner party talk. I didn't mean it.'

'Glad to hear it.'

We both laughed then and for a few minutes sat in amiable silence. How I wanted it to last, for us to go on being like that together, quiet and tender with each other, for the rest of the day, the week, forever, but there were things I needed to talk about.

Two nurse-aides came into the room, one carrying a vase of flowers and the other a bowl of grapes. 'From the team,' one of them said. 'With best wishes from all of us.' They nodded at me and left.

'Everyone here seems really nice,' I said.

'They are.'

We both watched the door for a couple of minutes as if expecting more of Chrissy's old colleagues to visit, but the corridor outside remained empty.

'Tell me more about Robbie. Why does he hate us so much?'

'He was just born bad I suppose. Some people are.'

'I wondered if, you know, something had happened to him, in Bendigo.'

Chrissy gave one her cynical snorts, then a spasm of pain made her scrunch up her face. She sank a little deeper into the pillows and briefly closed her eyes. I waited for her to recover. When she spoke again, her voice was almost spent. 'What are you looking for, Lexi? A convenient little cliché, that he was buggered by a scout master, or made to suck his teacher's cock? I'm sorry to disappoint you, but as far as I know, there was no execrable incident that screwed with his mind.'

'I thought maybe Dad's drinking.'

'That was never an issue. Dad had problems, sure, but he never took them out on us.'

'We should help him.'

'We can't. You can't. Mum and Dad tried, got him counselling, packed him off to some children's camp once, after he set fire to the maintenance shed at his school. That lasted three days before they sent him home again.'

'Was he, what do they call it, ADD or something? He must have some sort of mental condition.'

Chrissy gave a shallow laugh. 'Oh, there's a mental condition all right. You saw it.'

'I don't want to make fun of him. I want to understand.'

'There doesn't have to be an explanation. Rob is Rob. There's a screw loose. Always was. Always will be. People don't change, you know. They just become more of who they always were.'

She gave me a self-deprecating smile. 'Look at me. Living proof.'

Chrissy had the same Calvinistic attitude as Lauren. I wanted to believe people could change, grow into better human beings. 'It's a rather disheartening view, isn't it, to think there's nothing we can do to change our fate?'

'I find it kind of restful.' Chrissy's smile was sweet. It took me back years to when we both much younger, when I was only little and she was my fairy godmother. If she could help me realise my childish dreams back then, if only to play the part of Cinderella in a school play, surely together we could help our brother now.

'All the same,' I said, 'I can't help thinking there must be some way we can help him. He is our brother after all.'

'No.' Chrissy glared at me, as much as a person with two black eyes can glare. 'Don't you even think about going there, and if you're considering visiting him in prison, don't. Just don't. He's poisonous.'

I didn't immediately answer and Chrissy held my eye. 'I need you to promise, because don't you get it yet, Lexi? To Robbie, you are just another rabbit.'

An astonishing thought occurred to me. 'Don't tell me that's why you moved in up the road. Really? To keep an eye on me? Because you thought Robbie was around?'

'Didn't work though, did it?' She closed her eyes again and this time they stayed closed.

I went back to my own bed for a rest. My head ached and I could feel the ten-piece rock band inside my skull picking up their instruments for more raving. I desperately needed to sleep, but it eluded me; there was too much to think about.

Two hours later, Conor came to collect me and I checked out.

54

The next afternoon we returned to the hospital to collect Chrissy. I asked Conor to drop me at the door so I could talk to her alone while he parked the car.

Chrissy was looking stronger. Someone had replenished the bowl of white grapes and she had it on the bed beside her. I was pleased to see that this time she was eating them. I pulled a chair to the side of the bed and she passed the bowl to me and for the next little while we shared the fruit until most of it was eaten.

'Why did you tell me Peter had found someone else? Sophie says he expected you to join him in Doha.'

'I needed a break.'

'Really? Is that all? It's been an age, Chrissy, months and months.'

'You wouldn't understand. Conor is always there for you, but Peter would go off on assignment to god knows where, leaving me on my own for weeks. What sort of marriage is that? I suppose I wanted him to see how it felt if I cleared off for a while.'

'You should have said. And surely, you made your point months ago. Why didn't you go? I'd love to visit the Middle East.'

'What would I do in Qatar? It's hardly the most congenial corner of the world. And anyway, Pete would be somewhere else half the time, chasing ambulances for Al Jazeera.'

'But his cheque book. The one for his business. How come you've got it? You weren't really broke, were you?' A picture of the place she'd rented up the road in Mitchell Street came into my mind; how expensive it looked, how upmarket.

Chrissy didn't answer and I didn't push it. I had other more pressing questions.

'Robbie said Mum was pregnant with me because you pricked a hole in her diaphragm. Is that true?'

'Not all this again.' Chrissy put the empty bowl back on the table beside her bed. 'You've seen how he is. Whatever he told you, about whatever, whenever, it's all twisted nonsense. He made that hole. Haven't you got that by now?'

The dish she'd put on the table was perched precariously on top of a saucer and I moved it to safer ground, at the same time rearranging the other bits and bobs on the table – a water jug and glass, tea cup, a plate with two biscuits on it – but without actually thinking about them. My mind was on other things.

'What was the deal with the rulers?'

'What rulers?'

'The ones you took. When you were at school.'

I could see Chrissy was genuinely mystified. She put her hand up to scratch the side of her head, bringing it away again when her fingers met thick bandage. After a few minutes she remembered. 'Lord, fancy bringing those up. I'd forgotten all about them.' She assumed a contrite expression but we both knew it was false. She gave up any pretence at remorse and gave me a lopsided grin instead. 'Rob started it, then challenged me to me to nick as many as he did.'

'And did you? Pinch as many as Robbie?'

'More.' Chrissy must have thought I'd disapprove because she made a little huffing noise of impatience. 'We were kids. You never steal anything?'

I nodded. The lipsticks and those black stockings weren't the only things I'd ever nabbed. On another occasion, around the same time, I pilfered a box of crayons from the mall. Mum found out. This was before I'd used them which was just as well because Mum marched me back to the mall and into the shop I'd nicked them from, then stood back and watched, tight-lipped, while I returned them to the owner, apologised, and offered to help in the store. I never stole anything again after that.

'I'm sorry. I seemed to have got everything terribly mixed up.'

Chrissy reached out and put her hand over mine. 'You weren't to know. And anyway, none of it matters any more.'

'What about …?' I started to say something, but really, was stumped for words and at a loss as to how to finish the sentence, so I didn't. The thought came to me about what Matisse had once said, that if he could say things in words, he'd have no reason to paint. Then I thought about more recent occurrences that still mattered, to me: Steve, and Conor and why she had to hurt me … but while I needed to discuss these with Chrissy, I decided they were no-go areas, for now anyway. There would be time enough later, when we both recovered and might, just might, be able to talk properly about all these things and then, god willing, put it all behind us.

'I wish you'd talked to me more, been more honest, especially about Robbie.'

'I tried. You didn't want to listen.'

The memory of my conversation with Lauren, when we'd decided Chrissy was a sociopath, made me cringe. 'I'm sorry, about everything. You must think me a complete dolt.'

'Stop saying sorry.'

Chrissy pulled at the bedding and patted the blanket smooth across the bed. 'You've always had this dippy idea that we're alike. We're not. I'm difficult to live with and know it. You have to live your life and let me live mine.' She was rueful, as if thinking, like me, of those few years when our lives overlapped, when we both lived at home in Bendigo.

'I only wanted …'

'It's not all about you, Lexi.'

My demeanour must have been pathetically crestfallen because she gave me an encouraging smile. 'How the troubles rain down.'

When I didn't reply – how could I forget her contribution to my troubles? – she suggested we spend some time away together. 'In the summer, let's go to Bali for two weeks, just you and me,' she said. 'We'll stay in a remote spa somewhere and surrender ourselves to some serious pampering. What do you say?'

Any residual rancour I felt towards her evaporated and I basked in the promise of a shared holiday. Her solicitude that day was what I had most missed during the entire length of her stay with us. I wondered briefly where Conor had got to, at the same relieved he'd left us alone together.

Blood had seeped through the bandage around Chrissy's head and dried to the colour of old metal, but I leaned over and kissed her on the side of her head anyway.

'You always were a funny thing,' she said. And then. 'Let's go for a walk.'

'Are you sure, are you ready? What about where …?' I couldn't bring myself to say the word "stabbed", or refer directly to the wound Robbie had inflicted on her, but Chrissy knew what I meant.

'It's not so bad. Only five stitches. He missed the vital bits.' She gave me a wry smile. 'Typical of our brother to miss the stuff that matters.'

She pushed back the bed clothes and slowly brought her legs over the side of the bed and sat there for a couple of minutes, dangling her feet on the floor as if testing the water. I found the bag of clothes Sophie had brought, took out Chrissy's dressing gown and helped her into it.

A nurse came by as we were leaving the ward. She gave us

247

a dubious look, but didn't suggest Chrissy return to bed. I half expected her to issue a directive, that we take things slowly, but there was no need, Chrissy and I were moving at a snail's pace. Now and then, Chrissy stopped, holding a hand against her side, where Robbie had knifed her, and her face would tighten with pain. Then she'd give me a nudge and we'd move on again. A five-minute walk to the front entrance took us nearly forty minutes and when we got there, we both had to stop and rest. I was discouraging Chrissy from venturing any further, and looking around for a wheelchair to take her back to her room, when Conor arrived.

The three of us were on our way back to Chrissy's room, Conor and I on either side to assist her if she needed it, when without warning, my sister collapsed. She just sagged suddenly and before I knew what was happening, was on her knees and then slumped on the floor. Conor grabbed hold of her and supported her, but she seemed unaware of him. Her head lolled against him and her eyelids fluttered uncontrollably.

I yelled for help and people came running: two nurses and a doctor. One of the nurses pushed a red call button on the wall and within moments, aides arrived with a gurney and a load of scary-looking medical equipment. Conor and I had hardly stepped out of the way before they lifted Chrissy onto the stretcher, placed an oxygen mask over her face and whisked her away.

The doctor went with them, and one of the nurses. And me. I ran alongside the gurney. 'What's wrong with her? She was ... she was ... we were ...'

Conor gripped my arm. 'Slow down, Lex, you're babbling.'

I stopped and watched the gurney disappear down the corridor. The other nurse came to my side. 'You're one of the women from that incident out by Cliff Drive?'

I nodded.

'Best you wait here for now,' she said.

'I need to know what's happened.'

248

'Your sister suffered a trauma to the head. It's possible, but not at all certain, that she's suffered an intracerebral haemorrhage.'

'I don't know what that means.'

'It means bleeding inside the brain.'

'And …?'

The nurse was silent for a minute, obviously reluctant to say any more. When at last she spoke, her voice lost its official edge and she was more comforting. 'We don't know yet if that's the case with your sister.' She turned to go but I put a hand on her arm and insisted she explain fully.

'What exactly does "bleeding inside the brain" mean?'

The nurse studied my face, no doubt gauging how little she could get away with telling me. 'Cerebral haemorrhaging prevents oxygen getting to the brain. When that happens, brain cells start to die.'

I knew what that meant. Brain damage. I pushed from my mind images of Chrissy in a wheelchair, dribbling into a food tray. 'But we're in a hospital, so you can fix it, right?'

'She's in theatre now. Try not to worry. It may not be severe.'

Chrissy will be all right. Chrissy will be all right. I repeated the phrase silently, over and over until it became an incantation. Please, please God, let her get through this.

The nurse must have seen how anxious I was because although she remained non-committal, she assumed a professionally reassuring tone. 'Try not to worry. She's in safe hands.'

Two hours later, Doctor Chatwal came to tell me my sister was dead.

I felt numb.

Chrissy, Christine. My sister Chrissy. Lost and found and lost again. It might just as well have been me they pumped full of anaesthetic because I was so stupefied I couldn't even cry.

55

Back in Glebe, I kept walking in and out of Conor's study, going over and over the events and conversations of Chrissy's stay, and that Skype call with Robbie when I'd felt so happy, and so suddenly, inexplicably bilious. That had been a visceral reaction to seeing my brother's face again and I hadn't had a clue.

I was back at the kitchen table, my laptop open, exactly as I'd been that day, but this time, instead of being fooled by Robbie's mendacity, I was making arrangements for Chrissy's funeral.

The funeral directors had given me a template for the service sheet, but I wanted to design something original, and special. It was the least I could do. Sophie had undertaken to write a notice for the local press, and let Peter and Chrissy's friends know. We'd both agreed on the format for the funeral and while Sophie searched through the photos at their place, I trawled my memory bank for early happy occasions with Chrissy – barbecues by the pool at her place, walks in the national park, picnics for Sophie at Balmoral Beach.

I was absorbed in these memories when Lauren called on the house phone. 'I've been trying for ages to call you on your mobile, but it keeps telling me there's no provider,' she said.

'I got a new phone.'

'We need to talk.'

'Sure. You don't sound yourself. Is everything all right?'

'It's your sister.' Before I could even begin to tell Lauren Chrissy had died, she blurted out that Conor and Chrissy were an item.

I had a moment of Stygian paralysis. Then I wanted to tell Lauren to shut up, shut up, shut up. Whatever she had to say, I didn't want to know.

Lauren's voice broke through. '… in a restaurant. They were all over each other. Lexi? Are you still there?'

'When was this?'

'Just the other day, I was …'

I stopped listening. My head was ringing with Conor's lies: he'd said it was a one-off thing, that it had ended before it began.

'I have to go. Chrissy's not … she died.' I choked back a sob. 'The funeral's next week. I'll call you.' I put the phone down before it burst into flames and torched the house, and me with it.

So, Chrissy and Conor *had* been seeing each other. In that way.

There was no undoing what Lauren had told me and I didn't want to be there when Conor got home so I abandoned the notes I was writing for Chrissy's funeral and left the house.

Outside it was cold and I'd left my coat behind but I didn't care. I didn't care if I fell into the gutter and succumbed to pneumonia. This wasn't about Chrissy. She was dead. She couldn't upset me any more, or protect me, and nor could we go to Bali together and put the whole shitty business behind us. No, this was about Conor. He'd lied to me, betrayed me, betrayed *us*.

Death is surely kinder than divorce, widowhood more merciful than rejection.

I walked without thinking where I was going, so febrile I could barely carry myself around. The prospect of drugs was very attractive to me, something completely mind-altering like LSD or heroin. Any delirium would be better than this agitation. But where does one get drugs? I hadn't an inkling and given I was a middle-class professional woman living in a steadily gentrifying neighbourhood, I was unlikely to ever find out.

The only time I'd come close to feeling so gutted was when Mum died. And again, this time as then, the only relief came from watching movies, so I walked all the way down Broadway and then along George Street to Event Cinemas. There was a film about Winston Churchill playing but it was called *The Darkest Hour* and given I was wallowing in my own leaden hours, the title turned me right off. I don't remember what the first movie I watched was called and under normal circumstances it wasn't something I'd pay to see. It was a dull story about a woman on a train blubbering all the time about what a hard time she was having. *Welcome to my world, girl.*

When that film was finished, I went back to reception and bought a ticket to see another. This time it was *Phantom Thread*. As long as I could sit in a darkened cinema, absorbed in other people's dramas I could keep at bay harrowing thoughts about my own. Sometimes this worked and sometimes it didn't. There was one scene which resonated painfully with me, a tender moment between the ageing fashion designer and the young waitress. Every piece of me, the waitress says, she gives to him. I saw in those two actors Conor and my sister, eating together, laughing together, making love. Well, I had given every piece of me to Conor. The lines of that song, the Bryan Adams one Conor and I had so often listened to together, came back to taunt me.

I sighed, so loudly that someone in the row behind shooshed at me.

'Shoosh yourself,' I said.

That day everyone, and I include myself, was detestable to me and most of all myself. Lauren's courage put me to shame. She'd had the moxie to tell me about Conor and Chrissy and I'd been too spineless to let her know about Steve's infidelity. I still didn't know whether or not I'd done the right thing.

I blamed Conor, then Chrissy, then ached for her, then blamed them both. I would now never be able to confront my sister with this, or understand her motives. If it would bring her back, I'd happily let her have Conor. Although maybe not. I didn't even ask myself what Conor wanted in all this. I didn't want to see or think about him.

I got up and left that theatre and went into another. On the screen five guys were brawling in a pub. I wished I could do that, lose my rag completely, physically the way men do, hit, punch, and box each other until we all felt better.

It was nearly half an hour into the film when a man came in and sat down a few seats away from me. Why is it that in an almost empty theatre, or on an empty bus or train, someone has to take the seat close by or adjacent to yours? I snuck a dekko at him. It was hard to tell what he looked like, old anyway, maybe as old my dad would be if he were still alive. Our eyes met, then we both looked away, back at the screen. Maybe this man saw that I was crying and maybe he smelled vulnerability on me because a few minutes later he moved to the seat next to mine. I got up and left.

By now it was nearly ten o'clock. The sky was a flat grey stone. All around me office blocks towered like giant sentinels, dark apart from the floors being cleaned, or where people without homes to go to were working late. I didn't feel as if I had a home to go to either.

At street level, it was bright with shop windows, neon signs, traffic lights, headlights but I saw none of it. Sydney had faded to a watermark on sullied parchment.

I passed a homeless man camped in a doorway under his cardboard bivouac and ruminatively smoking the remains of a found cigarette. He reached out a gnarled and indigent hand to me and I gave him thirty-three dollars and sixty cents; it was all that was left in my wallet. When I moved on, I bumped into a couple of people. They grumbled at me, something like 'watch where you're going bitch' and I wanted to call out after them: Sorry, sorry, I'm not myself.

I did not feel normal.

What is normal anyway? Who is the person who can answer that? A psychologist or a philosopher? Some spiritual guru? The priest at Lauren's church? Freud would have us all twitching at various degrees of neurosis but what did he know?

I wandered in a stupor along George Street, realising too late that I was passing the Marble Bar where only months before, Conor and I had spent a late night, celebrating my birthday. I hurried past, towards the Town Hall where I turned the corner into Park Street, heading for Hyde Park. I didn't go in. Instead I stood at the intersection of Park and Elizabeth. I couldn't decide which way to go. I breathed in deeply, but there was no air. My chest felt tight and hard, with fear and indecision. It was now well after midnight and still I didn't want to return home to Glebe.

Maybe Freud was right and everyone *is* crazy.

A light rain began to fall, turning down the volume of the world while the pneumatic whine of my dislocation remained on high.

Those were my last days in the neighbourhood.

Half of me longed to stay. The other half needed desperately to go.

56

Chrissy's funeral was held at the Memorial Gardens in Leura. We'd had to wait ten days while Sophie tracked down her father and he was able to get a flight home.

Peter Everson was a year or so older than my sister and they'd met at an art gallery function in Katoomba. He was tall, with a long craggy face, blue affable eyes, and a soft voice that had the merest trace of a Lancashire accent. His hair seemed always in need of brushing and he wore his clothes loose, as if he thought they might fill out his lean frame. Despite his dishevelled appearance there was an air of distinction about my brother-in-law and when he spoke, people took notice.

It wasn't a religious ceremony. Chrissy had been agnostic and used to say she wanted to be buried, without any fanfare, in a sack somewhere under a tree in the Blue Mountains. I'd never taken this seriously. Given how much attention my sister gave her wardrobe, the importance she placed on always looking chic, ending up in a hessian sack was hardly her style. A gunny bag certainly wasn't my choice of shroud and I wouldn't let it be hers.

And, anyway, funerals are for the living, aren't they? Chrissy had gone – her absence so complete it stunned me – and saying goodbye, finding some sort of closure, demanded ritual. It necessitated poetry. Sophie had agreed with this, and Peter too, so there were songs, and poems, and periods of meditative silence.

The celebrant was an amiable middle-aged woman wearing a tailored black trouser suit, with grey hair cut in a smooth wave to her neck and softened with a purple tint. She welcomed us with genuine sympathy and led the proceedings without once making us feel we weren't in charge.

We sat up the front, by the coffin, Peter and Sophie, Conor and I.

I was stony-faced, holding myself in, determined to keep thoughts of Conor at bay and give all my attention to saying goodbye to Chrissy.

Afternoon light filtered through green and red stained-glass windows. No sounds entered the room from outside and inside there was only the occasional noise of people behind us, shifting in their seats, and the voice of whoever was speaking.

Sophie read a verse by Tennyson. The only line I remember is something like this: 'May there be no moaning, when I put out to sea.' I liked that bit about no moaning.

Peter gave the eulogy, his face grey with grief and tiredness. Jet lag would have exacerbated his shock. He spoke of his profound sorrow at Chrissy's death and his repugnance at the manner of it. 'So much killing in the world,' he said in a low mournful voice, almost as if he were talking to himself at that point, 'and to suffer violence in one's home, at the hand of a relative, is surely the worst kind.' In a stronger voice, he spoke of his dismay at being widowed a second time, adding that there would be no third partner. Chrissy, he said, had been an unforeseen gift, one he hadn't expected to find. 'We had our ups and downs, what couple doesn't, but Chrissy was my mate, my friend and confidant, irreplaceable.' He finished by quoting Aristotle: 'Love is composed of a single soul inhabiting two bodies.' I was thinking what a romantic notion that was, and how I'd once believed in it, when Peter said: 'And now, without Chrissy, I am only half a man.'

His words were moving and sincere. How could Chrissy ever have doubted him?

A couple of times during Peter's eulogy to his wife, he faltered, particularly when he spoke of his regret at being so often out of the country, and in retrospect how selfish he'd been, but throughout, his face struck me as illumined with love. And it struck me then, listening to him talk about my sister and their life together, how little we can ever know of what goes on between couples. Marriage is a province full of secrets.

It wasn't until I got up to speak and turned to face the room that I noticed how many people were there. The place was full and, other than Lauren and Steve, I didn't know any of them. I hadn't known until that day, and for Chrissy's sake was pleased to learn, that she'd had a lot of friends.

I'd prepared some words to say, but when it came time for me to speak, I knew they'd make me cry, so I recited a poem instead. That was easier. And faster. My face was still a fright of bruises and I'd have preferred not to be seen, but there was no way out of it. I had to speak, for Chrissy. On the web I'd found a poem that appealed to me and I recited that. I wished I could have found something Chrissy liked but I didn't even know whether or not she enjoyed poetry and if she did, what her favourites were. At school I was never particularly good at understanding poetry, but when I'd thought about what I might read for Chrissy, these two verses by Shelley seemed fitting:

Is it that in some brighter sphere
We part from friends we meet with here?
Or do we see the Future pass
Over the Present's dusky glass?

Or what is that makes us seem
To patch up fragments of a dream,
Part of which comes true, and part
Beats and trembles in the heart?

Conor and I had driven to Katoomba that morning, hardly speaking and when we did, only for me to ask that we stop for a coffee and for Conor to ask how many people were expected to show up for the funeral.

We drove home in a similar vein. Conor put my lack of conversation down to grief. He was half right. Now and then he glanced at me and once or twice reached out to take my hand. I let him hold it, but only briefly, and when he squeezed it, did not, could not, respond.

57

When we arrived back at Mitchell Street, I told Conor I needed to clear my head. What I didn't tell him was that I needed time alone, away from *him*, to figure out what it was exactly that I wanted, and to make some decisions, about us, but mainly about me. It was late, after eight. I got out of the car and without looking at him or saying anything more, headed off down the road. He called after me, wanting to know when I'd be back, but I pretended not to have heard.

I was no Arthur Stace, wandering the streets touting messages of eternity, let alone being consoled by them. Religion held no solace for me. I saw no comfort anywhere and wasn't interested in eternity unless it was ready to swallow me up and let me disappear.

I walked until my feet ached as much as my heart.

What I most wanted that night was to forge myself a new identity, take a one-way ticket to somewhere anywhere else, erase from Sydney the woman who had once been Lexi Madison married to Conor Devlin. The woman who once had a family and now had no one.

It was after one in the morning when I at last crept back into the house and into Conor's study to sleep, shutting the door firmly behind me in a silent message that no one else was to open it. Conor didn't take the hint. He was already dressed for work when he poked his head into the room and asked after me. As if he cared. As if I gave a damn.

'Where have you been?"

At first, I ignored him, didn't turn around, didn't even open my eyes.

'Lex?'

Still, I didn't move, still so stung by his betrayal that I wasn't sure I could speak but in the end I did. 'More to the point, Conor, where have *you* been?'

'In bed, where do you think? Wondering where the hell you've been all night.'

He came into the room and I was acutely aware of him standing by the bed for a few minutes. The atmosphere in the room was brittle.

'I trusted you, Conor. I fucking trusted you.'

He didn't say any more and I knew then that Conor knew I knew. Our marriage was a drained waterbed. There was nothing more we could say to each other.

As soon as I heard the front door close, I got up and had a long hot shower, dressed as if I were going to a job interview, in my best navy pants, white blouse, and a green jacket. I was hoping that if I dressed more smartly than I felt, my mood might catch up with the clothes. I made myself scrambled eggs and ate half of them, then rooted out my old sports bag and crammed a change of clothes into it, along with my toiletries and laptop, a book of drawings I'd done during my student days, and a package of photos.

The photos made me stop. I sat on the bed and sorted through them. A dozen or so were pictures of my wedding, taken in the Botanic Gardens under a stand of jacaranda trees that were in full flower. Conor was wearing a grey linen suit, with a white shirt and bluey-grey tie that perfectly matched his eyes, and a white rose bud in the buttonhole. I wore a cream silk tea dress with broderie anglaise, and my hair pinned up with a circlet of white and orange rose buds. Some of the photos showed us beaming at the camera, in others lovingly at each other. We were an attractive couple, but it was those trees with their vibrant, almost violent bursts of purple that stole the show, as if in some shivery way, they were warning us that we might not last.

I left the wedding photos behind. There was nothing in the house I wanted, not a single souvenir to remind me of the leprous year I'd just endured. I stuffed nearly everything I owned – my shoes and clothes, including the silk tea dress, books, sewing kit, even my painting paraphernalia – into five black bin bags and lugged them to the front gate.

Only one item remained in the wardrobe: the green cashmere cardigan that Chrissy had given me. I buried my face in the soft cloth. My feelings for my sister vacillated between disgust and regret, and between love and remorse. Why, why, why had she slept with Conor? I laid the cardigan on the bed, spread the sleeves, then found some sheets of tissue paper and placed them over the wool, before folding the sleeves in and turning it into a compact roll which I packed in my bag. I did all this in slow motion as if I didn't want the task to end. That cardigan was all I had of her.

In our bedroom I arranged a keepsake for Conor.

When we started out in our careers and one or other of us would be struggling at work, Lauren and I used to ask: what would a man do? And we'd both giggle and say: piss against the desk and walk on. During that egregious morning I couldn't think of a better strategy. On the top shelf of my wardrobe, hidden from Conor at the back, I'd been saving new lingerie, pearly-cream silk, for a romantic weekend away together. Ha bloody ha to that. I removed the bra and panties from their wrapping and laid them on the floor. Then I squatted and peed on them, and put them back in the wardrobe. After that I picked up the scissors again and cut the crotch from every pair of Conor's twelve pairs of navy Calvin Klein underpants. These weren't some of my proudest acts and I admit they were brainless and spiteful but by then I'd sort of lost my grip on reason.

58

While I waited for a taxi, I drank a glass of water and for a minute or two considered leaving a note for Conor, but there were no more words for him in me. I wasn't the same woman he'd met that day in the bookstore and didn't want to be. I knew that sooner or later we'd have to talk, but first I needed to be on my own for a while.

I observed the keys on the table, not even remotely nostalgic for the joy I'd felt the day Conor handed them to me. We were finished. I picked up my bags and left the house, studiously avoiding looking at my mural along the hallway. It pained me to leave that behind, but I'd do another one, something even better, somewhere else.

When the cab turned up, I jammed three of the bin bags in the boot and the other two on the back seat, and while the cabbie waited, dropped them all off at the nearest St Vinnie's store. I was just getting back into the taxi when I changed my mind about my painting gear and went back to where I'd put the bags. Fortunately, I knew which bag the stuff was in and that my paints were all near the top. I left my jars of gesso and varnish there because I didn't have room for them. Same with a roll of canvas and a pack of stretcher bars, but I grabbed my four best Galeria brushes and rummaged through a dozen tubes of acrylic paint to rescue my favourite colours:

cadmium red and yellow oxide, Prussian blue and raw sienna. There was a tube of brilliant violet which I used to like, a lot, but it reminded me of my wedding day, so I left it.

Back in the taxi, it was all I could do to fit what I'd recouped into my sports bag. I ended up with tubes of paint eased into every available crevice. The driver, with a studiously neutral expression, watched me in his rear-vision mirror. I tilted my chin at him and we carried on into town.

No one had seen me go. Our neighbours were all either at work or study. Even on the weekends sometimes, you could walk down our street and not see a soul. If it wasn't for voices drifting across back fences, or a group of kids going past on bikes now and then, you'd wonder if anyone else lived there. All the buzz in the neighbourhood was down Glebe Point Road at the markets, and the shops where students hung around the cafés and the second-hand bookshops.

I took my last long look at Glebe, laid-back and blowsy under an uncaring sun, and knew before we'd even left it behind that the place I'd cherished was already indifferent to me.

About thirty minutes later I booked into the backpackers near Kings Cross. It was a two-storey Victorian villa with cast-iron lace across the upstairs balcony and largely hidden behind a leafy garden in a tree-lined street. I knew the place well because I'd spent a week there when I first arrived in Sydney, before I found a shared house to move into. On that initial stay, the hostel's proximity to shops and pubs, and a railway station, had ticked all the boxes. Another, major factor in its favour during that first stay had been its occupants – I'd wanted to meet people, make friends, build contacts – but it was the last thing I wanted on my second stay. I didn't want to see, talk, or encounter anyone at all and was pleased to get a room to myself at the back of the house.

I dropped my bag on the floor and flopped on the bed feeling tense and tearful. Outside a truck roared past and despite sun shining through the thin nylon curtains I heard what I thought was a low growl of thunder. After that I dozed off and when I woke a couple of hours later, the sky had clouded over and it was raining, fat drops of water spattering the windows. In the garden below, shrubs and trees gleamed in the rain and I could hear car tyres swishing through the wet. Sydney's commuters were heading home, out of the city and into the sprawl.

My phone juddered in my bag. I took it out, unmuted it and ran through my messages. It seemed as if days had passed since I'd even looked at my phone. Two from Conor. The first said: 'Can't we talk about this?' The next one: 'Come home, please.'

I texted back: 'It's over.'

Two minutes later I texted again: 'We'll talk, but not yet.'

There was a message from Lauren, suggesting dinner. I replied, saying it had to be that evening and really, really hoped she could make it. Then I went online and booked a one-way train ticket to Melbourne.

59

Lauren and I met for an early dinner at an Asian restaurant down the road from the hostel. I ordered a bowl of noodles with chilli prawns and pak choi, but I wasn't remotely hungry and only picked at the food. Lauren ate sticky glazed chicken and rice.

The place was packed and running at a high decibel. Voices ricocheted across the hard surfaces of wooden floors and tables and we had to almost shout to hear each other.

'Your poor face.'

'I got off lightly.'

We didn't speak for a short time and I guessed Lauren was thinking about Chrissy, as I was.

'Here.' She took a package from her bag and pushed it across the table towards me. I opened it to find a bottle of L'Oréal Foundation. 'Should help cover those the bruises,' she said.

'Looks expensive.'

'It isn't, but it is waterproof.'

'Thanks, and thanks for being at the funeral.'

'I'm sorry about your sister.' Lauren put her palms together, as if she were about to pray, and held them against her lips. 'Wish I hadn't said anything now.'

'No, I'm glad you did. I needed to know.'

'Yes, I expect you did.'

Did I read in Lauren's clipped reply an unspoken reprimand? 'You know, don't you, about Chrissy and Steve?'

'He told me. Steve was an ass and we didn't speak for three days, but we got over it. We've the kids to think of. There was never any question of splitting up anyway. I love the man. He loves me.'

'Thank goodness it's out in the open.' I put my fork down. There was no point even pretending to eat. 'God, what a total screw-up it's all been.'

Lauren suggested wine, but I settled for mineral water. A glass of wine would have helped reduce the hubbub around us to an ambient buzz, but I'd been drinking far too much lately and decided to quit. 'I probably brought it on myself. After all, I did spend a night with her husband.'

'You didn't.' Lauren's eyebrows rose and her jaw dropped. If my disclosure offended her Christian sensibilities I didn't care; I was past having any secrets.

'I did but it's not what you think. It was years ago and all entirely innocent, although who knows, if he hadn't been my brother-in-law, I suppose we might have … it was that sort of evening.' I shrugged as if to shake myself free of this thought. 'No, I wouldn't have.'

Lauren waited for me to finish. I wondered if she thought I needed time to get something off my chest, to make a confession. I didn't.

'Although whether or not we had actually slept together is not the point. The point is that Chrissy believed we had. One injudicious night with Peter and it led to a huge, stupid misunderstanding.'

'That bad?'

'You have no idea. I might just as well have handed Chrissy a grenade. When she came to stay, she pulled the pin.' I rubbed my palms vigorously up and down against my face as if to erase the past, all of it.

'She was quite a bit older than you, wasn't she?'

I nodded. 'And I'm no psychologist, but I suppose living in the same house again pressed buttons.'

'You might say we're all sitting on hand grenades then, most of us anyway,' said Lauren. 'You know, old childhood injuries, whether or not they're real, family stuff just waiting to blow up in our faces. It can take ages for old grievances to surface. Decades usually.'

'You'd be happy if we all found God, wouldn't you?'

Lauren laughed. 'There are worse outcomes.'

'Like death?'

'Sorry, I didn't mean ...'

'No, it's fine,' I said, even though it wasn't.

Nothing may ever be right again. It was impossible to hold back more tears. Every little upset started them up again. I took out my handkerchief and wiped my eyes. Lauren waited quietly for me to recover. We sat there almost five minutes longer without speaking. I'd run out of words and was dog-tired, ready to get on the train and not have to think about anything for as many hours as it took to get to Melbourne.

'What will you do?'

'What I should have done years ago, rent a studio space somewhere and get back to painting.'

'Will that pay the rent?'

'No. I'll find a job, maybe part-time, but the art, I have to give it a go, for sanity's sake if nothing else.'

'I'm going to miss you,' said Lauren,

'And I you. God, will I miss you, Lauren, but we'll see each other. You'll be down to Melbourne, won't you? To visit your mum and dad.'

Lauren nodded. 'Yes, of course. Next month probably.'

We both knew it would be a long time, if ever, before I returned to Sydney. 'Can't see myself ever coming back here.'

'Won't you have to, to testify?'

This was a thought I'd pushed to the back of my mind and for a while I needed it to stay there. 'I'll cross that bridge when I have to.'

The walls of the restaurant were decorated with lacquer paintings. They were done on wood, some of them with mother of pearl inlay, or was it egg shell? I was tempted to go up and take a closer look, and see if I could figure out how they achieved that highly polished effect; I thought I could probably do something similar, using a varnish of shellac.

Lauren drew me back to our conversation. 'I've got something else for you. Don't take it the wrong way.'

I expected her to give me a copy of the Bible. Instead it was a self-help book, *Co-Dependent No More*. I'd be lying if I said I wasn't taken aback. 'Is that how you see me? You think I think I'm nothing without Conor?' Or without siblings. This thought came unbidden and made me pause.

'It has taken rather a long time for you to act, hasn't it?'

'Are you telling me now that you never liked Conor?'

'Admit it, Lexi, there were cracks.' Lauren smiled to remove the sting.

'You're right, and not just with Conor either.'

'Well, you know what they say about cracks.'

'They're where the light comes in.'

We both laughed.

'You're right though, Lauren. Now I think on it, when I look back, I see they've been there all the time, the cracks I mean.'

I started to open the book but Lauren stopped me. 'Later, when you're alone. Let's not waste this time together.'

Shortly after seven, she dropped me off in Kings Cross where I fetched my bag from the backpackers and set off down Darlinghurst Road, believing I had time and energy to walk to the central railway station. I had the time but not the energy. Within five minutes I stopped, swayed a little at the edge of the pavement and saw an alarming image of myself falling into the street in front of a bus or a semi-trailer. I conceded defeat, acknowledged I was too knackered to move another step under my own steam, and ordered an Uber.

60

Leaving Sydney felt like leaving my future behind.

If Mum were still alive, I'd have gone back to Bendigo, to our old house in Epsom, and holed out there for as long as it took for me to restore my equilibrium and reboot my life in some way. But Mum was dead and I was skint. That resolution of mine to adopt a more frugal lifestyle and save for an apartment was yet to kick in and I needed urgently to find a job. The scrap of paper Marley had given me, with the name of his friend on it, was in my wallet, but I hoped I wouldn't need it. I was grateful for Marley's help, but working for some tinpot suburban paper – I supposed that was where his friend worked – wasn't what I had in mind.

Not that I had anything particular in mind. I had no idea what was going to happen next in my life. I was grieving for Chrissy, and Robbie too in a warped kind of way, and felt the loss of Conor like an amputated limb. I repeated to myself, over and over, that I didn't need him, that it was time to follow my own dreams and not his, and that everything would be okay. This helped. Taking action was already making me feel a little stronger and I was collected enough to park the fears that come with uncertainty. Fear is the dark room where negatives are developed. I read that once, on a billboard outside a big stone church somewhere, and the message had stayed with me.

I took out the book Lauren had given me and dipped into it. At first, I wished she had given me the Bible instead, thinking – admittedly not for very long – that it may have been more useful. A maxim she'd quoted to me during our dinner was that the leopard cannot change its spots. It was from the Old Testament, she'd said, from the Book of Jeremiah. Lauren was referring to Conor, and to my siblings I suppose, and me as well probably. The proverb applies to all of us. No doubt the Good Book contains many other equally illuminating adages that might cast light on the human condition.

I was intrigued by Lauren's choice of gift, and trusted her enough to know she'd considered carefully what to give me. What had she seen in me that I hadn't? I opened the book at random and words and phrases like 'obsessing' and 'controlling' and 'the need to learn detachment' and 'know what you need' leapt from the page and I saw immediately that it might be worth reading.

I put the book back in my bag. A few minutes later I took it out again and appraised the photo of the author on the back cover: Melody Beattie. I made a pledge to us both that I'd read soon what she had to say.

What do I need? Conor and I had sought different things. I don't know how conscious this thought was at the time, but putting it into words now, it seems to me that he wanted sex and companionship while I wanted intimacy and friendship. For a long happy while, our needs had appeared to be the same.

The night train to Melbourne left shortly after eight-thirty in the evening. I stared vacantly through the window as we rattled out of the rail yards, across the southern suburbs until the pinpricks of urban light disappeared into the dark. I knew there were fields of wheat out there, and miles of bush and scrub, and the famous Ironbark Forest near Chiltern which Conor I always meant to visit, but it was a moonless night and too black to see anything.

As New South Wales receded into the night behind me, I couldn't help imagining myself stepping out of a Brett Whiteley painting and into a Peter Booth drawing.

With nothing visible out the windows, and too tired to read, I was left with my thoughts. Uncertainty didn't have to mean something bad was going to happen, but only that something *was* going to happen. It might just as well be something good.

The painter Frida Kahlo said that nothing is absolute, that everything changes and revolves. She also said something like this, that at the end of the day, we can endure much more than we than we think we can. And she would know.

These thoughts restored me sufficiently to realise I was famished. I went to the buffet car and bought a toasted cheese and ham sandwich and a large paper cup of hot chocolate.

It occurs to me now, that maybe if things had been different, if my sister hadn't behaved like such a blunt instrument, I may have believed what she'd tried to tell me about Robbie, although god knows, it would have helped if she'd been less abstruse about it all, told me more. And if I hadn't been so pig-headed myself, I might have paid more attention to the difficulties she was going through. I had, after all, suspected when she first phoned about coming to stay, that she was unhappy, but then, caught up in my own affairs, I'd thought no more about it.

I should have been more sympathetic.

Chrissy shouldn't have been such a bitch.

And who knows? It's an audacious thought, but, if my sister and I had got along better, we might have shared Conor, or Conor and Peter. No. Just Peter. I was over Conor. We might have had a polygamous marriage. In theory I'm not against the idea and people do, don't they? Wasn't there an actor once, Jack someone, who lived with two sisters? That may have been a mischievous rumour, but an arrangement like that, a *ménage à trois* let's say, appeals to a different, stronger me. I wouldn't have to be all things to my husband and he wouldn't have to be all things to me. I'm not sure humans are really cut out for monogamy. I'd go so far as to suggest that it's probably the worst way to live, especially for mothers and children. They say it takes a village to bring up a child. Perhaps it takes a group to make a marriage.

These considerations came to me much, much later, after I'd spent many months grappling with what had happened and came to accept that my happiness didn't have to end because my marriage to Conor had. On that night train out of Sydney, I was still in the grip of the monogamous ideal and saw my ruined marriage as a personal failure.

The carriage I was in was only half-full and I had a seat to myself. There was a boisterous family a few seats away from me, but I barely noticed them. After they went to the buffet car around ten o'clock, the carriage quietened and I managed to drift into sleep for a few hours.

When the sun rose around six-thirty I was wide awake. By seven the train was rumbling through bleak industrial parks towards winter and Flinders Street station at the end of Swanston Street.

That area of Swanston Street, where it meets the Yarra River, is a carbuncle on the city, a boulevard of cheap two-dollar shops on one side where homeless people bed down at night under cardboard shelters in filthy doorways. On the other side, with its condescending back to the street, stands St Paul's Cathedral. Only when you walk west towards Collins Street, into the business end of town, do you start seeing Melbourne's money and that's where I hoped I'd soon find a job.

It felt good to be back in Melbourne. I held my head high, put my shoulders back, and walked with more purpose than I'd felt in ages. I was ready for breakfast. In a café in Little Collins Street, I ordered a Danish pastry and an extra-large coffee and ruminated on the state of affairs, by which I mean my life, until the city woke up and I could get on with my day. Overnight I'd made decisions about what I needed to do and was eager now to put them into action.

At nine, I went in search of a hairdresser. I called in at three salons before I found one on Elizabeth Street that would give me an appointment there and then.

While I was in the salon, my phone rang. Straight away I recognised the number; it was the one Marley had given me, of his friend. Jackson. I didn't know if that was his first or last name. I accepted the call.

'Lexi?'

'Yes, but my name is Alexandra.' This was a spur of the moment decision, to start using my full name, Alexandra; it would help me draw a line between my new life from my old. Conor rarely used my full name, usually only when he felt he had a point to make and thought, invariably erroneously I might add, that I wasn't getting it. My name was nearly always shortened, by everyone who knew me, to Lexi, and Conor often truncated it even further to Lex.

Telling Jackson my name was Alexandra made me feel taller.

He came straight to the point and I liked that. 'Marley called. Recommended you. There's an opening here, if you're interested.' He was laconic, each word staccato as if he were almost too busy to make the call.

I was about to tell him I wasn't interested in working for a local paper when he said he worked in TV news and that they were looking for an environmental reporter.

'Didn't Marley say, I'm a graphic designer, not a journalist.'

'Said this was right up your street.'

What was Marley thinking? And yet . . .

'Someone who's prepared to kick butt for a decent story,' Jackson said. 'Get people to sit up and take notice. Specially around this whole climate change thing. And. Well. Marley says you know more than I do what we need to cover.'

Dear old Marley. He'd done me a huge favour and one day I'd repay him for it. Jackson and I agreed to meet, over lunch the next day.

When I walked out of the salon three hours later, I was a brunette and my hair was short, pixie style. I'd even had my eyebrows tinted to match and looked as different from the me who'd lived in Sydney as I needed to feel.

From Elizabeth Street I walked over to the State Library where there were patches of lawn outside, and trees. The lunch time crowd was spilling out of offices and lecture halls, and I was lucky to find a half-empty bench. Pigeons darted in and wandered about, confident of crumbs. Trams squealed along Swanston Street and somewhere nearby, a car alarm went off.

I went over the conversation I'd had with Jackson, knowing I'd already decided to take the job. As long as I was making decisions and acting on them, I was keeping depression at bay. But only just. Ever since Lauren's phone call, which had confirmed Conor's affair with Chrissy, my self-assurance had been ebbing. I'd quickly grown mistrustful again, and found it difficult to make eye contact, especially with men. I was making a conscious effort to rise above this, to maintain an approximation at least of confidence, but each day I'd hunkered a little further down inside my skin.

When we married, I'd been so sure I'd somehow conjured up from my imaginings, from my own power, the life I shared with Conor in Glebe. This now struck me as hubristic. And childish. Clearly, I'd got everything wrong, made terrible decisions. I had to re-learn myself, find my way back to optimism. As things turned out, this was to take me more than a year, during which Conor and I began filing through the legal morass of divorce.

In the meantime, I faked it. Every other day I reminded myself of something else Frida Kahlo said, that little by little, we should be able to solve any problems and survive. Compared with Frida's suffering, after that dreadful crippling accident she had, my troubles were negligible. I knew I'd be all right, and that whatever happened next was my responsibility. Reminding myself of this buoyed me.

I hadn't meant to, but I'd left my art books behind in Mitchell

Street. Even if I'd remembered at the time, they would have been too heavy to bring away with me anyway, but I knew I'd regret them sooner or later. They were still under my side of the bed and I wondered how long it would take Conor to find them there.

Another thought came to me, on that first day back in Melbourne, that leaving my future behind was probably a good thing. I'd once congratulated myself for learning how to live in the present, but half the text book had been missing. To live happily in the here and now – to not carry around at every instant the weight of what went before or expectations about something that might not even happen – I had to leave the future behind as well as the past. I knew as I strove to adopt this frame of mind, that nothing was so bad that it wouldn't, given time, get better.

The promise of a job prompted me to take a tram to Fitzroy Street and find a second-hand clothing shop and I was about to step on a tram when I changed my mind. I wasn't in the mood that day for someone else's cast-offs. I made a pact with myself that I'd get back to dressing sustainably, just as soon as, but right then, I had a yen for *new* clothes that no one else had ever worn before, clothes just for me.

I turned back towards the CBD and then reconsidered; I'd be letting myself down if I suddenly, after five years of re-homing cast-offs, bought new. I went online and searched for a second-hand boutique that sold upmarket clothes. I didn't need labels, I wasn't into Gucci or Prada just because they were Gucci and Prada, but I did want nice outfits, something classical that would last more than one season. I googled quality-second-hand-clothes-Melbourne and found a couple of boutiques with prices so outrageous I almost changed my mind for the third time, but stopped short. Now wasn't the time to compromise my beliefs. What sort of environmental reporter would I be if I couldn't walk the talk. Here was my chance to show people that having a social conscience doesn't mean you have to look daggy. With this in mind, I eschewed the charity shops I usually visited and set off for those boutiques instead. The pre-loved clothes I found there were just what I was looking for.

I didn't want to admit it to myself, but in the recesses of my mind, as I selected clothes and tried them on, I was asking myself: what would Chrissy choose? Whether consciously or not, her casual-chic style influenced me and I left the first store with two dresses I knew she'd like for herself, one blue and the other green, both made from a soft wool-mix fabric. In the second shop, I purchased a blue linen herringbone jacket that I would keep for spring, and, best of all, an almost new cashmere coat. It was another Perri Cutten, only this time it was a dark viridian green, a perfect match with both dresses.

After my shopping spree, I took the new me into the nearest liquor store, bought a bottle of Bollinger, and caught a tram down to St Kilda, one of my favourite parts of the city. It's a scruffy suburb prowling along the edge of Port Phillip Bay, Melbourne's own tattered Glebe, and I'd always said that if I'd stayed in the city after I finished uni, that's where I'd rent a place.

St Kilda was where my friend Dion lived, in a shared house not far from the water. He said to me once, and I hoped he meant it, that if I ever needed it and wherever he lived, that's where I'd find a place to crash.

AUTHOR'S NOTE

The germ of this novel, the bacillus which spread to infect Lexi Maddison's life, began when a friend mentioned to me that one in twenty-five Americans is a sociopath. At the time, we were picking over the 2016 election in the US, trying and failing to understand how low America has fallen.

That chilling statistic, that so many outwardly ordinary people are actually sociopathic, astounded me. I purchased a copy of Martha Stout's *The Sociopath Next Door* and was both repelled and fascinated by what she had to say.

I began macabrely imagining what it would be like to find myself grappling with a sociopath. Would I know before it was too late that it was *Atrax robustus* smiling at me from across the room, or from a computer screen?

I am indebted to Norman Bilbrough for his advice and encouragement; and to Anna Bruce, Anna Mahoney, Pania Parry and Shirley Walden who gave me constructive and supportive feedback on early drafts. My heartfelt thanks to Andrea Coppock for her masterly editing, and to the team at Mary Egan Publishing whose contribution was, as always, impeccable.

Patricia Donovan